Forgotten

Shifters of Moonrise: Book 1

R.A. Beckem

For those who lose themselves in books on purpose.
May the Males of Moonrise steal you away all over again.

Contents

Content and Trigger Warnings

WELCOME TO MOONRISE, YOU CHAOTIC CREATURE.

Before you sprint into this book like Kara running from her problems, here's the official list of "stuff my lawyer (aka common sense) says I need to warn you about."

You're here because:

- You saw "wolf shifter" and your inner goblin whispered *"Yes... bite marks."*

- You're in my writing community and I've trauma-bonded you into this.

- You're my family and I love you but please don't text me about the spice.

Whatever group you're in—*welcome!* Let's do this.

LANGUAGE: There is cussing. A lot of it. Zander alone could make a sailor say "sir, calm down." I mean... look at the chapter titles. Nothing was safe.

SEXUAL CONTENT: Ohhhh sweet summer child. This is open-door romance. Wide open. Like "Kara literally cannot catch a break or a breath" open.

You'll find:

- Outdoor moments, because nature said "sure why not."

- Oral, because Zander Holt is an overachiever.

- A shower scene, because these two can't even bathe peacefully.

Yes, it's on-page. No, I didn't hold back. Yes, your Kindle might judge you.

VIOLENCE: Listen. These men have the emotional regulation of a blender at full speed. They're wolf shifters. They fight. They growl. They throw each other into trees for fun. Nothing violent happens **between the main couple**, because we respect boundaries around here... unlike Zander, who respects *nothing* except Kara's safety and maybe her thighs.

MILD TORTURE: Barely there. Honestly, it's the PG-13 version of torture.

MURDER: Ah yes. The Moonrise tradition. There's murder! Lots of it mentioned, most of it happens in wolf form, and at one point somebody's head goes *yeet* in a direction no head should go. You'll be fine. Probably.

Alright, heathen.

You survived the warning page. Now go meet Zander and Kara—and may the Moonrise gods have mercy on your heart rate.

I'm sorry, your what?

KARA

"RUN!"

The word screams in my head as I sprint through this forest. *Why am I running?* God, I wish I knew. But this feeling in the pit of my stomach—the one right next to the stitch in my side—tells me I need to keep moving.

The world blurs as I run faster than I think I've ever run before, but I don't think it's going to matter. Making the one move that every horror movie pegs as idiotic, I look back. Almost like karma is ready to bite me in the ass, my foot catches on a root and I fall. Hard.

"Dammit!" My ankle—while I don't think it's broken—hurts like a bitch. My knees and hands are absolutely shredded. At this point, I should just let whatever it is catch me. Can't be worse than this, right?

The snap of a twig comes from my left, and the panic I was feeling ratchets up another notch. It's too close, and I'm too tired to get up and keep moving.

"Kara!" That voice. I know it. *I think?* It's that weird nagging in the back of my mind that tells me that the voice is someone I know and should trust. But part of me can't do that anymore. The birds that were chirping moments ago seem to have gone quiet. Like an idiot, I stay right where I am, erratically scanning left and right. Hoping to pinpoint the source of the voice that seems to be my salvation and destruction all rolled into one.

"Kara! Come on! Where are you, love?"

Before I can even think to respond, run, or whatever I was gearing up to do, a man—no, a *mountain*—comes into the clearing I've found myself sprawled out in. He's massive. Tall in that dangerous kind of way. Muscled in all the right places. But it's his eyes. Even in this darker corner of the woods, I can see just how green they are, and I'm transfixed. His shaggy, brown-blond hair looks like it could use a cut, but in the best way. His strong jaw and broad shoulders add to the rugged mountain aura he's throwing.

Those same features give me pause. It's terrifying in a way that I can't even explain. It's that fear you get when your whole world has been turned upside down, and you can't figure out which way is up. I probably should have noticed that fear before his eyes and size, but here we are.

My eyes trail down his bare chest and keep going. Shit. He's naked—birthday suit, hung-like-an-ox, naked—and my mouth goes dry.

"There you are," he says, surprisingly gentle as he steps closer and looks down at me. Then he realizes what I'm staring at, and the laugh he barks out startles me. I snap my eyes up to his, and his smile could power cities.

"You're allowed to look, you know. Part of the perks of being my mate."

I swallow—hard—and my mouth drops open like a fish searching for water. "I'm sorry, your *what*?" I stammer as I try to figure out what the hell is going on.

"Your mate..." he says with a touch of trepidation. "You know, married—well, not yet, but soon—and bonded together for life. Ring any bells?" His smile fades as quickly as it had appeared, replaced with concern. And is that...confusion?

"Umm, no!" I say, a bit more forcefully than I intended, just now realizing I'm still sprawled out on the ground. I crawl backward before scurrying to my feet. Or I try to. Fucking hell, my ankle might actually be broken. I almost fall again as I try to put weight on it.

"Whoa there, spitfire." Mountain man wraps his arms around me before I absolutely faceplant. "I got you." Freezing in his embrace for just a moment, I begin to flail.

"And you can let go now!" I say as I hobble out of his arms with less grace than I would have liked. Even though he lets me escape his grasp, it's definitely not his first choice.

Turning to face him with my arms up like I have any chance of fending him off, I scan the tree line to hopefully find some sort of exit. "Listen, I have no clue who you are. I've been running through this damn forest for what feels like hours. All I remember is that I am freaked the fuck out. Then you show up, buck-ass naked, and expect me to accept that I'm your mate—whatever the fuck that is. I think the fuck not!" The last part comes out as more of a screech than just words.

"You...you don't remember me?" He's back to that too gentle, kind of worried tone, and I don't like how it makes me feel. *Why don't I like it?* "Kara, I..."

"No! No, no, no! Seriously, this is not okay. And could you please put some clothes on?" Why am I so focused on his beautiful body?

He chuckles this time. "I can't do that 'cause they kind of got ripped up when I took off after you, but how about I stand over here?" He backs up with his hands up in surrender, and puts himself behind a stump. "Will this work?"

"Sure, fine." It's not fine, but what choice do I have? Glaring at this man who so clearly knows me, but I have no recollection of him, I add, "But you better start explaining how the hell you know me, and why I have no idea who you are!" Oh, good. The panic is back. At least that's something relatively familiar in this sea of blank chaos.

That gentle, kind look gets fully replaced by confusion and resignation. Keeping his hands up as if to show me he means no harm, he begins, "Okay, umm, my name is Zander Holt, and I'm the Alpha of our pack—have been since my father died four years ago. We met a little over two months ago when we were both at an Alpha meeting." Sighing, he adds, "I have zero clue why you don't know who I am."

"Pack?" Now I'm the one with trepidation and confusion in my voice. "What the hell are you talking about, and how have we only known each other for two months and you are calling me your mate?" This is too much.

"Oh.. okay. Before I answer, can you answer something for me?" he—Zander—says with an almost pleading look in his eyes. That look...it makes me want to do anything he says.

"Sure."

"Do you know what a shifter is?" He's so gentle that it scares me.

"No...should I?"

"Fucking hell!" Zander throws his hands up and yells, "I knew there was something seriously wrong with that bitch!" He looks at me and his eyes flash yellow, making him look like some sort of monster. I stumble back into a tree, and oh good, the panic is now even stronger. The shift in his demeanor almost gives me whiplash.

"Shit, sorry. My wolf is riding me pretty hard, and he gets pissed if something fucks with, well, anything." Again, Zander puts his arms up in a surrendering, placating way.

"Listen, I don't know what the hell you're on, but I'm out!" I turn to run—or more accurately, hobble—away, but Zander grabs my wrist, making me turn back to look at him. A jolt of what I can only describe as an electrical zing goes through my body, but I don't have the time or energy to process that.

"Okay, hang on, I'm sorry. This is a lot, I know. But at least give me time to explain. I'm not the enemy. This witch showed up on our pack grounds, and she left when we tried to get rid of her—but warned us that everything would change. We had no idea what she meant, but I think I'm starting to figure it out." He's talking crazy fast now, like he's scared that I'll bolt. And he's right. I'm about five seconds away from trying to break from his grip and getting the hell out of here.

The problem is, I don't actually want to leave him. This dual sensation is almost too much.

"Just...come back with me. We will figure this out, I promise." He's pleading now. I look up into those emerald pools and see it: he's telling the truth. I have no clue how I know, but he is. I don't know who I am—or what I am. Because apparently *that* matters. I have zero clue who he is or what the hell a shifter is.

I still don't understand why he's buck-ass naked and doesn't seem to care. *God, what have I gotten myself into?*

The reality is I have nowhere to go, and I don't even know where I am. He doesn't seem to want to hurt me, so maybe I should take a chance. The only time I've felt even remotely calm is when he's touching me, and that panics me, too. So here we go.

I breathe out a heavy sigh. My shoulders sag and I look up at him again. "Okay, but no funny business! And I want you dressed ASAP. This is way too much."

Zander closes his eyes and seems to breathe for the first time since we started talking. "Yes, of course. Let's get you back to the pack house. You'll be safe there, and we can figure out what to do about everything else after that."

Without breaking contact, Zander turns to head back the way he came. I take a step and attempt to put weight on my ankle. The yelp I let out is enough for Zander to whip around so fast I almost don't track it. In the next breath, I'm scooped up and cradled to his hard, muscular chest.

"What are you doing?" I ask incredulously. I take a breath in and get a whiff of his scent, freshly tilled soil and a hint of cinnamon. I melt into his embrace, but the next moment, I realize what I'm doing, and start to panic again. *God, this panicking thing is getting old fast.* I try to get down, but Zander's hold tightens.

"You can't walk, and it will be faster if I carry you," he says without even looking at me. But he's stiffened, and his muscles ripple with so much strength it makes me—nope, not going there.

"Fine, but no funny business," I say again. What the fuck is wrong with me?

"Yep, no funny business." He chuckles and starts walking again, heading back the way we came.

CHAPTER TWO

It's a wolf!

ZANDER

How the hell does she not remember me? I carry her through the woods, cradled against my chest while her wildflower and vanilla scent assaults me. We lapse into silence, probably because she's confused and terrified. And I have absolutely no idea how to fix this.

I'm the Alpha of Moonrise Pack. I'm supposed to fix every problem the pack has—or at least have a damn good idea where to start. Especially when it comes to my mate; except I've got jack shit for ideas. She's my other half. The part of me that was missing for the whole of the thirty years of my life before we met.

Just three days ago, we were talking about what the future of our packs looks like. She is the daughter of another Alpha, and was set to take over her own pack when her father is ready to step down.

Now we're here. Me with every memory of us, our pack, *everything*! My wolf growls before he practically yells in my head. *Mine! Hurt!* I growl and my eyes flash yellow.

"Whoa there, mountain man! I'm letting you carry me 'cause I can't walk. Doesn't mean I want to be ripped apart." The panic and worry she's projecting is again growing to the level it was back in the clearing.

"Sorry," I say for what feels like the tenth time in as many minutes. I'm freaking her out, and I don't know how to stop. I take a few deep breaths and glance down at her in my arms. Her rich, ginger hair cascades down her back and over my arms. Her normally caramel eyes are dulled and look anywhere but at me, and it's killing me.

"What's the last thing you remember?" I know I said we'd go back to the pack house and talk more there, but I need to figure this out. It's destroying me that she doesn't know me—know *us*.

"You mean before you ran me down and I about died from a damn tree root?" Kara quips.

I sigh again, trying to keep my attitude out of my tone. "Yes, before I ran you down and you about died." *Shit, that was not how I meant to say it.* Sarcasm, it's going to get me killed one of these days.

Those caramel eyes turn on me, flashing disdain before she sighs and her shoulders fall. "Nothing. The first thing I remember is telling myself to run, and being completely terrified."

Shit, shit, shit! This isn't some weird amnesia thing. I reach out to Damien and Kai, my second and third, through the pack link to let them know I have found Kara. Kai is the first to reply.

Is she okay? Safe? What happened? Are you on your way back? What do you need from us? I roll my eyes as he does his usual thing and bombards me with every question in his head. He's been my best friend since we were kids, but damn, the questions!

We're on our way back. She's injured, but we'll talk when we get there, I reply to both of them, even though only Kai has acknowledged me.

We'll meet you back at the pack house. Damien went North and will take a minute to get back, Kai says quickly. I can tell he wants to ask more questions, but doesn't.

That's when I realize the thing that's been eating at me since I caught up to Kara—the same thing my wolf has been angry about. I can't feel her wolf. At all. I try to speak to Kara through the bond—but nothing. Zip. FUCK! This is even worse than I thought! I don't even think her wolf is actively part of her right now. I pick up my pace. I could shift and get us there faster, but as jumpy as she is, I don't think that will go over well.

After the longest ten minutes of my life, we break through the trees and walk towards the pack house. Kai is standing on the lawn in front of the house, waiting for us with his signature grin plastered on his face. He's as tall as me, though not nearly as muscled. His lean frame is just a sign he's not Alpha, but Beta. His long, brown hair is actually tied back today.

As soon as I make it to the patio, Kara starts squirming out of my arms, and I place her in a chair in hopes that she will sit and let us figure this whole mess out—but I should have known better. The second I step away, she's up and trying to find an exit. She has that panicked look in her eyes again.

"Hey, hey, it's okay. Remember we said we would try to figure out what's going on? I just thought you'd be more comfortable in a chair with that ankle of yours." I raise my hands in a gesture of surrender.

"Yeah, you did. But you neglected to mention other giant men would be around. Seems like this is just some sort of bait and switch bullshit," Kara snaps at me with that newfound sarcastic edge I can't help but find attractive, even in this insane situation we're in.

"Well, yeah," Kai responds before I can. "Obviously I'd be here. Although, I've never been called giant before." He smirks at Kara like he always does, not realizing that this could be the most volatile we've ever seen her.

"And who the fuck are you?" Kara quips, hands going to her hips in defiance.

Kai's face falls, and he looks at her before his gaze swings to me, like I have all the answers. Before I have a chance to explain, Damien bursts through the trees in wolf form, and I mentally curse. *Nope, now she'll be the most volatile.* Why the fuck didn't I ask him to shift before he got back here?

Kara screams. Actually screams. She also forgets she almost broke her ankle half an hour ago, and takes off in a poor attempt of a run. She takes all of four steps before I grab her around the waist and begin to start from square one with her like I did in the forest. At the same time, I speak to Damien through our bond to shift and find clothes for both of us, like yesterday.

"Hey, it's okay. I promise. No one here will hurt you. You have my word. You're safe. Please, give us a chance to help you," I say the words as gently as I can, cooing to her like I would to a small child. The worst part is, every second, she slips further and further away from the woman who makes me whole.

Thankfully, Kara stops screaming and trying to get away, but is shaking like a leaf. And shit, are those tears? What the fuck do I do with tears?

"It's a wolf. A fucking wolf, and none of you seem to care!" Kara says almost frantically between breaths that come way too fast for my liking. She looks over her shoulder around my body, and she gasps. Without even turning around, I know what she saw. Damien shifted back to his human form and is walking towards the back door of the pack house.

"Where's the wolf? It was right there..." Kara whispers. Well, at least she's not crying. I'll take what I can get at the moment.

"Wait, he's naked," she says with a gasp. "You're naked." She looks up at me like she's just put two and two together, and I know what's coming at this point.

Panic and a new attempt to bolt. Fuck my life.

"Oh my God! What the hell is this? Let me go!" Kara starts flailing and scratching me. What's crazy is, I'm actually upset her nails aren't lengthening into claws. If they did, I'd know it was going to be okay. Right now, I don't know anything.

"Please, it will be okay, I promise," I coo into her ear, trying to get through the blind panic that has taken over her again.

CHAPTER THREE

Left panic

ZANDER

THIS PANIC IN HER eyes—it's exactly the same panic Carmen said Kara had on her face before she bolted. Carmen is Kara's best friend. A five-foot nothin' spitfire that upended her own life to follow her best friend to a new pack without a question. She's the one that came barging into my office while I was in a meeting with Damien and Kai about that crazy witch we found on our land, and basically screamed at us that Kara bolted! Just remembering that look in Carmen's eyes will haunt me.

———

"SHE'S GONE!" CARMEN SCREAMED. "She just got this wild look in her eyes. Like she had no idea where she was, and just ran! Nothing I did would stop her!" She collapsed to the floor and started sobbing.

"Who's gone?" Damien was the first of us to gain their bearings, as per usual. He's always the business-first one out of our trio. That's why he's my second.

"Kara!" Carmen said between sobs. "She just left."

"What? Where?" It's all I could string together as I fought with every ounce of my strength to keep from shifting. I jumped to my feet and headed towards the door, fighting with all my strength to keep my wolf at bay. My thoughts derailed on my mate and where she could be.

Ever since we found our mate, my wolf had been riding me like no other. I'd never been this volatile. According to my father, it was what happens to newly mated shifters until their mate goes into their first heat, and the bond is cemented. It can take days, weeks, or months. There's no timeline. And I'm an Alpha, so my volatility is more than most. Dad said it was three months for him and mom, and he about killed his best friend for giving her a hug one time

I BLINK AND REMEMBER I'm trying to calm down my beautiful, albeit frantic, mate.

"Kara, honey, please just let me help. Please," I beg her. I don't know what else to do at this point. The last time I begged for anything was the day my father died. We had been injured on a scouting mission. A mission that shouldn't have been a problem. But something happened, and it went south fast. His injuries were too severe for even his enhanced healing to fix, and we weren't near any healers. I still remember that day four years ago like it was yesterday. I begged for him to come back to me, just like I'm begging Kara now.

Kara starts sobbing. She's left the panic and has moved to terror. My heart shatters. There is no fixing this right now, is there?

Damien appears out of nowhere, fully dressed—thank fuck—and has a pair of gym shorts in his hand for me. He looks at the scene in front of him, and has one hell of a confused look on his face. It's at that moment I realize I should have told them what's going on way before this moment. But I was so concerned with Kara, I didn't even think about it.

What the hell is going on? Damien asks me through the bond.

I'd like to know too, Kai chimes in.

I close my eyes, praying for strength to say the words that have been breaking me for the last half hour. *She doesn't know who she is, who we are, or even what she is.*

The witch! Kai's eyes go wide as he puts it together way faster than even I did. Thankfully, he's still using the bond link.

What do we do? I have never felt so helpless. Even when my mom died. This is a new level of torture.

What about the safe house in town? We can put her up there. She'll still be somewhere we can monitor, but she'll feel like we are giving her space. Damien, ever the pragmatic one, states matter-of-factly.

That could work. We just have to convince her, I say back. Kara is looking at me now, and I realize none of us have said anything for the last minute or two, and it's freaking her out. Not enough to try to get away, but actually the opposite. She's frozen in place—eyes darting between us.

"How about this," I offer on a sigh. "How about Kai—that's the one who was here when we got here—takes you to an apartment we have in town where you can relax, take a shower, eat, whatever you need. Then, when you're ready, we can figure this out together. How does that sound?"

"You're not going to keep me prisoner?" Kara asks, genuinely surprised by my suggestion.

Is that what she thinks is going on? Shit, this is so much worse than I thought. I'm still holding her in my arms, but she stopped fighting a while ago. I lean back to look into her eyes.

"No, of course not. We just want you to be comfortable, and it's obvious being around me, well us, is a lot right now. I want you to have what you need." *Resigned, I might add.* "Even space."

She closes her eyes and takes a deep breath. I hold mine, praying this will work.

"Okay," Kara says so quietly that if I didn't have the hearing I do, I would have missed it. "I'll go. That seems like a safer option, anyway. He's not some crazed monster-wolf thing."

Don't even say anything, I growl through the bond to both Damien and Kai. Luckily, they have the sense to keep their mouths shut and not show their thoughts on their faces.

"Come on," Kai tentatively reaches a hand towards her, and I have to fight back a growl as she takes his hand. At any other time, I would have ripped off Kai's—or any man's, for that matter—head off for touching what's mine. But right now, that will make everything worse.

Kai leads Kara to the front of the house towards his massive truck he swears he 'has to have 'cause it picks up chicks and dicks.'

As Kara climbs into the front passenger seat, I can't help but feel like my world is falling apart, and there is nothing I can do about it. But this is for the best, I think. Hell, I don't even know what 'the best' is right now.

They take off down the drive, and Damien looks at me.

"You better explain what the hell is going on, 'cause if this is going to affect the pack, I need to know." Damien growls.

"Come on, I need a drink. I'll tell you everything," I respond in kind, because sometimes his pack-first mentality really pisses me off.

We head inside and I do just that, explain what I know. Which isn't much.

CHAPTER FOUR

Not some crazed monster–wolf thing

KARA

TEN MINUTES EARLIER

"Where's the wolf? It was right there..." I whisper, because at this point, I'm all cried out. There's so much happening all at once, and I don't know what to focus on. A wolf came out of the woods, but now a man has taken his...oh, *shit*. My mind reels as I start to put the pieces together.

There's no way.

"Wait, he's naked," I gasp at Zander, who looks just as terrified as me, but why would he be so? "You're naked."

What the actual fuck? He's a fucking wolf, too! He has to be. Renewing my efforts to get away, the absolute panic I was feeling in the woods is back. "Oh my God, what the hell is this? Let me go!" I scream at him, flailing my arms and trying to scratch him or whatever else I can do to make him let me go. I dig my nails into his massive arms, trying to get some sort of purchase. If I can just...get...myself...free... But this mountain man isn't even budging. GAH!

"Please, it will be okay, I promise," Zander whispers into my ear what I'm sure is meant to placate me and calm me down. "Kara, honey, please let me help. Please." Why does he sound almost desperate? Like he genuinely cares? He's maintaining his notion that we are mates—*bonded*. Isn't that the term he used? There's a part of me that seems to recognize him, but I have no connection to him. Zero.

The war inside me continues to rage as I try to find some sort of foothold in my own mind. I start sobbing because this whole situation is just too much. I'm tired, but I'm also terrified—my mind feels like a muddled mess. The wolf-man thing shows back up fully clothed, and has clothes for Zander, too. He looks confused, and just stares at Zander, not even saying anything.

The three men don't speak a word, but their focus on each other intensifies while their eyes go hazy. It feels like time stops. The strangeness of the situation is enough to calm me and dry my tears. I know I'm staring, but the freakiness of the situation makes it impossible to turn away. *What the fuck is going on?*

Zander looks back down at me and sighs. "How about this? How about Kai—that's the one who was here when we got here—takes you to an apartment we have in town where you can relax, take a shower, eat, whatever you need. Then, when you're ready, we can figure this out together. How does that sound?"

I stare back in shock. This isn't a hostage situation. "You're not going to keep me prisoner?" I ask between heaving breaths that are way too shallow for the amount of oxygen I need to make my brain work through what he's saying.

"No, of course not. We just want you to be comfortable, and it's obvious being around me, well us, is a lot right now. I want you to have what you need." Zander closes his eyes like he's praying for strength. "Even space."

I close my eyes and take the first deep, calming breath I've taken in probably the last twenty minutes. The reality is this is my only option, and might be my only way to get out of here. "Okay," I whisper, because words are beyond me right now. I'm too wrung out. "I'll go. That seems like a safer option, anyway. He's not some crazed monster-wolf thing." At least I hope he's not.

Kai slowly reaches a hand towards me like I will freak out again, and I just might, honestly. "Come on." Zander stiffens, which confuses me even more. I glance up at him before taking Kai's waiting hand. The look on Zander's face is a mix of anger and true fear. I don't get it.

Kai leads me around the front of the house towards the drive and one of the biggest trucks I've ever seen. It would be impressive if I wasn't so...well, everything.

He opens the passenger door for me, and I climb into the cab. As Kai walks around, I catch a glimpse of Zander and the other broody one. Zander looks like his life is ending, and the broody one looks confused and pissed. Both reactions seem strange.

Kai climbs into the driver's seat and looks over. "Ready?"

"Sure," I snip. "Not like I have a choice."

Kai looks at me with a quizzical look before he replies, "You have all the choices. It just feels like you don't right now. Let's get you to that apartment, and you'll feel better. Yeah?"

I take another deep breath as I nod. Kai puts the truck into drive, and we take off down the winding lane towards, hopefully, freedom.

CHAPTER FIVE

The fastest, if not dumbest, way

KARA

WE SIT IN SILENCE during the twenty-minute drive. I've glanced over multiple times, and Kai looks like he wants to say something. I finally can't take it anymore. "What is it?"

"Nothing. Just trying to figure out what's going on." He smiles at me in a familiar way that makes me more uncomfortable.

"Same, this whole thing just seems wrong," I reply.

"Zander really is trying to help. He's kind of an ass, but he cares." That's supposed to make me feel better?

"Sure, whatever you say."

"It's true. He's the Alpha. It's his nature."

"I have no idea what that means. But fine, let's just say I believe you. This is all still too much."

Kai glances over at me with a smile that seems genuine. "I get it. That's why we're going to the apartment, so you have space and time."

All I can do is nod while I look around as we drive. I need to get away, and I don't know this area at all. As we pull into the parking lot, I continue to stare straight ahead, wracking my brain for a way to escape. The engine cuts off, and after a moment of silence, I glance over at Kai who is staring at me expectantly. "What?" I ask.

"Wait here, I want to make sure the place is still secure for you, then you can come up and get settled."

There's no way he's going to leave me alone. I stare at him for probably too long, but finally nod and say, "Yeah, that's fine," while I try to hide my renewed excitement.

Jumping out of the truck, Kai heads towards the door, and I watch him until he goes inside. I close my eyes and take a deep breath, trying to calm my racing heart. Opening my eyes, I scan the area, making sure it's clear before I throw the door open and half fall, half jump out of the truck. *Why is this damn truck so big?* Stumbling to my feet, I take off in some semblance of a run—or try to. *Damn ankle.*

I take off down the street and realize I need to stop trying to run. Between my half-ass attempt to run and frantic scanning for somewhere to go, people are starting to stare. I slow down and take the next corner, looking around for something Flower shop, drug store, hardware store, *there!* Gas station. This is a stupid idea, but what other choice do I have?

Walking into the station parking lot, I scan for someone to ask for help. Noticing a trucker headed back to his truck, I make my way towards him since he doesn't seem that murderous. *Most serial killers look like they won't kill you, but they still do,* says that voice in my head, but it doesn't matter. I need to get far away from here, and this seems like the fastest, if not dumbest, way.

I tentatively approach him, and he looks up as I walk up to him. "Can I help you, miss?"

"Umm, yeah. I was wondering if you would be willing to drive me to the next town over, or further if you can. I'm running from my crazy ex, and I don't have any way to get out of here." I look around like I'm scared someone will see me.

Because, yeah, I am—I'm not actually pretending. The *crazy ex* part might or might not be a lie. That part is to be determined.

"I normally don't give rides to people," he states flatly, and my shoulders fall. I knew this was a dumb idea. "But, you seem genuinely in need of some help, so get in. I can take you as far as Gray's Creek. That's about forty-five minutes south of here."

"Oh my God, thank you." I smile like a crazy person, but I'm just riding this good luck train and seeing where it leads.

He walks me over to the passenger door and opens it for me. I climb in while he gets back around to the driver's side, and pray to whatever power runs the universe that I'm not going to be some statistic.

As we drive down the road, I slowly calm down and my adrenaline starts to crash. I know I need to stay awake, but it's a true struggle. My leg starts vibrating and I once again am wide awake. Adrenaline pumping, I pull what I realize is a phone out, and see a picture of Kai on the screen. He's calling! Immediate decline!

Nope, nope. Nope! I turn the phone off as quickly as I can and shove it in my back pocket.

"You alright over there?" the driver guy questions.

I jump at his words, but recover quickly. "Yeah, sorry. Just the ex. I didn't realize I hadn't turned my phone off."

He regards me with curiosity, but doesn't pry. When we arrive in Gray's Creek, he asks if there is anywhere I want him to drop me off to.

"Is there a motel somewhere? I just want to get cleaned up and sleep for a bit."

"Yeah, just up the way," he replies and pulls over along the road in front of a run-down motel. "Do you have any money?" He looks over at me and I stare at him. Crap. How the fuck did I not think about paying for things?

My shoulders sag in a mix of disappointment and frustration. "No, I didn't even think about that when I ran."

He pulls out his wallet and hands me a couple hundred dollars. "Here, I don't know what you're running from, but whatever it is seems like it's not great. Take this. It's not a lot, but it will buy you a room for the night, and maybe a good meal and a bus ticket out of here."

I give him a watery smile as I accept his generosity. "Thank you. I truly don't know how I would even have made it this far without you."

"You're welcome. Just, how about not hitchhiking anymore? It's not actually that safe." He chuckles as I get out of the truck and limp my way to the front office, to hopefully get a room and figure out what the hell to do next.

I lay down on the bed and stare up at the stain-covered ceiling. God, I wish I could just remember anything before the damn woods. It's not like I've forgotten how to function in society. I just don't know who I am or what any of it means. Curling onto my side, I try to make sense of what I should be doing as tears start coming faster and faster. My reality comes crashing down around me. The confusion, pain, heartache—which I can't understand—and utter desolation of my situation hits me with the force of a tsunami.

Minutes—hours?—later, my eyes are puffy and my chest hurts. But I roll off the bed and head to the bathroom for a much-needed shower. I strip out of my disgusting clothes and realize I have nothing else to wear. I'm going to have to figure that out, too. For the first time since this whole mess started, I look at my reflection in the bathroom mirror and let out a small scream.

Oh my God. I look horrible. No wonder that trucker looked at me with pity and the front desk worker asked if I wanted the police. TWICE! I don't just have puffy eyes and red cheeks from crying. I look like someone just tried to chase me through the woods.

Ha! That's ironic.

I go to turn on the shower, and the water barely gets above tepid. It's fine, whatever. After longer than I wanted, the water is cold and my hair and body are finally clean. I can't go putting my gross clothes back on, so I wrap myself in a towel that has seen better days and slide under the itchy, thirty-year-old covers.

Tomorrow, I'll have to figure out food and clothes. I have about a hundred and sixty-five dollars left after paying thirty-five dollars for the room for the night. I'm pretty sure the front desk person gave me some crazy discount, but I'm grateful for it. I'll find some food and get some clean clothes. Maybe spend a second night here. Guaranteed bed and all. Then I'll find a bus station and just go somewhere. It's not hard to hide your identity when you don't even know it.

I fall asleep to the sounds of the people next door having a much better time than I am.

CHAPTER SIX

His phone is in pieces, again

ZANDER

SITTING IN MY OFFICE—THE place this whole mess started in—I lean back in my chair, away from my desk. Closing my eyes, I lean my head back and take a deep breath, trying to center myself. *It's not working.* The desk has way too many pressing matters I need to deal with, but there is nothing that I can do because of where my mind is. It's singularly focused on Kara. Is she okay? I know she's scared—that's damn obvious. How's Kai dealing with her? I know I picked Kai to take her because Damien would have made things so much worse. I love the man like my brother, but he has zero ability to separate the safety of the pack from anything else.

"Let me get this straight." Damien cuts through my brooding thoughts from the sofa on the other side of the room. "That witch we ran off our lands two days ago? She's the reason Kara doesn't have any memory of herself or us?" The contemplative broody male across from me stares me down like I have all the answers and I'm keeping them from him.

"That's my guess," I say with a sigh that comes from my soul. It causes Damien to shift uncomfortably. It's only then I realize I'm projecting. My dominance as an Alpha is oozing out of me unconsciously. I'm so wound up and worried that my normal handle on my wolf is fraying at an alarming rate.

Find her! my wolf practically snarls in my head.

I will, I reply in the same tone. My wolf and I don't verbally communicate often. When we do, it's usually when the short leash I keep him on—and my temper—is fraying.

"Sorry," I say as I pull back on the aura and make a conscious effort to lock it down. "This whole thing has me so fucked."

"I understand that," Damien says as he visibly relaxes, but maintains an edge to his tone I don't like. "You haven't completed your bond yet, so you're already on edge, and this isn't helping the situation. Stands to reason you'd be testy."

"Testy? That's what you're going with?" I raise my eyebrow at him.

"Yes, testy." The sarcasm practically rolls off of him. "You're more than a little distracted, throwing your aura around like it's nothing. You were already on edge before all this, and now it's worse," he says with a chuckle. What the fuck is wrong with this man?

It's been about thirty minutes since they left, meaning they should be there by now. Kai should be texting or calling with an update soon. He's too far to use the pack link. Before my thoughts fully form, my phone rings, and I answer without looking.

"Well?" It's all I say before Kai's frantic and nervous voice comes on the phone.

"She's gone." I stand up, the force causing the chair to fall back behind me, and Damien jumps to his feet, too.

"What the hell did you just say?" I seethe, my vision starting to go red. My wolf is so close to the surface right now, he might force a shift—and then we'd all be fucked. Grabbing onto the last piece of my control, I take a couple breaths while waiting for Kai's response.

Kai audibly gulps and takes a breath before continuing, "I went into the apartment to make sure it was secure, and when I came out, the door to my truck was open and Kara was gone. I tried to track her, but there's nothing. I couldn't pick up her scent. Nothing. I'm sorry, Zander. I really fucked up here. What do you want me to do?"

He keeps talking, trying to get me to respond, but I don't hear him. My vision fully turns red, and I throw the phone at the wall, shattering it. I turn around and slam my fist into the wall so hard the plaster cracks and my knuckles split, but I keep punching. When that doesn't calm me down, I turn around, only to see Damien has moved closer to me while still maintaining some distance. As my second, he's the only one who has a chance of keeping me from falling off the ledge of my sanity. But I don't think even he can stop what's about to happen.

Damien draws his phone out and answers without taking his eyes off me. Doesn't he know looking me in the eye right now is a dumbass move? For that, I want to hurt him just like I'm hurt. I step towards him, but at the last second, I turn towards my desk and with an unholy howl, I flip it—my computer and the papers fly in every direction.

In the back of my mind, I make note of Damien talking to someone on the phone. Probably Kai, the motherfucker. I'm going to kill him when he gets back here. He fucked everything up more than it already was. He let my mate run away.

"Yeah, he's taking it as well as you'd expect," Damien says, almost casually. "So far we've lost the wall, his desk, and his phone is in pieces—again."

I turn on him. What the hell does it matter if my desk is destroyed? Kara is gone. We have no way of tracking her. As I stalk towards him, my vision goes completely red. What gives him the right to be so nonchalant about this? My mate is alone and scared, and I can't do a goddamned thing about it—I vaguely notice my wolf hasn't fully taken over and let me rage.

"I'm going to call you back. Keep searching and let me know if you find anything," Damien says before he sets his phone on the bookcase near him—never taking his eyes off me. He's got half a brain at least because he isn't looking directly at my eyes now, but it's still challenging my wolf—and I might just let my wolf have this one.

"Brother," Damien raises his hands in surrender, "You don't want to do this. We need you to get a grip on your wolf so we can figure out how to find Kara. That's what you want, right? To find your mate and bring her back safely?"

I take another menacing step towards Damien and growl, "I want her back *now*. She's mine." My voice is layered with a deeper one. There's a lisp to my words, and I realize my canines have elongated just like my claws on my fingers. My wolf is just below the surface, and I don't know if I can keep him at bay much longer. I don't know if I want to.

I've always been more volatile than most. Alpha genes tend to do that to you. Then I found my mate, and it got worse. Now she's gone because of some damned witch and the stupidity of my so-called friend—not just my friend, my third!

Damien and I circle each other, him as non-threateningly as he can, and me trying to rein in my control so I don't kill my best friend. I need to get a hold of myself.

"I know she's yours. She's important to me, too. She's our Luna. *We* need her to keep the pack stable and balanced. We just need to figure out a way to find her." Damien's words finally cut through the haze, and the reality of what he's saying makes it to my brain. I don't just need her, the pack does, too. So does her father's pack. He might still be leading it, but I know he was looking forward to stepping down when Kara was ready.

I stop. Just stop. I try to breathe through the constant panic and fear that's gripped me for the last few hours. We need to get her back, but me going off the rails isn't going to accomplish that.

"We need to find her," I repeat.

"We will. We need to get Callum here. He will find her or at least give us a starting point," Damien says as he reaches for his phone again, looks down briefly to find the contact, and makes the call. Callum must be too far away for the pack link to work, or he's ignoring it.

I stalk to the other side of the room and grab my bottle of Four Roses Single Barrel, and pour myself a three-finger pour. Thank fuck I didn't destroy my bar.

I turn back towards Damien who raises an eyebrow at me. I shrug and drink half of it down in one go.

"I need you to get to the pack house ASAP, and bring your laptop and whatever else you need to track someone," Damien tells Callum. Callum is in my inner circle, and a world-class computer whiz—more accurately, a hacker. Probably half the stuff he does is illegal, but I don't give a shit. He keeps our tech in tip-top shape and knows his way around the finance world. He's partially the reason our pack has gone from one of the midrange packs wealth-wise to one of the top packs.

"I don't care what you need to bring, just get your ass here now. Alpha needs your unique skill set like yesterday," Damien all but growls into the phone and hangs up. Oh, so he *is* affected by this whole thing.

"Callum said he's got to run by his house to grab the stuff, but will be here in thirty minutes. Do you really think alcohol is a good idea right now? It usually makes it easier for your wolf to force a shift." Damien is the only one in this pack that has the balls to say shit like that to me.

"Probably not, but if I don't do something to calm myself down, I'll shift. And I don't know if I'll be able to wrestle control back anytime soon," I say with a sigh. The reality of my own words is a punch to the gut. I'm close to breaking. I need to get my shit together.

"Well, you've got less than thirty minutes before Callum gets here and to get yourself under a semblance of control, otherwise you risk killing the one person we know who can figure out where Kara went," Damien says as he sits back down, like the last ten minutes didn't happen.

I shoot back the other half of my drink and refill my glass before I stalk back over to my desk—well, what's left of my desk. My chair is also in shambles. I really liked that desk, too. Making a mental note to deal with this mess tomorrow, I grit my teeth and say, "Maybe we should go wait in the hall so we can head to the security room when Callum gets here."

"Sounds good to me." Damien stands and heads to the hall without even looking back. The fucker has a death wish, but knows I won't actually kill him—might punch him in the back of the head to prove a point though. Then again, maybe I won't. I groan and follow him out, finishing my whiskey and putting the glass on a side table as I walk out of the room.

Twenty-five minutes later, Callum walks in with his normal devil-may-care expression. He may be a tech guru, but like the rest of us, he's built like a brick wall. His leaner build, blond hair, and blue eyes make him the most eligible bachelor in our pack. His smile falters when he takes in the look on both our faces.

"What happened?" Callum asks as he looks between us.

The quick explanation Damien gives has Callum turning almost green. I stand off to the side, silently waiting for Damien to shut up.

"Oh shit," Callum says, almost refusing to believe what he's heard. I know he's realized the seriousness of this whole fucking mess. "The way Damien talked on the phone, it sounded bad so I brought all the stuff I would need for any type of tracking. I'll do what I can to find her, Alpha," he adds the last part because I know my aura isn't really under control, and it makes him nervous.

We head over to the security room, and Callum gets to work, setting up and plugging God knows what together to make the computer do what he wants.

"Where was the last place anyone saw Kara?" Callum asks no one in particular as he begins typing away at his computer.

"At the safe house on Grand in town," Damien says. "Kai was taking her there for..." He trails off, and I jump in.

"Something happened, and Kara got spooked and ran. We have no way of tracking her through normal means," I say through gritted teeth.

"Zander, pull it back," Damien says with a sigh, and I realize he's talking about my aura. I take a breath and pull it back in, then see Callum visibly relax. Cal is a Gamma, so he's not as strong as Day or K, and the aura hits him harder. He's technically my fifth.

"Okay, I have a starting point, so I'm going to tap into every camera I can so we can get an idea of where she went," Callum says and goes back to his computer. "This could take me a bit because that's the area of town with the least cameras, so I'll have to be thorough with each one."

"Just find her, please," I say and fall into the other chair to wait.

Chapter Seven

Hobo chic

Kara

I WAKE UP THE next morning after what feels like the worst night of sleep of my life. I can't shake the feeling that the dreams that plagued me were not dreams, but memories. But no matter how hard I try to remember as I lay here, I can't.

My reality crashes back around me as the light of the dawn seeps through the crack in the curtains. I formulate a basic plan with simple steps. Small victories equal happiness, right? Step one, figure out how to clean my clothes so I don't look like a complete hobo. Step two, find something to eat. Step three, figure out where to go next.

Last night, I thought I might stay here another night so I could get a better grip on my circumstances, but I think I'm going to find the bus station and head somewhere else. The less time I'm in one place, the better.

I groan and drag myself out of bed, wrapping the towel I used as makeshift night clothes around myself and head towards my pile of discarded clothes on the floor. The leggings I was wearing yesterday seem mostly just dirty, except for a couple of rips where the ground decided to come up and claw me. It doesn't look horrible, I guess. I shake them and most of the dried dirt flies off in the dust cloud, so I call that good. My underwear and bra are going to have to do.

My shirt is a whole other story. When I pick it up, I realize just how bad of a shape it's in. Luckily, it was a baggy tee, so I do some fancy ripping and tying to create some sort of half-assed intentional mess of a shirt. Hobo chic. Good enough for a girl on the run.

I pick up the rest of the cash and the phone I have yet to turn back on. I'll sell it to someone and get some more cash—at least I think I will. Taking a last look back at the safe haven I've had for the last fifteen hours, I head to the front office to check out and see if they can give me some direction.

Ten minutes later, I'm walking down the sidewalk towards a diner that the front desk worker recommended. I know I look crazy, but honestly, I can't help it. As I walk down the street, it's impossible not to constantly look around.

Maybe you shouldn't be looking around like a crazy person if you don't want to be noticed, a small voice in my head that doesn't quite sound like myself says with so much attitude I almost flinch. As weird and uncomfortable as it makes me, the strange voice is right. I need to act like I'm just a girl headed to a diner for breakfast—at the ass crack of dawn. What could go wrong?

I walk up to the front door of South Side Diner, take a deep breath, and walk in. It's still early, so the only customers are the old men drinking coffee in the corner. A middle-aged woman who looks like she's seen a lot, but has a kind face, looks up from where she's refilling the coffee of some of the men.

"Welcome in, hun. Take a seat anywhere and I'll be over with a menu and some coffee," she says as she raises the coffee carafe in indication.

Looking around, I choose a booth near the back corner, away from the windows. I might not have a quick exit if I need it, but I'm also not going to be spotted by a passerby.

Just as I sit down with a defeated sigh, the server comes over with a coffee cup and a menu. "Hi, hun, I'm Susan. What can I get ya started with?" After she sets down the menu and coffee, she looks up at me with a smile that falters as she takes me in. Recovering quickly, the look of sympathy doesn't leave her eyes.

"Umm," I say, taking a brief look at the menu and deciding on the first thing that sounds halfway decent, but also cheap. "I'll just take two eggs scrambled, and two pieces of bacon, please."

"Sure, hun. Anything besides coffee to drink? OJ? Coke?"

That all costs money, and I can't afford to waste what little I have left. "How about just a water?"

"Of course." A knowing look crosses her face. *Is it that obvious?* That I'm some scared girl that doesn't know what to do or where to turn? "I'll get that put in for you and bring you over a water."

She turns with a smile and heads to turn in the ticket to the kitchen. I sit and stare at the coffee in front of me. The swirling steam coming off it entrances me for just a moment while I sit and think about how I'm ever going to get through the next steps of this crazy plan.

A few minutes later, Susan is back with my water and a plate of food. My eggs and bacon sit nicely next to a few pieces of toast, two links of sausage, and a bowl of fruit. I look up at her with a mix of confusion, fear, and a hint of hope.

"I know you didn't order all this, but don't worry. It's on the house. I get it. Something happened, and you're scared and running. You need more than two eggs and a couple pieces of bacon." She looks at me with more care and sympathy than I feel I deserve, but I'm grateful nonetheless.

"Thank you." The burning in my eyes is the only warning I get before a single tear falls down my face.

"Don't worry about it. Eat up." She smiles and turns with her coffee carafe in hand, heading back over to the men and their coffee club.

I take a deep breath as I pick up my fork and begin to eat the first meal I think I've had in ages—*when was the last time I ate?*—hoping this is a sign of things to come.

Susan pops back over as I'm finishing up. "How was that?" She smiles.

"Really good, thank you."

Susan looks around like she's looking for something or someone, but turns to me and asks, "Where are you headed, if you don't mind my asking?"

"I...don't know," I say honestly. "I hitchhiked here, and don't know where to go next. I was hoping to get to a bus station and head out of town. But I'm not sure where it is."

"You're actually not far from it. About two blocks north of here. I know a bus leaves in a little over an hour for Frankfort. It's the closest city to here. I have a friend that lives there and owns a bar. They are always looking for help. I'll give her a call and pretend you're my cousin. Give you a good recommendation. I'm sure she will give you a chance. What's your name, sweetie?" She rattles off so much information that my head swims.

I stutter for a moment before I answer, "Kara, my name is Kara Holt." I pause at that, because my last name isn't Holt, but it's the name I seem to have to give. Like it's correct, but new.

"Well Kara, I hope you find your way." She takes out her notepad and writes down her friend's name, phone number, and the bar's address. Susan rips it out and hands it to me with a smile that says so much. *I see you. I understand you. I was in your shoes once.* While I don't think she was in my exact situation, I think she did go on the run at some point and landed here.

"Thank you, again. How much do I owe you for breakfast?"

"I told you. It's on the house. Now get moving. You don't want to miss that bus." Susan smiles and waves towards the door.

I smile too, get up, and head towards the door. I turn around and say goodbye to my new friend with a wave, and head out into the morning towards the bus station and apparently, a potential job.

Four hours later, I step off a bus in Frankfort with a paper clutched in my hand that gives me all the basic info of Susan's friend, Ada, and a general idea of where I need to go. I don't even get ten steps from the bus when a woman in her mid-forties approaches me with a smile. "Are you Kara?"

"Umm, yes..." I say with a lot of apprehension. This could go one of two ways.

"I'm Ada. Susan called me and said you were going to be coming in on this bus, so I thought it would be easier to meet you and help you get settled." Ada is tall and willowy, but has a smile that makes you want to be near her. At the same time, you can tell she owns a bar. She's intense.

"Oh, that was nice of her," I awkwardly respond. At least this isn't someone trying to take me back.

Ada smiles again. "Susan said you were a bit skittish. Seems there's a lot going on that you need a bit of help through. I get it, sometimes we all just need a hand. Especially when we are running with no place to go. Come on, my car is just over there. I've got an extra bedroom, and I think I even have some clothes that will fit. Let's go get you settled, then I'll take you by the bar and introduce you to my staff."

I freeze. "Wait! Just like that? You don't even know me. I could be some crazed serial killer or something?" I say, shocked by this whole exchange. I put my hands up like I'm trying to defend myself. Ada is a lot, and I don't even know what to do with it.

"Honey, it's okay. I was in your shoes once. So was Susan. We made a promise to each other that if we ever came across another young woman who seemed like she needed help escaping whatever was going on, we would help."

She wraps her arms around my shoulders in a protective hug that makes me melt. I don't have any other options, so I might as well.

We head across town to a townhome that gives off a comfortable vibe. As I walk in, I notice how little green grass and trees are around. It's all concrete and stone. I don't know why, but it makes my chest ache. Like part of me is missing nature. I shake off the strange feeling and follow Ada inside.

"Now I know it's not much, but it's home. There is a spare room upstairs and a bathroom right next to it. That will be where you are. I'll rummage around and find some clothes I think will work until we can get you to a store and get you some of your own things." Ada talks while she points things out, and I follow like a lost puppy. "Like I said, it's my bar. So of course you can have a job. Have you ever been a server?"

Ada keeps going without waiting for me to answer. She's a force of nature, and it's all I can do to orbit around her. "No matter, it's pretty easy. You just take orders, and the bartenders will make everything. We might stick you behind the bar some if you're comfortable. We split tips between servers and bartenders, but you'll make plenty to get yourself on your feet soon enough."

It's so much to process. Just last night, my world was crashing down around me. I still have no idea who I am or what is going on, but at least this will help—I think.

"Why don't you head upstairs and take a shower? I'll put some clothes on your bed, then we will head to the bar." Ada looks back at me with another one of those *everything is okay* smiles.

I smile back at her with a nod, and head for the stairs. This shower feels ten times better than the one I had last night. The water is a better temperature. The shampoo and soap smell like heaven. I just stand in the spray for a long while, letting the last twenty-four hours wash down the drain. I may be confused and lost, but with Ada, I feel found. Even if it's only temporary.

CHAPTER EIGHT

Fuck me sideways

ZANDER

I RUB MY EYES and stretch as the morning light spills in through the window of my office. Sitting in my chair and staring out at the forest around, I struggle to focus on anything in particular.

I didn't sleep a wink last night, and I can feel it. As a wolf, I don't need as much sleep as humans, but damn, not getting any still sucks. But how am I supposed to sleep when my mate is out there? My wolf hasn't calmed down since this whole damn mess started. He's riding me hard to just start looking for her. But I can't do that 'cause I have zero clue where to start.

Callum spent the entire night tracking Kara. I bugged him every fifteen minutes for the first couple hours, but Damien finally forced me to leave the security room because I was making everyone tense, and also making Callum's job ten times harder.

Sometime after midnight, I went to the gym with Damien, and we spent a few hours beating the shit out of each other. The only way either of us knows how to deal with the kind of pent-up aggression I'm feeling. We've been friends since we were just newly shifted. I've known I was an Alpha since I was born—family line and all that. But for most shifters, it's not until you shift for the first time that your strength within the pack begins to show. When Damien shifted for the first time, it was obvious he was strong. His parents presented him to my dad, the Alpha, because they knew he would need specialized training to hone the power he had.

I met him the same day. I was a year older, but my dad thought Damien would be a good sparring partner for me. He was right. What he didn't expect was the friendship and intense bond that was forged between us as we both got the shit beat out of us while we grew into the wolves we were meant to be. I knew before we even graduated high school that Damien would be my second.

The memories of our time growing up in this intense, crazy world help ground me as the chaos around me keeps pressing in.

"Alpha?" I turn when I hear Kai address me formally from the door. I haven't directly spoken to him since he got back around 2:00 a.m. He had been scouring the area trying to find and fix his fuck up. Am I still pissed? Absolutely. But I also know the whole reason he went into the apartment first was because he was doing the one thing he's done since Kara came to our pack. He took up the mantle of her personal guard almost immediately, so it was natural for him to want to secure the place before she went in. In the light of the morning, I realize he was only doing his job.

I groan, rubbing my eyes again. "What is it, Kai? And you know you don't have to call me that when it's just us."

"I wasn't sure if you were still planning on ripping my head off, so I figured I'd be safe," he says with a half-smile and a chuckle.

"Nope, you get to keep your head, but I'd probably still maintain distance. My wolf isn't as forgiving as I am," I reply with a half-hearted attempt at humor.

"Noted." Kai shifts uncomfortably. He knows how bad he fucked up, and I'm sure he doesn't fully believe I won't murder him where he stands. But, like Damien, Kai is bonded to me. We met after high school, but we clicked immediately. His sardonic, easygoing nature is the exact opposite of Damien's. My father always told me I needed balance in my inner circle to lead well, and Kai is that balance. I need both of them to run this pack. So killing either one would put a small damper on that.

"What do you want, Kai?" I ask with a sigh, rubbing the bridge of my nose to ward off the headache that's developed from lack of sleep.

"Right, yeah," he starts at my words. "Callum thinks he tracked Kara to Gray's Creek. He found her on the security feeds of different cameras in town and saw her getting into a semi. He caught the DOT tag and company name, and was able to hack the GPS system and track it to Gray's Creek. It stopped on the side of the road for like five minutes before it drove off. It was stopped in front of a motel..."

Kai keeps talking, but I just stop. I freeze on his words that we have an idea of where she was at least last evening. I'm barreling through the door before I even register I've moved, and Kai is right behind me.

"Alpha!" he says as he tries to keep up with me while I barrel through the foyer and out the front door. "She's not there anymore! We've tracked her to a couple other locations this morning."

"Fine," I growl as Damien and Callum come running outside as well. I'm halfway to my truck before I actually think about what he says. I turn to them, knowing my eyes just flashed with my wolf, and take a step towards them. "What are you saying? You lost her again?"

They freeze, but it's Damien who takes a step towards me. The only one who has a chance in hell to face my wolf if he forces his way to the surface. I've been halfway to a shift since yesterday, and this might just push my wolf too far.

"Callum tracked her via the cameras in town to a diner, then about an hour later, she walked out and headed towards what we're guessing was the bus station." Damien drops his eyes away from mine, but doesn't back down.

Callum chimes in, "My next task is to go and hack those cameras and see if I can figure out what bus she's planning to get on. I'll relay what I find."

Without another word, I turn and head to my truck, Damien and Kai on my heels. "No," I say, and they both freeze mid-step.

"Not you, Kai." Kai flinches, but that's his only reaction. "I'm fine with you coming, but I don't know what my wolf is going to do in close proximity to the person he perceives lost her. And besides, I need someone to stay here.

'Cause I'm not coming back till I have her, and someone needs to keep this place running."

"Zander, if we aren't coming back for a while, we need to grab the go bags before we leave," Damien says in his levelheaded *security-first* voice that only pisses me off. Only because he's fucking right and I know it.

I turn around and head back to the pack house to grab my go bag with Damien on my heels. Of course, my new phone chooses that exact moment to ring. Damien, in his wisdom, keeps spare phones around because I seem to break mine regularly. At some point last night, he fished my SIM card out of my old phone and put it in the new one. Growling, I fish the thing out of my pocket and groan when I see who's calling. Kara's dad, David. I was really hoping I wouldn't have to deal with this.

I answer while I rub my eyes with what I hope is a normal tone. "Hi, sir, what can I do for you?"

"Where's my daughter, Zander?" No pretense, just straight to the point. "She was supposed to call us last night, but didn't. We've tried calling her phone and texting both last night and this morning. When she didn't answer last night, I was hoping it was because you two were just busy, but her phone is now going straight to voicemail. So WHERE IS SHE!" He finishes on what can only be described as a gravelly yell.

This is one of those times I really wish I would have found my mate in any-one other than another alpha's daughter. Because this conversation is going to implode epically as soon as I open my mouth. Do I lie and say she's sleeping and forgot to charge her phone? Maybe I go with she's hanging out with Carmen and they obviously got distracted, again. It's happened before, so it's plausible. I take another breath and look up at the ceiling, bracing for the reality that's going to smash me upside the head. If I lie to this man, it will only end badly.

"We don't know," I say with a grimace, knowing the next words I say will make things ten times worse. I rush on before he has time to say anything. "Something happened to her yesterday, and she forgot who and what she was. While trying to get her to a safe house away from us because we were scaring her, she bolted.

Kara is currently on the run. Be we have a tentative location for her and are heading to retrieve her now."

"You *what now*?" David's voice is nothing but rage, and I can tell his canines have lowered. "I hear what you're saying, but you need to tell me again and with as much detail as you can before I end you and your whole pack."

Fuck me sideways. This is exactly why I didn't want to tell him in the first place.

In the background, a lot of scuffling and words are exchanged, presumably between Kara's parents, before a softer voice joins the call. "Zander, honey. What happened? Why does David look like he's going to destroy half my house?" Kara's mom, Francine Lancaster—Franny—says into the phone with a lot more gentleness than I deserve at this point.

I'm actually really glad she took the phone, because I think I'll be able to explain everything, and it will actually be absorbed by someone other than the giant alphahole that is my would-be father-in-law. I get it, I'm the same way. A raging temper that is only partially in check at the best of times is just part of being an Alpha. We all sit on the edge of a knife, and it doesn't take much to cut us.

I relay as much of the story as I possibly can, ending with saying we're going after her, and I know Franny's heart is in her throat. She's barely able to respond when she says, "I know you'll get her back, Zander. What can we do to help?"

"At this point, I have no idea. Callum is still trying to figure out where she's headed, and you guys are an hour and a half in the wrong direction to intercept her. Hang tight and I'll keep you updated."

"Honey, you know that's not going to work for David. He needs to be part of this. Also, I would prefer my house to still be standing at the end of the day."

"Why don't you guys come here and help Kai while I'm gone. He's not had to run the place without Damien or I before, and it would be helpful for someone who understands pack structure to be here." I know Kai doesn't actually need the help, but it will keep them occupied and make them feel helpful.

Kai looks at me and I speak through the bond while I'm talking to Franny. *Just humor them. They might actually be slightly helpful. Just don't let them tell the whole damn pack what happened.*

Kai nods and goes back to the security room to update Callum that the in-laws are coming to town. I snort at my own joke.

"I'll find her and bring her back," I say into the phone. "Trust me."

"I know you will, Zander. The alternative isn't acceptable," Franny says coldly, and I remember why exactly she's the Luna of Shadow Creek Pack.

I end the call and look towards Damien who has both our bags in his hands. "Let's go."

Chapter Nine

Desperate and cracking

ZANDER

"Stop fidgeting," Damien says, exasperated from the driver's seat as we head down the road. "What the hell is the problem now?"

For the last twenty minutes, we've been driving in relative silence, Damien cutting me glances as I constantly shift in my seat. I'm on edge, and he knows it. "What if we can't find her? She's been in Gray's Creek since last night, but what if we can't find her now?" I'm starting to lose my shit, and I know it. I'm desperate and cracking. Damien is the only one that sees this venerable side of me, but I still hate it.

"She won't be," Damien responds, and I whip my head towards him. If he wasn't driving, I would have clocked him.

"What the hell does that mean?" Anger takes the primary position on my emotional rollercoaster.

Damien rolls his eyes at my outburst, but responds anyway. "She's resourceful. Always has been. And she's likable. I don't think either of those traits disappeared with this mess. My guess is she will have already moved on by the time we get there. But we will be able to get a trail of where she went."

I go to argue with him, but he's right. Kara is so many things, and this memory issue isn't going to stop her from using the skills she needs to survive. Her getting away from us is proof of that. Like it or not, Damien is my second because he always has a level head. Even when I lose my shit. It pisses me off more often than not, but it's true.

"Fucking hell." I rub my hands down my face. I don't think I've ever felt this out of control.

"We will find her. But we also need to talk about the witch." Damien jumps topics like it's the weather, and it just frustrates me more.

"What about the damn witch?" I growl.

"What if the only way to get Kara back to herself is to find this witch and force the reverse of the spell, curse, whatever the hell it is? I mean, let's be honest, we should have known that pushing her off our lands would have repercussions." He glances at me with a half chuckle. "Not that any of us thought it would be Kara who would take the brunt of this."

"Of course we didn't think it would be her. She wasn't even fucking there."

"But you were. It's not a secret that you found your mate, even if you haven't finished the bond. Wolves change when they find their mate. Attitude, smell, everything. You become a new person. Witches have a sixth sense. I'm sure she knew. It probably didn't take her long to figure out who, especially since you're the Alpha of Moonrise Pack."

I want to be mad at him, but everything he says is true. Alpha matches are widely known because they can change the power of the packs. Especially our match. I'm a current Alpha, and Kara's the daughter of an Alpha, and will become an Alpha in her own right if she doesn't pass it to her younger brother.

"So you think that finding Kara needs to happen at the same time as finding the witch." It's not a question, because I'm in full agreement.

He answers anyway, "Yes, which is why before I left, I gave Kai instructions to start looking into the witch, and when Kara's parents arrive, they will help."

I grunt in acknowledgement of what he said, but don't respond. Honestly, I could give a flying fuck if we find the witch or not. Kara is my priority. My entire world shifted when I found her, and I don't think I can deal with a world without her in it.

As I'm left alone with my thoughts and Damien bringing up the witch, I can't help but let my mind drift back to that night.

—————

Alpha, there's been a breach of the parameter on the south side of the pack lands, *one of my enforcers relays to me via the pack link.*

Have you contained it? *I ask as I get up out of bed. Kara mumbles something as she rolls towards where I was. I take my pillow and give it to her. Snuggling down with it, she breathes in my scent and relaxes back into sleep. I don't want to leave her, but when my enforcers reach out to me specifically when I'm not on rotation, I know something is seriously wrong. I bend down to kiss the top of her head, breathing in her wildflower and vanilla scent. It centers me for whatever is to come. I dress quickly in gym shorts since I know I'll be shifting once I head out the door.*

Damien meets me in the foyer dressed similar to me. Low slung sweatpants hug his frame and a murderous look is on his face. This man would destroy the world to protect his pack. I can't imagine how insane he will become when he finally finds his mate.

"Do you have a general location?" I ask as I stalk past him towards the front door.

"Southside of the pack lands near the lake about a quarter mile past the south end homes," Damien says as he follows. "Kai was notified first as it's his night, but once he got out there and realized it's a bigger problem, he had Marcus wake us."

I reach out to Kai. Any update?

From what I understand, a female crossed the border about ten minutes ago. Scent makes me think she's a witch. I've been tracking her for the last five minutes, and I'm closing in, but I think you should deal with this one. I sense she's strong *Kai relays along with this location.*

I look at Damien, and he nods, dropping his sweatpants; I do the same with my shorts. We need to get there fast, and shifting is the quickest way. Shifting overtakes each of us as easily as taking our next breath. As the two most powerful wolves in the pack, our wolves are just as massive as we are in human form. Mine is a deep brown, and his is a tawny color. We grab our clothes with our teeth and head out to rendezvous with Kai.

A couple minutes later, I get my first scent of the witch. Her power is a tangible thing in the air. Why is she here? Damien skirts to the right and I take the left. I know Kai is in the front, coming from that way. We have her blocked in.

As I approach, I drop my shorts and shift back, taking a quick second to throw them on. I break into the clearing, and she's standing in the middle like she's been waiting for us to come to her. She's tall with long, blonde hair, but I can tell it's a glamour to hide her age. That kind of power doesn't come without time. Her eyes bore into me.

"What are you doing on my lands in the middle of the night? If you wanted to meet, you know the proper channels," I say, barely containing my rage.

"I didn't feel like the 'proper channels' would be the best way to convey my message," she replies with an air I don't like.

Raising my eyebrow in response, I chance a glance around and see that both Damien and Kai have also moved in. There's nowhere for her to go.

"I have been contracted to give you a message, Zander, Alpha of Moonrise Pack. You've not been in power long, but your power grows more each day. That power has created enemies, and you cannot afford to have them now more than ever." She stares straight at me—more like through me.

It's only now I realize we've actually cornered her only about twenty feet from our borders. If she crosses back onto neutral ground, there's nothing we can do. I step to the right to block that from happening, and she matches my movements, staying facing me fully.

"Is that supposed to scare me?"

"It's a warning, one you should heed."

"And what if I don't?" I scoff, crossing my arms over my chest and bracing my legs apart.

"Then the problem you will face will tear you apart." With that, she bolts towards the border faster than I would have ever guessed she could move. I lunge, but miss by inches as she breaches the border and stops. As she turns back towards me, she gives me a smile that is nothing but cold, calculating menace.

"Remember what I said," she says as she turns away and fucking vanishes.

Damien and Kai step up to my sides, and all three of us just stare at where the witch was before. Not knowing what the hell she meant about anything she said, but knowing it's not good.

CHAPTER TEN

Punch first, ask questions later

ZANDER

"Z? YOU WITH ME?" Damien asks from the driver's seat. As I refocus on my surroundings, I realize we are at the hotel Callum had pegged as where Kara stayed last night.

Everything in me screams to find her. It's not even the fact that she ran from me that fills me with rage anymore. It's that ache in my chest. Our bond. It's so new, but it's already grown so much that being without her just hurts. I don't understand how she's not feeling that same ache. Maybe since her wolf is suppressed, it's also suppressing the way she feels?

"Alright, let's go talk to the front desk. Maybe we will get lucky and she stuck around an extra day to get her bearings," I say with a defeated sigh.

"Doubtful. Like I said, she's resourceful. She will have already moved on, so we need to get a timeline to figure out how far behind we are," Damien says as he climbs out of the truck and makes his way to the front office. I follow on his heels, knowing he's going to be the one to have to speak. I'll punch first and ask questions later.

As we walk into the office, the guy behind the counter acknowledges us without even looking up from his computer. "How can I help you? Check in isn't for another few hours." On the last word, he finally looks up and visibly shudders. Typical reaction. It's not like we're normal-looking guys. Both of us have a good five inches on the guy and probably fifty pounds of muscle.

"We're not here to cause trouble, just needing some info on my friend's missing..." Damien pauses before continuing, obviously trying to figure out the right word to use with the human so it won't sound wild. "Fiancé," he finishes.

"Why are you looking for her—I mean, I don't know of anyone," the poor boy stutters.

"Where did she go?" I slam my hands on the counter, and it cracks. Damien glances at me with a raised eyebrow, and looks back at the kid who probably will shit his pants by the end of this conversation if I don't kill him first.

"She was hurt in a pretty bad accident last night, so she probably looked scratched up. Maybe even had a limp. She didn't have her cell on her, so we're assuming she came here and stayed before going somewhere else. How about you tell us where she went and we leave here with no issues?" Damien says as smoothly as he can.

"Listen, I can't just tell two random guys where a hurt girl went. What if you're abusing her?"

With that statement, I see red. I reach over the counter and grab the guy by his shirt collar. "Listen here, buddy. My fiancé is hurt and scared, and all I want is to find her and bring her home so I can help her. I would never hurt her, and the fact that you even imply that makes me want to hurt you. So be a good boy and tell me where she went before someone actually does get hurt," I growl, and I know my eyes have shifted colors. The poor bastard pisses himself.

"Okay, okay! I'll tell you, just don't hurt me!" he says with absolute terror on his face. "She wanted to know somewhere to get breakfast, so I told her to go to the diner down the street. She went down there, and about forty minutes later, I saw her walk out and head further down the street. I'm guessing the bus station. I swear, that's all I know."

I shove him backward into the chair he had vacated when we walked in. "Thank you." Without another word, Damien and I turn around and head back to the truck. Before we even get there, Damien is on the phone with Callum.

"Check the bus station footage. We got a lead that she was probably headed there." He waits for a response and continues, "We just need to know which bus she got on. I'm guessing there's only a few out of here daily, so it shouldn't be hard. We can drive faster than buses, and if she didn't leave too far ahead of us, we can beat her to her destination."

We climb in the truck and wait for Callum to do his magic. Five minutes later, the messages come through on my phone. I read them out loud to Damien who is doing some sort of research on his phone.

> **Frankfort. Bus left two hours ago**

> **Since I know the bus, I'll be able to tap the cameras when she gets off and figure out where she goes from there.**

Damien looks up from his phone at me. "We're behind her by two hours. We most likely won't be able to catch up before she arrives in Frankfort. Callum will be able to track her. What do you want to do?"

This is exactly the situation I didn't want to be in. She's out of our reach, and if she gets to a city, it's going to be next to impossible to track her quickly. Time wasn't on our side from the start, and now it's fucked us. I throw my phone on the floorboards of the truck and wrench the door open. I jump out of the truck, stripping off my shirt and take off down the roads towards the wood—fuck my pants, I'll get new ones later.

Luckily, this area is surrounded by woods, and there's no close pack lands. This is neutral territory.

The minute I cross into the woods, I shift. I'm done feeling, done controlling my wolf, done with it all. I knew shifting in this heightened state was a risk. My wolf might not give control back to me, but I don't care. Damien and Kai can handle things. I just need to be gone. Is this childish and pathetic? Probably. But with Kara gone, with no chance of finding her any time soon, I can't deal with any of it.

I faintly hear Damien in the background screaming into my head through the pack link, but I ignore him. As I run through the woods, I feel my wolf force take more and more control away, and I let him. My heart is already shattered, now my control might as well follow. My last thought before I let my wolf completely take over?

Don't kill anyone.

CHAPTER ELEVEN

Unless he's meeting someone

KARA

WHO WOULD HAVE THOUGHT that I actually have a knack for serving drinks and interacting with people? Not me. Or at least not the me that showed up in Frankfort—scared, alone, and confused as hell. Has it only been ten days since my world came crashing down around me? Seems like it's been a lifetime already. And yet, it feels like it all happened ten minutes ago.

I stand to the side of the bar, waiting for Christy to make the round of drinks table three wants, and rub my chest for what feels like the tenth time in the last hour. This weird, dull ache has been living there just under my ribs since yesterday. It's not painful, but it is concerning. Not like I'd know if this is something I'd dealt with before or anything. But here we are.

Christy sets the three beers and one water on the bar before looking at me. "You good?"

"Hmm?" I respond, realizing I'm staring off into space again. "Oh, yeah, I'm fine. Just indigestion or something. Probably just need to drink some water."

Christy raises an eyebrow at me, but doesn't comment as I take the drinks, load up my tray, and head to the table of who I've quickly learned are the annoying regulars who come in three to four times a week, but tip like shit. I plaster on a smile that I'm sure doesn't reach my eyes and set the drinks down in front of the men. I'm sure at some point in their lives they were attractive, but these sixty-somethings have been ridden hard and put away wet. It would be better if they realized it, too. Because the way they leer and try to cop a feel of every female in this place is gross.

"Anything else, guys?" I ask with a saccharine sweet smile that I'm sure will give me the typical less than one dollar tip.

"Not right now, honey, but we will be looking for you when we're ready for more," says the one I've dubbed *Creep One*.

"Great, I'll be by in a little while," I say as I back away, 'cause like hell they are getting anywhere near my ass. I made that mistake once, and never again. Ugh...the creep factor is high tonight, and it's only 6:00 p.m.

As I head to another table to clear it, I notice someone walk in, and pray they go sit at the bar. I know it's early, but I'm exhausted. I've been exhausted for days now. Heading back up to the bar to drop off the glasses so Christy can throw them in the sink, I glance at the person who decided to NOT sit at the bar, and chose the table in the corner.

"Are you sure you're okay?" Christy asks me as she takes the glasses. "You just seem tired and keep rubbing your sternum like whatever is bothering you will be rubbed away if you keep at it. It's not a good look, and our tips are going to tank. You're not pregnant, are you?"

"God, no! I've just been tired the last few days, not sleeping well. It's catching up with me. I've only taken one day off since I started. I'm sure that's it. The chest thing is something that started yesterday. Like I said, I'm fine." I sound like I'm certain it's nothing, but honestly, I might have a fatal disease and wouldn't have a clue.

"Well, you better perk yourself up and go help that guy who just came in. He's a new face, so maybe if you put on that charm, you'll get a decent tip out of him. Unless he's meeting someone." She rolls her eyes and goes back to the patrons at the bar.

I finally turn fully and start walking over to the man in the corner, coming up short. There's no way in hell. *Zander.* No, no, no, no. Why? I turn around, and that's when I realize he's staring right at me. I guess I'm not turning and bailing, am I?

Taking a breath and releasing it slowly, I start walking again, right up to his table. His piercing stare is almost too much. "Hi," I squeak out. *That's great. Good job, Kara.*

"Hey." He smiles, and it's one of those genuine smiles that makes a person look good. Wait, what? Oh, who am I kidding. He's fucking hot, but he still freaks me the fuck out.

"What are you doing here?" I try to glare at him, but I'm sure I end up looking stupid.

"I came to talk. Just talk. The way things were left, I think I made everything worse, and we need to clear the air," Zander responds in a smooth tone. "I didn't handle any of what happened well."

"Well, I guess talking is a thing that can happen, maybe. But to stay, you need to order something," I reply with a hint of annoyance.

Zander smiles again. "I'll just take a Coke."

"Right, okay, yeah. I'll be back." I turn around and practically run to the bar. Christy is smirking as I approach, because of course she is.

"Don't," I say with bite. "One Coke."

She just chuckles and gets the drink for me. I bring it back to Zander, who hasn't taken his eyes off me since he walked in, apparently. "I need to go check on my other tables. I'll be back."

"Sure," is all Zander responds, and I don't know how to take that.

Heading over to the creepy regulars, I can feel Zander tracking my every move. It's this feeling of being watched, but not in a bad way. More of a protector way. Unnerving, but I guess it's nice.

"Still doing okay, fellas?" I ask with every ounce of patience I can muster.

"Another round, sweetheart," Creep Two pipes up.

"Coming right up," I say and back away before they get any ideas.

I make it back to the bar, and Christy must have heard because she's already pouring the beer. "Thanks, Christy."

"No problem, I'll do anything to get them to their three beers each so they leave." Christy eyes them and grimaces.

"Agreed." Picking up the tray, I head back to the men from hell. "Here you go."

"Thanks, honey," Creep One says. I smile and turn around without thinking, but then he immediately grabs my ass. I swing away as fast as I can, but not fast enough. Before I can even get my hand raised to slap him, the guy is shoved back in his chair.

I stumble back myself and realize Zander has stepped in. *Oh shit.* I may not be his biggest fan right now or want him anywhere near me, but this is not going to end well for the creepy guy.

"Do not *ever* lay a hand on her," Zander says as he leans over the table and glares daggers at the man.

"Cool it, kid. I didn't know she was taken." The guy throws his hands up in a surrender gesture, and I almost laugh.

"*Kid?* Just because you're obviously much older than I am doesn't give you a right to touch any woman without her consent. And she clearly didn't give it. Now I'll pay your tab, but you can move on." Zander's voice takes on a lethal edge that I shouldn't find attractive, but here we are.

"Since when did this bar get bouncers?" Creep One's buddy, the one who's normally quiet but laughs and smiles at everything that happens, asks no one in particular.

"Since today. Now there's the door. Use it!" Zander eyes flash, and I've never seen those three creeps move so fast in my life.

They leave the bar, and I hear clapping behind me. Christy is grinning like a loon and doing some sort of slow clap. The patrons at the bar are chuckling, and I'm standing here like what the fuck just happened.

"No one touches you." Zander turns to me, but it's not menace that I feel from him now. It's that same protectiveness. In the next breath, he smiles sheepishly and says, "I knocked my drink over when I got up. Can I get a mop to clean it up? Only fair since I ran off your customers."

"Umm, sure. And don't worry about running them off. I'm sure they will be back in a few days. They are regulars, and always a pain in the ass. They are usually gone by seven every night they come in, though." Apparently, rambling is my defense mechanism.

Grabbing the mop and bucket from behind the bar, I head back to the spill. "Here," Zander says, reaching for the mop. "Seriously, I made the mess, I'll clean it up." Deciding not to fight him on this, he cleans the floor while I wipe down the table.

"Can we talk now?" Zander asks once we're finished and I've returned with a new Coke.

"I can't, I'm working." It's the truth, but not the whole truth. I just can't deal with all this right now.

"I'll wait till you're ready," Zander responds like he wasn't expecting anything less.

And he does just that. He waits till the end of my shift, continually ordering soda, staying completely sober, even as the place gets busy for a Thursday night. As my shift ends, he asks again, and I tell him no as I climb into Ada's car and leave.

CHAPTER TWELVE

God, what have I done?

KARA

THE NEXT DAY, HE'S back again, and somehow shows up about forty-five minutes after my shift starts. This time, he sits at the bar as I'm working a bartending shift instead of serving. It's Friday, so the place is crazy busy, but my avenging angel is always present, running off the scum.

"Who the hell is that guy?" Christy asks when we're both at the other end of the bar, making drinks.

"Someone I was running from." The second the words leave my mouth, I realize how bad that sounds. I can't let Christy believe Zander is abusive, 'cause he's far from it. "Not bad running or anything. Just a lot was going on and I needed space. So I left without telling him where I was going, and he figured it out. Now he's hanging around trying to get me to sit down and talk, and I've been avoiding him."

"Well, if he keeps running off the crap people, he can stay as long as he wants." She laughs and goes back to her customers.

I glance over at where Zander is sitting, and yet again, realize he's staring right at me. Why is him being here causing me to be so conflicted? Part of me really doesn't want him around. My brain blames him for being the catalyst of this whole mess. But my body and soul don't feel that way. I don't know how they feel, but it's definitely not *kick him out*, which confuses me.

Before Zander has a chance to say anything about his empty drink, I walk over and grab the soda dispenser. Leaning over the bar, I fill it up, doing my best to avoid eye contact. Because I don't need another thing that confuses the hell out of me.

"Thanks, Kara," Zander says with a hint of trepidation. Is he nervous that I'm going to bolt again? I'm at my job. "Can we please just take five minutes and talk? I really think it will help both of us."

I sigh and glance up at those beautiful, green eyes. They're pleading with me. Why does it feel so much better when he's around? I've had a lot of time to just think since everything transpired a few weeks ago. Even though I was freaked the fuck out and panicking because I didn't have a clue who I or anyone else was. Okay, I still don't know. Even back then, I had this gut feeling that I was safe with him. When I left him, that feeling left, too.

Now that he's back in my life, I don't feel so lost and confused. And that fact alone confuses the hell out of me. Come to think of it, that weird pain in my chest has subsided, too. Jesus Christ, what the hell does *that* mean?

Okay fine, maybe I need answers, and he's the only one that can give them to me. But I sure as hell am not going to give him any kind of gratification in that.

"Fine, I'll give you five minutes when I go on my break in an hour. But we're staying in a public place, and I reserve the right to walk away if I want," I say with a heavy amount of doubt.

Zander lights up like he's a child and I just handed him the Christmas present he's been wanting all year. "Perfect, fine, yeah. Whatever makes you comfortable," he rushes out like I'm going to change my mind.

"Until then, I have work to do." I turn around and realize my heart is racing. Quickly, I start focusing on other customers and try to forget I just gave the guy who's upended my world five minutes of my time. *God, what have I done?*

My nerves ratchet up as my break draws closer. Let's be honest, I don't want to talk to Zander. His intensity freaks me out. But there's a part of me that revels in his protective side when it comes to perceived threats against me from the asshole patrons.

My heart skips a beat when I catch his eye. He pointedly glances at the clock on the wall behind the bar, like he's been counting down the minutes till my break. I take a deep breath and walk over to where Christy is cleaning up a table. *Here goes nothing.*

"Christy, I'm going to take my break. But I'm going to use that table in the corner 'cause I promised Zander I'd speak to him, and want to be somewhere you can see me."

"Alright, hun. I'm sure you'll be fine, but I'll have my eye on you," Christy responds with a wink—a fucking wink!

"Right, yeah." I roll my eyes and head around the bar to where Zander is sitting, and motion him to follow me.

CHAPTER THIRTEEN

Stop it, emotions

KARA

WITHOUT PROTEST, ZANDER GETS off his stool and follows me to the back corner of the bar where there is an empty table. I might have left it dirty so people would be less likely to sit at it. It's Friday, so we're busy, but definitely not anywhere as busy as we could be. It's still early. I don't work the closing shift tonight so I won't get the good tips, but I actually get to bed at a decent hour. So win!

We both sit, and I stare at him without saying a word. He's the one who wanted to chat, so he can lead this little exchange. He doesn't disappoint, and immediately starts verbally vomiting.

"Okay, I know you said I only get five minutes of your time, so I'm going to get through this as quickly as I can. You can ask or say whatever you want."

"Mmhmm." I raise an eyebrow.

"You had your memory and apparently part of what makes you, well *you*, wiped by a witch who has some sort of vendetta against my pack. We think so. And because you are important to me, you were the target, even though I technically was the actual target. I understand why you ran from me. I handled everything really bad when you first were, umm, affected." The pleading look in his eyes and the almost manic way he's talking is practically bipolar.

"Okay?" I respond with a whole lot of confusion and skepticism.

"Yeah, I know this sounds insane, but there's more," Zander says quickly, as if realizing that if he says much else that's too far out there, I'm going to bolt. He's not wrong.

"Go on."

Zander leans forward to be closer to me, like he can't help it, and continues. "Right after you left, we did try to track you, but you were able to evade us. It only was a few days ago that Callum, our tech guy, got a positive hit on where you were. I knew I had to be the one to make contact with you, and hopefully make this better."

"Better, huh?"

"Yes, anyway, I have a question. Have you been noticing anything that seems off? Pain that is completely unexplained, exhaustion that doesn't seem like any amount of sleep fixes it. Anything like that?" he rushes on.

Oh look, that weird panic I had way back when all this started has decided to show up again. 'Cause what the fuck?

I look away from Zander, but reply, "Yeah, a few days ago a weird tightness in my chest started, and I've definitely not been running at full capacity. But it got better yesterday, and has been a lot less since then."

Zander visibly relaxes. "I'm glad it's gotten better. It's the same for me."

"I'm sorry, what?" I whip my head back around to face him fully.

"You remember back when we were in the woods, and before I realized how bad your memory problems were, I said we were mates?"

"Vaguely, I've tried to forget most of that day," I respond, but in actuality, I've gone back to that day like a broken record ever since.

"Apparently, there's a part of being mates that actually makes it impossible for them to be separate for any extended length of time. I assumed that you would only have just been noticing the effects recently, because that part of you is suppressed. I've been miserable for a while now," Zander says the last part like he's talking about the weather and something earth-shattering.

"What do you mean, you've been miserable for a while?" I am well and truly lost and I genuinely don't think anything he says will clear this up.

"I mean, for the last week, when I finally came back to myself..."

"Wait! Came back to yourself? Like the wolf thing?" I ask, whispering the last part.

"Yeah, the *wolf thing*," he responds just as quietly. "For the last week, I've been dealing with a pain, emptiness in my chest, constant exhaustion, and my mood has been more shitty than normal. Well, my mood has been shit since you left, if I'm being honest. It's the reason when mates find each other, they immediately merge their lives."

Before I have a change to question *that* piece of information, he continues, "I used to think it was just a tradition, but apparently there's actually a reason. Our bond isn't just mental, it's also physical. I've been doing a lot better since I came into the bar yesterday and you were here. That's part of the reason I haven't left. I felt like I was whole again. I could tell you were uncomfortable, so I didn't want to be in the way, but I couldn't leave you." Zander finally ends the word vomit and looks at me expectantly.

What the hell am I supposed to say or do with that info? I was in pain. It wasn't unbearable, but not great either. When Zander showed up yesterday, it dulled, and today, it's almost gone. I mean, obviously I know the whole wolf thing might be true. He said we were mates almost immediately, and has stuck with that. I can't deny there is some sort of pull towards him. But it's not anything close to lust, let alone love.

"So what does this mean for me?" It's the only thing I can come up with that doesn't completely give away my spiraling thoughts.

Zander takes another deep breath and says, "I'd like you to come back with me."

My face must give away the panic that's quickly rising in my gut, because he immediately followed that statement with, "Just so that we're near each other. I know you don't feel the pull like I do, but I'm going to be honest, it's nice not feeling like my insides are going to rip out every second."

"Well, that's...umm...descriptive."

"Yeah, that was probably not the best explanation, but it's the only way I can think to explain what it feels like when you're not around me. I'm not saying we have to spend every second together, but I always wondered why mated pairs never spent much time apart. Apparently, this is the reason. It physically sucks," Zander explains, and I get what he's saying, but I don't want to believe it.

"Listen, I fully understand where you're coming from, but I'm not really on board with going back with you. I feel like I was just getting some sense of normalcy here, and you show up and upend everything again. Okay, that sounds crazy, 'cause I still don't have any recollection from before the woods, but I feel like being on my own is a good thing." Oh good, now I'm the one word vomiting.

Here's the thing. I actually can see myself going back with him, but I can't give him that. Not now. Not yet. Not after all this bullshit.

Zander looks me straight in the eye, and the look of defeat quickly morphs into determination. It's that determined look that causes me to stop and think again. But I can't give in this easily, can I?

"Okay, I understand. But I'm not giving up. I'll leave you to finish your shift today, but will you please turn your phone back on so I can at least know you're safe? Will you give me that?" Zander's determination bleeds into every word.

Sighing, I think about the fact that he came all this way, and is hanging around with the hope I'll go back with him. So much rides on him right now, that I guess I can give him this one.

"Fine, I'll turn my phone back on as soon as I get back to...where I'm staying. I don't keep it with me since I don't want to use it."

Zander's face lights up in a way that makes my chest hurt. *Stop it, emotions. You're not supposed to be part of this.* This is a decision that will give him something while keeping me in control. Right? Yeah, that's what I'm going with.

"Thank you, I really appreciate that," he begins. "I'm going to warn you. When you turn your phone on, it's probably going to blow up with about a thousand messages. Not just from me, but from Carmen, your parents, and about fifty other people that are all worried about you."

"What. The. Fuck," I say as my jaw hits the floor.

"Yeah," Zander replies sheepishly. "I know it's a lot. Maybe turn the thing on and stick it in a drawer for a while so it doesn't bother you?"

"You're not going to show up where I'm staying, are you?" I ask, realizing what I just agreed to.

"No, absolutely not. You said what you wanted, and I won't betray that. You don't want me following you around, so I won't. This is the only place I'll turn up. But I won't stop that. I need to see you."

"Okay, fine, but I need to get back to work now. I'll see you later, I guess." I get up, dazed, and head back to the bar because I need to get busy doing something.

When I get home, I follow through on my promise and grab the phone that's been off for almost two weeks now. I take a deep breath and turn the phone on. Staring at it as it starts up, I genuinely wonder what is going to happen. Forty-five seconds later, the phone starts chirping like someone lit in on fire. Five, ten, thirty, fifty, one hundred messages, and it just keeps going.

"What the actual hell? He wasn't kidding!"

I throw the phone on my bed and smother it with my pillow to muffle the noise, then go shower. I have the day off tomorrow, so I know I won't see Zander. He promised he would not bother me outside the Tipsy Mule. I'm going to have to tackle all those messages, but I think I'm going to talk to Ada first.

This shower is so much like the first shower I took in that crappy motel. That one washed off the panic and confusion of that day. This one washes away the confusion of Zander's revelations. I let the water run down my body and think about everything that's happened since that day in the woods. So much, and yet so little.

Finishing up in the shower, I walk back into my bedroom, and see that my phone has stopped screaming at me. I move the pillow and pick up the phone, looking at the screen. Four hundred and seventy-five messages, and sixty voicemails. I don't even look at how many app notifications I have. I guess I can start with looking at who the voicemails are from? *I don't have to listen to them,* I reason.

Opening the voicemail screen, I scroll all the way to the oldest one. It's from my dad. The next four are from my mom. Back to dad for the next three. As

I keep scrolling, it's a mixture of them. Then there's someone I have labeled as *Bestie*, a few random names I don't recognize, and then as I get closer to the current date, Zander. There's one from each of the last five days, including today. I decide to listen to that one.

Hey, Kara, I know you probably just turned your phone back on, and it's probably overwhelming with the amount of messages and voicemails you have. I'm not helping, I know. But I've been calling your phone and leaving you a message every day, so I figured I would continue. You might want to go back and listen to the others first.

I pause the voicemail recording and let out the breath I didn't know I was holding. He sounds so sure of himself, but also nervous. Like he's worried everything will fall apart. Does he not realize it already has? Hitting play, I resume listening.

But, if you don't and you're listening to this one first, I guess I'll just say that the others are from a desperate man who just wants his mate back. I'm still that desperate man, but I'm going to take a different approach. I know everything I said today was a lot. It might be too much for you to deal with, and you might never come back to me, but I really hope you do. Even if it's to help piece back your memories and help you gain what you lost. Even if I'm not part of it. So if you are still listening, just know I'm here in whatever way you'll let me. Talk soon.

I open my eyes I didn't know I had closed and realize I'm sitting on my bed, cradling the phone in my hands. He just offered what I didn't think I needed. A way to rebuild what I lost without the titles or push for more. This whole thing just got so much more complicated. I don't have the bandwidth to process this right now.

I set the phone down on my side table, and just like the first night I ran, I wrap the towel tighter around myself and lay down under the covers. At least this time the covers aren't scratchy and no one is screwing on the other side of the wall.

Chapter Fourteen

You sound like my mother

ZANDER

I know I told Kara I would leave her alone everywhere except for the bar, but I can't help checking up on her. Thanks to Callum's techno detective skills and convincing Kara to turn her phone back on, I know where she's been staying. I also know she's safe in the townhome of one Ada Christianson. The way she got connected with Ada was through the server at the diner Kara had breakfast at that first morning after she left.

I'm not going to bother her, but I'm sitting in my truck just down the street. Just staring at the house, hoping to catch a glimpse of her. Let's be fucking honest—I'm stalking her. I've lost my mind. I left Damien and Kara's parents in charge, and have been doing nothing the past two weeks.

As I sit here brooding for what feels like hours, my phone rings from where it's sitting in the center counsel. Looking down, I hope it's Kara, but know it's not. Of course, it's Damien.

"What is it?" I ask. Pleasantries are beyond me at this point.

"Let me guess. You're sitting outside the house she's staying in because she isn't at the bar," Damien replies with a hint of annoyance. This whole thing has been stressing him out. Dude needs to find his own mate, 'cause he needs a reality check. Or maybe I need one, hell if I know.

"Yes I am, I need to know she's safe," I say.

"She is obviously safe. She's been doing nothing but going between work and that house since she got to Frankfort. Now that Callum knows where she is, he's been able to track her movements with the city cameras. But she's not why I called,' Damien drones on.

"So why did you call?" I ask as I drag my hand down my face.

"You need to think about coming back to the pack and actually running things around here. It's been nearly two weeks. The first week you went completely off grid and your wolf was fully in control. Once you got back, we had narrowed down where Kara was, and you headed to Frankfort alone," Damien continues. "Just because she's your mate doesn't mean you can neglect your other duties."

"You sound like my mother," I deadpan.

"Funny, considering I've never met her."

"Have you talked to David about what's actually going on, or do you assume that I'm intentionally neglecting my duties to the pack? Because I'm not. David explained why my moods were getting worse. Why I'm exhausted. Why I've been in physical pain. It's not because I miss her. I do, but that's not it," I bark at Damien. He may be my best friend, but he's just dense.

"I spoke with him, and he explained the bond isn't just a mental thing, it's physical, too. Until the bond is solidified, separation doesn't go over well. It's better afterward, but can still cause problems," Damien fills in like he's reading a text book.

"Yeah, and yesterday, I walked into the bar for the first time and saw her. The relief I felt almost brought me to my knees. I noticed she was dealing with the same thing, too, but not as much. I'm guessing that's because her wolf is suppressed. We spoke this afternoon for a while, and I explained a lot to her. Asked her to come back with me. I think she will, I just need to give her time." I know I'm rambling, but I can't give up on this, on us. Damien just needs to get that through his head. I won't be the Alpha I need or want to be without her.

"So, what you're saying is that I need to keep doing what I'm doing, and you'll be home when you're home? That sounds pathetic, but fine. Callum is working on a lead on the witch, and we should have more on that in a day or so." Damien is lucky he's my best friend, 'cause fucking hell.

"Good. If all goes well, *we* will be home in a couple days, too." I hang up because I truly don't want to kill my best friend, but I might head back early to do it.

I drop my phone in the passenger seat and slam my head back into the headrest. Closing my eyes, I take a breath and pray that maybe she will listen to the voicemails I've been leaving her. With that thought, I grab my phone and go to the Friend Finder app. "Thank fuck!" She turned on her phone. Her location is pinging again. With a sigh of relief, I put my phone down and turn the truck on. I can head to the hotel knowing I can at least trust where she's at.

Back in my hotel room, I lay down on my bed and open the Finder app for what feels like the hundredth time since I realized Kara turned her phone on. There's something about just knowing where she is that relaxes me. Putting my phone down, I think back a week to when my wolf finally seeded control back to me. It was David who met me on the lawn of the pack house.

***

I WALK OUT OF *the woods in wolf form. My wolf has been in control for the past few days and finally seeded control back to me. He had gotten us back into the pack lands and about a mile from the pack house before he let me control anything. Obviously, he was done leading and wanted to rest.*

I look up and see David, Kara's dad, standing on the lawn, a stoic statue of power. How could he not be? He's the current Alpha of Shadow Creek Pack, the largest pack in the region. He doesn't say a word as I approach, still in wolf form. Instead, he holds out a pair of shorts for me. I shift and put them on without saying anything, either.

What am I supposed to say? His daughter was cursed and ran away on my watch. I lost my shit when I couldn't bring her back like I thought I could, and let my wolf take over. I don't even know how many days it's been, but I feel like I'm being stabbed in my chest. I'm exhausted.

"David..." I begin, but he puts his hand up to silence me. He still hasn't spoken, and I feel like I'm sixteen again and my father is mad at me for screwing up for the thousandth time.

"Has the pain started?" David asks. That's not what I figured he would start with. I come up short and just stare at him for a minute.

"Has the pain started?" he repeats.

"There's an ache in my chest that makes me feel like I'm being stabbed. But it's been a while since I spent that much time in wolf form. I just figured it was a side effect."

"It's not that simple. There's a reason that when wolves find their mates, they move in together pretty quickly. At this point, it just feels like a tradition, but it's actually a lot more than that. Being a mate is physical, emotional, and mental. The physical part makes you want to be around the other person. It's because until the bond is finished, separation of length can get painful. It's how the wolves keep you with your mate. They can't fully mate till we do. That's what's happening. Because you're an Alpha, it hits harder and faster. Your mood has been shit since this started, and I'm guessing it's not getting better."

I have nothing to say to that. He's not yelling and freaking out like he did on the phone, and that worries me more. Why isn't he pissed?

"Okay, why aren't you pissed off and yelling at me?" I'll admit, I'm afraid of the answer.

He sighs and says, "Oh, I'm fucking furious. You fucking lost my daughter, then went broody Alpha and abandoned your pack to your second. But Damien and Kai have been running things pretty well. And Franny has been keeping me in check."

"So what do we do? What do I do?" I ask, feeling property chastised. I'm the Alpha of my pack, and I feel like I'm just a pup again.

"We do nothing. But you are going to talk to your inner circle. Get an update on where things stand and make a plan to get Kara back. We know where she is, but figured you would need to be the one to bring her home."

"You know where she is?"

"Yeah, and if you would have had your shit together, you could have already gone to see her."

"How? Wait, when did you figure it out?"

"I didn't, it was Callum. He's damn handy with a computer. I need someone like him in my pack. He figured it out two days ago. We've been keeping tabs on her, but haven't made contact. I've been sending a few of my trusted pack members to keep watch, but no one has spoken to her. She doesn't recognize them at all."

"That makes sense with all she's dealing with." My problems feel so small now that I've taken my feelings out of it and looked at the situation logically.

"With you being her mate, we think you'll be the only one to break through to her. Even with her suppressed wolf, we think she will feel enough of your connection to come back."

"What about the witch? Any progress on that front?"

"Some, but nothing of note. Like I said, go have your inner circle update you. We will regroup and you can make a plan to go bring my daughter home," David concludes and turns towards the house without another word.

I TAKE ONE LAST look at my phone and do something I didn't think I'd do until she gave me the go ahead.

> **Hey Kara, I'm sure you're probably sleeping, but I wanted to let you know I'm here if you want to talk**
> **- Z**

CHAPTER FIFTEEN

Firefly

KARA

I WAKE UP WITH the light of the dawn. Even though I've been working wild excessive hours at the Tipsy Mule, I still can't seem to sleep if the sun is up. At least I'm off today. Well, most of the day. I didn't tell Zander because I didn't want him to show up, but one of the other servers needed to be off, so I picked up half her shift. I go in at 6:00 p.m. It's not that I'm trying to ignore him, but being around him is so overwhelming. My mind doesn't know him, but I can tell my body and heart does. The dual emotions make me crazy.

Groaning, I roll over to my side table and grab my phone. I hadn't looked at the messages last night because there were so many. But this morning, with fresh eyes, I decide to at least look at the main screen and see who I have to deal with.

Multiple messages from my parents, the person labeled Bestie, and a ton of unknowns. Well, not really unknowns. They all have contact info, but I don't have a clue who they are. But the interesting thing is there's only one from Zander. And it's from last night.

> Hey Kara, I'm sure you're probably sleeping, but I wanted to just let you know I'm here if you want to talk - Z.

I just stare at my phone. I can't deny that this man is trying. He's hurting, too. I guess I need to give it to him that he has this relationship with me that I don't remember, and he's trying to find some sort of semblance of that relationship again.

How am I supposed to respond? Tell him, *oh good, I'm glad someone is here that knows more about me than I do right now. And now they want to talk to me so everything will come rushing back*? Yeah, that's way too bitchy. Oh wait, I know. *Oh Zander, just being around you makes everything so much better!* Too much? Yep, I'm officially spiraling.

Sighing, I just keep it simple.

> **Thanks. I have a lot to think about today. I'm sure I'll see you at the bar tomorrow. We can talk more then.**

His reply comes almost instantly. It's wild because it's not even 7:00 a.m.

> **I'll see you then. Like I said, whatever you need, I'm here.**

I should have expected that response. Looking through other messages, I should have gathered most of them would be the typical *where are you?* and *come home*. Or even *we miss you*. I guess it's nice to know I'm missed. But other than that, nothing earth-shattering, thank God.

I set my phone down, get dressed, and head down to the kitchen where Ada is already up and making breakfast. I don't think this woman ever sleeps.

"Morning, Ada," I say with a sleepy smile. This woman has been a real hero the last couple weeks. Never wavering, never questioning. Always willing to listen to anything, but also willing to call me out on shit.

"Morning, dear. How'd ya sleep last night?" she replies from over at the stove where she's flipping pancakes.

"Actually, I don't feel as exhausted as I have the last few days." With that sentence, I flop into a chair at the table and realize what I just said. Jesus, this whole mate-bond-pain thing is really fucked up, but how am I supposed to talk to anyone about this?

"That's good to hear. Christy messaged me last night and said that you and the guy who's been hanging around the bar talked for a while. You know, the guy who's become our unofficial bouncer. How'd that go? I know you were avoiding him like the plague," Ada responds, and if there's one thing I've learned about her, it's that she may not be a physically intimidating lady, but she's fierce and doesn't sugarcoat anything.

"Uh, well. I'm sure Christy told you he's the guy I was running from. But I swear, it's not because he was abusive or anything. I needed to just be by myself for a while, and the only way I thought I could make that happen was running. Which I did, and now he found me and is wanting to be part of my life, but isn't pushing for things to go back to what they were. But I don't know what I'm going to do."

I pause to take a breath, glancing up at Ada to see her staring at me. I look out the big window in the kitchen and continue, "I turned my phone back on last night and found so many voicemails and messages from all these people who care about me. It's so overwhelming, and I don't know what to do with any of it."

Looking back over at Ada, she's smiling when she says, "So your past has caught up with your present, and you're trying to figure out what your future is." It's not a question—it doesn't need to be.

I sigh and look at my hands in my lap. "Yeah, I feel like if I go back, I'll have to deal with more than I want to right now. But there's this part of me that feels like going back will help piece me back together."

Over the last few weeks, we've talked about feeling lost and not feeling like myself. Through it all, Ada's been kind and understanding. Never pushing for details I wasn't willing to share.

"Well, I can't tell you what you should do, but based on what I know of you, you'll make the decision that makes the most sense for you in the moment, and go full on with it. You'll be okay. Now eat your pancakes," Ada says with all the mother energy she has.

"Yes, mom." I laugh, digging into the best blueberry pancakes I've ever had, I think.

After breakfast, I head back up to my room and decide to listen to some of the most recent voicemails. I figure the ones from the first few days will be full of frantic people and not make anything better. One that sticks out to me is from my dad.

Hey firefly, I'm sure you're still off trying to find yourself, and I get it. Callum, the tech guy I told you about in a different message, has tracked where you have been staying and working. I've been keeping tabs on you from a distance. I know you don't know me or anyone, but you're still my little girl, so I have to protect you. Zander is heading to Frankfort to find you and hopefully bring you home. You guys are good together, and will both be stronger together if you can get past this whole mess. It's not your fault. Honestly, I'm not surprised you ran after everything that happened and how it was handled. I love you, firefly. Come home.

That nickname. It's a flash of a memory of a feeling. While I have no memory of him, just having him call me firefly does something to me. I find myself tearing up, which blows my mind.

The other voice message that sticks out is from 'Bestie,' who I now know is Carmen.

Bitch! I can't believe you haven't come home yet. Okay, fine, I get it. The guys explained it to me, but I don't understand. Supposedly, this damn witch is pissed at the Moonrise Pack and because Z is the Alpha and freshly mated, she took out her witch woo-woo shit on you. What the fuck is that nonsense? I miss you, boo. You're my girl. I came to this damn pack with you, and then you left me to deal with these men on my own. Damien is such a pain with his rules and pack-first BS, Kai won't stop flirting with me—and everyone else—and Callum, well, never mind him. It's whatever. I know you don't remember us, but we love you, girl. We miss you. Come home.

While I have no idea who this girl is, I can tell why we're friends. Her personality reminds me a lot of Christy. We must be really close.

I spend the rest of the morning and most of the afternoon sorting through messages and looking at the photos on my phone, praying something sparks a memory, but nothing concrete ever emerges. Just feelings and random emotions. Maybe Zander is right—everything is still there, just buried.

As it gets closer to evening, I get ready for my shift and Ada takes me to the bar. For whatever reason, I bring my phone with me and leave it on. Do I want Zander to find me? I didn't think I did when I woke up this morning, but the fact that my phone is sitting next to the register and is on makes me think I do want him to find me. Who would have thought?

Tonight, I'm working with a whole slew of people since it's Saturday night and we're open till 3:00 a.m. Yay, late nights. At least the tips will be good and I'm not on tending duty, so I just have to avoid getting my ass groped more than once.

Three hours into my shift, the place is packed, but nothing crazy has happened yet. It's still early for the bar scene to make me too insane. I turn around from cleaning up a table of empty bottles and glasses and yelp. Zander is here, and he's standing less than two feet from me. How the hell did he not only get in here, but this close before I realized it?

"You're not where you're supposed to be," he says with a hint of amusement. No anger at all, just interest.

"Umm yeah, I picked up a shift last minute and didn't think you needed to know." I know the squeak of my words is pathetic, but I can't change it.

"Yet, you bring your phone. The phone you've had off for almost two weeks and only just turned on. The phone that is currently still on. You wanted me to track you down." He says the words with relish. The smile on his face is pure male arrogance.

Shit, he's that perceptive? "Umm, no?" Well, damn. That was not supposed to come out as a question.

"It's fine, Kara. I'm not going to get in the way of your tips. Just know I'm glad you wanted me to be around. I wanted to be around you, too. I'll be in the back corner. Won't even sit in your section tonight," Zander says with the sweetest smile I've ever seen.

"No, here, this table is open," I rush out before I can even think about what I'm doing. *What the fuck, Kara? You want him near you now?* Jesus Christ.

His grin turns into a full-blown smile, and Zander passes by me, heading to the table I pointed out. As he passes, our arms brush and a wave of what I can only describe as relief mixed with peace washes over my whole body. It takes everything in me not to turn into a puddle on the floor. *What the hell was that?*

Zander turns around just in time to catch the look of confusion on my face, and I walk away as fast as I can. "Coke, right?" I ask over my shoulder.

"Yeah, thanks," Zander says with a knowing expression. I am well and truly screwed.

CHAPTER SIXTEEN

Friends, fuck buddies, and flings

ZANDER

THAT TOUCH. OKAY, I may have guessed something like that would happen since we've been physically apart for so long, but the electric jolt it gave me could have powered cities. Okay, maybe not *cities*, but damn. I should have *accidentally* brushed up against her a lot sooner than now.

This time was technically an accident. As I turn back to look at Kara, I see her confusion, and the smirk that comes across my face says it all. *Yeah, babe, I felt that, too.* But she's pretending nothing happened so I will too, for now.

As the night progresses, she keeps her distance with her body, but her eyes never stray too far away from me. We've locked eyes so many times it's like we've had full conversations without words. At first, Kara would look away the second we made eye contact. But, the more it happens, the more her eyes linger on me. Maybe I'm closer to her coming back with me than I realized?

Kara keeps my drink full, which is the only time she speaks to me—only pleasantries, but I'll take it. But now, it's after midnight and I'm starving. Giving in, I order chicken strips and some fries. I really should remember to eat.

I genuinely thought about leaving a couple times to give Kara some space, but the jerks that haunt this place are pissing me off. I've thrown out three 'men' who copped feels of not just Kara, but every female in here. There's been a few others for whom I've just had to stand up, and they've bolted or immediately apologized. Guess it's a good thing the whole Alpha aura doesn't just work on shifters. Granted, a few of them have come in tonight, too. They've been on their best behavior.

It didn't take long to realize they were David's men playing backup for me. I knew the second they walked in. One thing about shifters, we smell a lot different than humans. So unless we are intentionally masking our scent, we're pretty easy to pick out of the crowd. At least with each other. Humans don't have the same senses we do. It was also obvious they knew I would be there because they acknowledged me almost immediately, but stayed out of my way. Deference to another alpha, especially their Alpha's daughter's mate, runs deep.

By the time it's last call at 2:30 a.m., Kara has gone from bewildered, to flabbergasted, to downright frustrated. On top of that, she looks like she could fall over at any second, and it's taking everything in my power to not swoop in and help her. I know us being in close proximity has helped, but we haven't touched or been physical, and that's what really keeps the pain and fatigue away. When you overwork yourself, it hits harder.

As patrons pay their tabs and begin clearing out, I get up to go wait in my truck. Okay, maybe I'm still hoping that Kara will miraculously change her mind tonight and want to come home with me, but I'm not holding my breath. I'm pretty sure she's leaning towards coming back, but I don't think she's there yet.

"Where are you going?" a voice calls from behind the bar. I turn around, and it's one of the bartenders raising an eyebrow at me.

"I was going to go 'cause you're closing." I shrug. I'm not going to be in the way of them leaving on time.

"Just park it. Friends, fuck buddies, and flings get to hang while we close up. I'm not sure what you are, but..." She shrugs and turns back to what she was doing.

Sitting back down, I look over at Kara—who had been clearing off the last table—and she is staring at the gal behind the bar. Her face is incredulous, and I can't help the shit-eating grin I know I'm now sporting. This is too good.

She marches over to the bar and has a whisper-yell conversation with the bartender, but I only pick up every few words.

"What the hell, Lauren?"

"What...oh, come on!"

"Absolutely not...what? No way!" Kara responds.

"It's fine," Lauren whispers, before glancing over at me and shooting me a wink with a thumbs up.

I'm not exactly sure what just happened, but I think I owe Lauren. I laugh out loud and nod my head in acknowledgement to her. If Kara wasn't off-kilter before, she is now. Maybe I'll be able to convince her. Just as I have that thought, I remember back to when I found her in the woods. The only reason she came with me was because she was off-kilter. Damnit! I can't do that to her again. I'm absolutely not making her uncomfortable.

Thirty minutes later, the place is cleaned up and the main door is locked. Servers and bartenders are starting to leave, and Kara comes over to me.

"Ready?" she asks, giving me a look that's half-exasperation and—I think I'm dreaming—it looks half happy, too. I'm still reeling from Lauren's declaration and Kara's reaction to it. But it looks like Kara is, as well.

"Yeah, I'm assuming your ride is outside?" I respond, getting up to follow her out the back door.

"Actually, you're it, buddy. Lauren was planning to give me a ride, but she bailed and said you are. She's already left. Bitch..." she finishes with a mumble. Kara's eyes keep darting around like she's trying to find someone to save her from this situation, but they keep coming back to me.

I chuckle and say, "Come on, my truck's around front."

CHAPTER SEVENTEEN

So, we're basically just dating?

ZANDER

I TAKE OVER LEADING the way to my truck and open the passenger door for her. Kara walks up to me, eyeing me suspiciously, but I just smile and hold the door open for her. As she climbs in, it takes all my will power to not help her. Shit, I'm going to be in close proximity to her. This is going to be rough.

Once she's in, I close the door and walk around to the driver's side. I didn't think I'd have to psyche myself up for the next fifteen minutes of the drive. Climbing in, I look over at Kara. The way she's staring out the front window makes me chuckle, because it looks as if turning her head would start World War III.

"You okay?" Am I smiling? Fuck, I don't want her uncomfortable.

Kara whips her head towards me. "Huh? Oh, yeah, fine."

"I'm just going to drive you back to where you're staying. Nothing else," I respond as Kara's face falls just slightly, but she recovers quickly. Did she want me to push for more? Jesus, now I'm the one getting emotional whiplash.

"Yeah, I know. It's just not how I thought tonight would go at all."

How did she think it would go? "It's a lot. We can just drive in silence. We don't need to talk."

"No, it's fine. Can you, umm..." she starts, but falters. "Can you tell me a bit more about why when we're apart for a while, like we were for the last couple weeks, it's physically painful? I just can't wrap my head around that."

"Sure," I reply with a smile. "But I'm going to warn you, I don't know too much more. It's a new thing for me, too." I start the engine and put the truck in drive.

"That's fine. I still don't have any memories from before you found me in the woods, but I keep getting these feelings and such. It's unnerving," Kara says with a shudder.

"I don't doubt it." I lapse into silence, trying to get my thoughts in order. I don't want to add to her confusion, but I'm not sure how to explain any of this.

How am I supposed to explain something to her that I really don't understand myself? How much is too much? Should I tell her she's literally my other half and I've been swimming in a sea of nothing since she left? Probably not. That will absolutely scare her away, and I don't want that.

"Okay, let me see." I begin as I drive towards the neighborhood where the townhome is.

"I should have guessed you knew where I'm staying," Kara comments without any heat.

Glancing over, I shrug and continue, "From what I understand, part of the mate bond is that it's not just a mental feeling, it's also physical and emotional. All three components create the bond. But in the beginning, before the bond is complete, the physical part is what keeps mates together. Our wolves need the bond more than us, so they are the ones who influence the reactions. Being separated causes pain, exhaustion, and can even cause sickness if left for too long without contact."

"Wait, what do you mean, before the bond's completed?" Kara cuts in.

"You caught that, huh?"

"Yeah, but what do you mean?"

I sigh and stare down the road as I drive. "When that whole mess happened two weeks ago, we had only been together for about two months. We didn't complete the bond yet, which is normal for shifters. It can take from weeks to months to complete it."

"So, we're basically just dating?" Kara asks. *Is that disappointment in her voice?*

"Well, not really. For shifters, when mates find each other and they both accept that the other is their mate, they're basically married in the eyes of the packs. The mate bond solidifies as the couple creates a deeper connection, and the bond ceremony is held when the couple feels ready to complete the bond. We're in that in-between period. We had accepted we are mates, but didn't complete the bond yet." As I finish my explanation, I hope to whatever god is out there that she doesn't panic.

Kara doesn't respond. Just sits there in silence. It stretches for more than a minute, and I can't help but glance over at her with increasing worry. The profile of her face is contemplative, but not panicky. *Did I say too much?*

"You okay?" I ask as I turn my attention back to the road.

Kara sighs, and I feel her looking at me. "Yeah, I guess I didn't realize how much my leaving affected you." She seems slightly dejected, and that's what worries me. "When I left, it was because I was freaked the fuck out. I didn't know who or what I was. Things just kept being thrown at me, and I couldn't handle it. Apparently, my self-preservation was to just run away."

"I didn't help that, did I?" I respond, because the last thing I want is for her to think she's the problem here.

"Actually, looking back, if I would have taken a second, you were just trying to help. I was just so far into flight mode I don't think it mattered," Kara says with more conviction.

"So what are you saying?" I can't be reading into this wrong. Is she actually leaning towards coming back with me?

"I'm saying maybe going back with you will help me figure things out," she says while looking at her hands.

Before I have time to process, let alone respond, to the best news I could have heard tonight, we arrive at the townhome. I pull the truck to the side of the road and throw it into park. Schooling my features the best I can, I turn and look at her.

Kara continues, "I'm not saying we're going back to whatever we were before all this insanity started. But, I'm saying I don't want to feel like shit while I try to find myself, and you might be the only person that could help me figure it out."

She's coming home! Holy shit! She's willingly coming back with me! It takes everything in my body to hold myself from grabbing her and hugging her like I would have before.

"Really? You'll come back with me?" Damn, that was a shocking amount of chill for how excited I am.

"Yeah, but not right now. I need to talk to Ada. She's done so much for me since I showed up in Frankfort," Kara says quietly.

"So when are you thinking?"

"Honestly, I think sooner rather than later. I'll text you tomorrow afternoon when to come over. I don't want to think about this too much. Well, too much more than I've already thought about it," Kara says, and I'm absolutely floored with her decision.

"Okay, awesome. I will...wait for your message," I say calmly, but internally, I'm losing my shit.

Kara reaches for the handle and opens the door. "Thanks for the ride. I'll see you tomorrow." She climbs out of the truck, and the *first date* nature of the moment isn't lost on me.

"Sleep well," I say as she turns back to shut the door. She smiles and walks into the townhome. I slam my head onto the headrest and grin like a madman.

Grabbing my phone from the center console, I pull up Damien's number and hit dial. I'm too shaky to even think of messaging anyone right now.

He answers on the third ring. "Z? What's wrong? It's almost four in the morning." There's worry laced in his tone.

"Nothing, nothing's wrong. She's coming home, Day. I don't know what exactly convinced her, but she agreed to come home!" I almost yell into the phone.

"Holy shit! Are you on your way to get her now, or what?"

"No, I just dropped her off at the townhome she's been staying at. Said she wanted to talk to the gal she's been staying with before we leave. She's going to message me tomorrow afternoon when she's ready to leave." The grin on my face almost hurts, it's so big.

"So what's the plan?" Damien replies. Damn him, always killing my buzz with logistics.

"I'm not ready to think about that yet. Just give me this for the moment. I'll call you in a few hours after I've slept for a bit. We'll figure this shit out then. But I just needed to tell someone."

"You sure she's not going to run again?" Damien kills my mood in a heartbeat.

"Yes, she's had her phone on for a couple days now, and I don't see her turning it off. It will be fine. Just start thinking about logistics and we will talk later. I'm headed to the hotel to sleep."

"Thanks for the update. And Z?"

"Yeah?"

"I'm glad you got your girl back," Damien says, shocking me.

"Thanks, Day, me too." I hang up.

It feels like a weight lifts off my shoulders and I drive back to my hotel. Tomorrow might actually be a decent day.

CHAPTER EIGHTEEN

Discombobulated

KARA

AFTER FALLING INTO BED last night and sleeping like the dead for most of the morning, I wake up and roll over to where my phone is laying on the nightstand. Honestly, I was half expecting at least one message from Zander, but the only messages I have are the ones I haven't read yet.

I roll back to my back and stare at the ceiling. *What have I gotten myself into?* I know that going back with Zander is the most reasonable choice to find the answers I desperately need—but going back with him also makes me feel like I failed on my own. It's the constant back-and-forth that is making me crazy.

The dream I had last night is fuzzy at best, but I know it was important. Like every time I've fallen asleep the last two weeks, I can't remember who was in the dream or what it was about, but the emotions were there. Last night was no different. The dream had to have been about Zander. When I woke up from it, I felt protected and safe. I even reached for the other side of my bed, as if I was reaching for someone.

Zander really has me discombobulated. But I know he's not going to do anything that would intentionally hurt me. Just in the few days since he's been back in my life, he's made that abundantly clear. My comfort comes first to him.

I think it was that realization that pushed me over the edge about going back with him. He cares for me, even though I am clueless how we fit together. It doesn't bother him.

I knew the bubble I created around myself these past few weeks had to pop eventually—I just didn't expect it to come so soon. Part of me thought I'd be here for a couple more weeks, then move on to my own place for a while. I never thought I'd be upending my world so soon. But here we are.

I hear Ada downstairs and know it's time to rip the Band-Aid off. Groaning, I climb out of bed and head to my bathroom to procrastinate for a bit longer before I dress and head downstairs.

I find Ada in the living room at her desk, organizing some papers. She always tries to get paperwork for the bar done on Sundays, as the bar's not open and she tries to catch up.

"I hear your guy friend brought you home last night," she says without even turning around. I swear, that woman could hear a pin drop in the next zip code.

"Umm, yeah. Lauren was supposed to give me a ride, then up and decided Zander could. She left before I realized, and it kind of just happened."

Finally deigning to turn around, Ada gives me a look that I can't actually decipher. She just stares at me like I have more to say, and she knows it. I mean, I do, but her already knowing what's coming is unnerving.

Resolved to just get it out, I begin, "I know when you took me in you said I could stay as long as I needed. It didn't matter my reasoning of being here or what my reasoning would be when I moved on. But I wanted you to know how grateful I am for you taking me in and giving me a job when I was alone and really confused."

All Ada does is raise an eyebrow, and I realize she already knows I'm leaving. *How the hell does she do that?*

Wringing my hands, I continue. "I came here 'cause I needed space from everything that was happening to and around me. I needed time to figure out my own head. I thought it would be longer, but circumstances changed. I'm leaving today. With Zander," I finish—finally making full eye contact.

"Lauren filled me in this morning that the vibe between you two seemed like it was correcting itself," she says with a hint of amusement. "I wouldn't be so on board, but I know you weren't running from an abusive situation. I could tell you just needed space for a while, and didn't know how to make that happen.

"Zander is a good guy. At least what I know of him, he is. I know we've talked about how I don't remember much from before that day, but one thing that's obvious is my heart and mind know Zander, and somehow know he won't hurt me. I think he's the best way to figuring out myself again." The rightness of what I'm saying washes over me. I don't think I fully believed it until I said it out loud to someone else.

"So when's he coming?" I love how straightforward Ada always is.

"He's waiting for my message. Then he'll come over and we'll be heading back to his home today," I say. This is the part I was worried about. I don't want to leave Ada with a bunch of shifts to fill.

"Perfect, I already have all your shifts covered for the week, so let's eat some lunch. You text him, and then we'll pack up the stuff you've collected the last few weeks," Ada responds, with only care in her words.

I stare dumbfounded for a moment, but quickly recover and pull my phone out to message Zander.

> **I spoke with Ada. Everything is good. You can come over whenever you're ready. I just need to eat something and pack up the few things I have.**

His reply comes within a minute.

> **Give me an hour, and I'll be there.**

> **Alright, sounds good.**

"Zander says he'll be here in about an hour." I look up from my phone and tell Ada.

"Perfect, I can't wait to meet him," Ada responds as she pulls out leftovers for lunch.

An hour and fifteen minutes later, Zander is standing in the living room chatting easily with Ada, and I'm left wondering what I should be doing. I just awkwardly stand here, watching their conversation. So I announce, a bit too loudly, "I'm going to go grab my stuff from upstairs."

Zander looks over at me and asks, "Do you need any help?"

"No, no. It's like two bags. I got it," I reply and quickly head upstairs.

Twenty minutes later, the bags are in the back seat of the truck and I'm hugging Ada on the front step.

"You keep in touch. And if you need anything, you know where I am," she says as she gives me one more hug.

"I can't thank you enough for everything you've done for me," I tell her before turning towards the truck. Zander is waiting to help me in, just like last night. Except this time, I give him my hand and actually let him let me in.

Chapter Nineteen

So much for a happy reunion

Kara

The drive back to what Zander calls his *pack lands* takes about two hours, and it's super uneventful. Honestly, I'm grateful for that. We're about thirty minutes to our destination when Zander glances over and asks me, "Do you have any questions before we get there? We have a little bit of time, and I want to make sure you're comfortable."

Do I have questions? Absolutely! But I'm not sure how to approach any of them. Sighing, I start with the one that's bothering me the most. "Who's going to be there when we arrive?"

"Well, up until this morning, there have been about fifteen people staying at the pack house working on different aspects for the situation. But we made the call to limit it to people you've already met," Zander says as he keeps his eyes on the road.

"Oh, that's nice," I reply awkwardly.

"So that means my second and third will be there, Damien and Kai. Plus, one other person will be there. Carmen. I know you don't remember her, but she's been your best friend since you were pups—sorry, kids. This whole thing has been super hard on her. She asked if she could be there to help you transition and give you a friend," Zander continues.

"Oh, that's nice," I repeat.

"You already said that," Zander says with a chuckle.

"Yeah, sorry. I'm just processing, I think."

"That makes sense. We will figure this out," Zander says as he reaches over and puts his hand on my thigh, squeezing lightly. That electric shock happens again, and he jerks away. "Sorry, that was presumptive of me."

"It's fine," I tell him. "And thanks, I just don't want to be more trouble. I know I already made things really difficult."

"You did what you thought you had to. No one is mad at you. Just worried for you," he responds. "Let's just take it one step at a time, yeah?"

"Okay, yeah," I reply with a bit more conviction.

Twenty minutes later, we're parking in front of a massive house. This is the pack house? My house? It's more like a mansion. Only two stories, but it sprawls with a massive wraparound porch. There is a huge bay of windows that takes up both stories. How the hell is this place even real?

As we park in the massive circle drive, I notice three people standing on the front porch waiting for us. Two I've already met, albeit under stressful circumstances. Zander, ever the gentleman, jumps out of the truck and comes around to my side before I have a chance to get out.

"Thanks," I tell him as I take his hand and he helps me out. Looking around, I let out a sigh that helps settle my nerves. I know these people. Well, knew. They know me. *They won't hurt me. I'm safe.* I keep repeating my new mantra to myself as we walk up the path and come face to face.

"Hi." *Was that my voice?* It sounds so small.

"Hey, girlie. I'm glad you came back," the female—Carmen—says. I can tell she's doing everything in her power to not hug me. Carmen is shorter than me with dark brown, almost black hair. Her skin is the color of milk chocolate—is that even a color? Even though she's dwarfed by the men next to her, she emits a spitfire energy that commands space. I can just tell.

"Glad you came back," the broody one—Damien?—says as he nods in acknowledgement to Zander. If he didn't have that permanent scowl etched between his eyebrows, I'd say he was beautiful in a very typical way—blond hair, sea blue eyes.

The third one of the trio, Kai, has yet to meet mine or Zander's eyes. His hands are shoved deep in his pockets like he's doing everything he can to take up the least amount of space. He was the one who was 'in charge' when I bolted. I'm sure his life has been hell since then.

"Kai, I'm sorry. You didn't do anything wrong. I was running on adrenaline and fear, and you were just the unlucky one that had to deal with it," I tell him. He looks up with a sheepish smile and nods at me.

"Thanks. I'm sorry, too. I should have realized that you were scared more than I did at the time," Kai says, his soul-deep gray eyes imploring me to understand.

I glance over at Zander, and he's standing right next to me. A bit too close for comfort. Would it be rude to step away? I really don't want the zing thing to happen again. At least, not with an audience.

The silence between the five of us stretches to an awkward minute while we're all just waiting for someone to say something. *So much for a happy reunion.* I feel like maybe I should say something, but what? Luckily, it's Carmen who breaks the silence and the awkward spell we're all under.

"So, I have an idea, but you can totally say no if you want. Why don't you and I have a girls' night? Nothing big, just hanging out, eating some food, and chatting. Maybe a movie. I know you don't remember me, but we've been best friends for years. I think us hanging out will at least help you relax. I've already set you up a room."

The tension that was building amongst us visibly eases, but the tension in Zander increases. I guess there is still a part of him thinking we will be back to where we were before. But that's just not going to happen right now. As much as I just want to hole up in my room and not talk to anyone, maybe hanging out with someone will be good for me?

"Umm, sure. That sounds fun. I can't say I'll be great company, but I'd like to try," I finally respond.

"Great! I already ordered pizza, and these guys will leave us alone. I'm sure they have big bad Alpha pack business that we don't need to deal with," Carmen says, rolling her eyes at the guys and jumping forward to grab my arm. I don't know much about her, but I can tell she's the spitfire of our friendship, or was.

Carmen all but drags me into the house, calling over her shoulder, "If Kara has any bags, you can bring them to my room. But this is a girls' only night. Y'all have fun doing whatever it is you do."

With that, we head upstairs, Carmen chattering the whole time. Maybe if I just nod, smile, and say things randomly, I won't have to participate too much in the evening. I have a feeling she will tell me just about any story from our past she can think of to help with my memory.

The pizza arrives along with my bags in the hands of Zander thirty minutes later, and for the rest of the night, Carmen and I watch movies while she keeps me entertained with stories from our childhood. As the hours progress, the easy comradery of having Carmen around makes my first night back a lot easier to deal with. I fall asleep next to her on her bed as the moon shines in the window and think, *maybe this was a good call after all.*

Chapter Twenty

Define okay

ZANDER

Thirty Minutes Earlier

Well, fuck. Of course, Kara wouldn't immediately want to spend time with me. Why would she? I'm sitting in this weird middle ground of *I make her uncomfortable* and *I'm her safe place*. It's maddening. I watch as both girls head up the stairs to the second floor towards Carmen's room. Apparently, Kara's new room is right there, too. I don't know why I thought she would stay with me still. I had one goal: get her home. I did that. Now what?

Standing in the foyer next to Damien and Kai, I realize just how silent and broody both of them are. This whole situation really has us all fucked up. The grumpy act I expect from Day, but Kai? I can count on one hand how many times he's acted like this. The last two weeks have been hell for him.

Once the girls disappear past the landing and down the hall, I head to my office without looking back. I haven't even been here more than two hours since Damien and I left to find Kara two weeks ago. Per usual, the pack came together to repair my rage-fueled destruction. Sinking into my chair behind the desk, I wait for either of the guys to say something.

Kai and Damien sit on opposite ends of the couch, and it's Kai who speaks first.

"So she's okay?"

I roll my eyes and huff. "Define *okay*. Is she healthy and unharmed? Yes. Does she remember anything from before this mess? Nothing but random feelings. Is our connection still there? Yes. We both feel better being around each other and we did brush arms once last night. The shock of connection is definitely still present. Her wolf is suppressed, but I think she's still there, under the surface."

"Okay, so it's not horrible, but it's not great, either," Kai replies with his half-hearted attempt at a chuckle. Leave it to Kai to try to find levity in any situation.

"Sure, we can call it that." Damien rolls his eyes. "Now that Kara's home, what's our next step? We need to figure out who this witch is. David and I have been working on it for two weeks, and are nowhere closer to an answer than we were when she slipped back across the borders."

"Well, we just keep working on it. What other choice do we have?" I respond just as the driveway sensor goes off. I look up at the monitors on the wall next to my desk and see the pizza delivery driver heading towards the pack house. Standing, I head back out to collect Kara's bags and the pizza. I'll do anything to see her. Even if it's for thirty seconds as an errand boy.

The driver arrives with six pizzas, which confuses the hell out of me. Then he passes the delivery note to me. Four pizzas for Kai, Damien, and myself, and two for the girls. Also, that Carmen said I'd be paying. Should have known. I pay and tip the driver before heading back to the office to hand over the goods to the guys, then make my way up to Carmen's room.

When I knock on the door, it's Kara who answers. Just seeing her face relaxes something inside of me. When she sees it's me on the other side of the door, her face lights up before she schools her features.

The relief and joy I feel at her initial reaction almost makes me drop to my knees—or at least drop the pizzas. Thankfully, neither happens, and I pull myself together as I say, "I come bearing pizza and your bags. Would you like the bags with you or in your room?"

"Umm, I think I'll take them," Kara replies, reaching for the pizza first. She hands that off to Carmen and grabs the bags from me.

We both stand there awkwardly for a minute before I say, "Right, I'll be going. But Carmen knows how to work the intercom system, and you can text or call me if you need or want anything."

"Thanks. I think we're good. Umm, have a good night?" It comes out as a question, and I can tell she didn't mean it that way. She tries again with more conviction, "Sorry, have a good night."

"Right, yeah. Have a good night," I say, turning to head back downstairs.

Back in my office, I immediately head over to my bar. I've been hanging out at a bar for the better part of four days, but I've been stone-cold sober the whole time. I haven't touched alcohol since Kara left and I destroyed my office in a drunken Alpha rage. Not my best work. Tonight, though, I need a drink to get my mind off the fact that my mate is finally home and I can't be with her.

I pull out three glasses and reach for the nice rye whiskey. Filling the glasses, I turn and hand one to each of my boys.

"I know we have a ton of business to catch up on, so let's do that while we eat," I tell them. "When will David and Franny be back? I'm sure they want to see their daughter."

"Wednesday. David had some things in his own pack to take care of, and we all figured that will give Kara a bit more time to adjust," Damien replies.

"Makes sense, what about the rest of the pack? What do they know?" I ask, realizing I've completely neglected everything the last two weeks. I mentally slap myself. My dad would be furious with me if he was still alive. He wouldn't have ever allowed this. Granted, I wouldn't be Alpha, and probably would have had a lot more freedom, but still.

"We've been telling people that Kara had some business in her father's pack that needed her attention, and you went with her on account of your growing bond and to support a neighboring Alpha," Kai adds. "We figured that would be plausible. Both things would technically be true if that is what she was really doing."

"Right, good. What else do I need to know of the cover story? How are we dealing with things going forward?"

"Right now, we're just going to keep Kara sequestered until she's ready to visit the village. She wasn't super involved around the village yet anyway, so it should work. But she's going to have to figure out what she wants her new role to look like, and fast. You've technically been together for almost three months. Being an Alpha pairing, people will start questioning things. You're the Alpha, yes. But she's the Luna. The mother of the pack. If she's not a prominent figure in the pack soon..." Damien's voice trails off.

He doesn't need to complete the thought. I know he's right. A pack without a Luna isn't as strong as one with a Luna. That's why Alpha successors try to find their mates before they take over packs. My father found my mother at a mating circle. Something that packs put on to get matable males and females in one place to find matches.

There hasn't been a mating circle in years, and before my father died, he was considering hosting one so I could find my mate. I pushed back because I was only twenty-five. I had just become eligible to take over the pack, and I wasn't ready to find my mate. Most pack members start looking as soon as their wolf matures at twenty-one. I wasn't in any hurry. My father should have been alive for years more. Hell, he and my mom were together for fifteen years before he took over.

Then my father died three years ago, and I found myself an Alpha without a mate. A young Alpha, at that. I had so much still to learn, finding a mate dropped way down on my to-do list.

All that is to say, finding my mate didn't matter to me for my own selfish reasons. But my pack was, and still is, suffering because the role of Luna hasn't been filled in, well, twenty-four years. I was six when rogues killed my mother while she was visiting her family in Starfall Pack. The blessing in disguise is that I didn't go on that trip. I was my parents' only child, and if I would have been there, there's a possibility I would have been killed, too.

Twenty-four years of no motherly influence on the pack. While the Alpha is the strength of the pack, the Luna is the glue. Now that I've found my mate, the pack is restless to have that glue solidified again.

I know I've been quiet for a couple minutes, brooding over everything Day said. My guys learned a long time ago to give me time, and I'll reply eventually. But, it's Kai who breaks the silence first. "Once we uncover her memories and release her wolf, it will get easier. But until then, we will continue to search for the witch and keep our pack safe."

"That all sounds good, but let's move on to normal pack business for a bit. I need something normal to focus on." I sigh and get up to refill my drink.

For the next few hours, we work through all the things that make a pack run. Finances, births, deaths, problems, solutions, complaints, compliments, even requests to join and leave the pack. I lose myself in the mundane and try to forget that Kara is so close, but still so far away.

Just past midnight, we call it quits and I head up to my bedroom. My room feels empty without her, but as I climb into bed, I swear to myself that I'll make her fall in love with me again. Even the human way, if necessary. I'm not losing her. Not again.

CHAPTER TWENTY-ONE

You're not ready for that

KARA

OVER THE NEXT TWO days, I split my time between hanging out with Carmen and sitting in on a few meetings here and there because, as Zander says, *"There's a lot that you might want to know, and the easiest way to learn about things is to be there."* Truthfully, I don't know what's going on in the meetings, but being around people that genuinely want me there is nice. I didn't realize how hard I was working myself at the bar, so doing a lot less has been a nice change of pace.

Carmen is an absolute gem. If anyone has figured out how to balance still being my friend and not overwhelming me with the past, it's her. She just spends time with me, and the stories come naturally throughout our conversations.

Like now, we're outside lounging on the patio with books in our hands, and it's just comfortable. I get to a stopping point in the book I'm currently reading and look over to see her watching me. "What?" I ask her, confused.

"I was just thinking how we never used to get to do this. You were always so busy. Before you met Zander and we moved here, you were always with your dad, learning the ropes on how to be a badass Alpha," she muses.

"I was going to ask you about that. Why did you move with me?" It's one of those questions that's been plaguing me since Zander mentioned that Carmen is from my old pack, too. There's a story there. It's big. I can see it in her eyes just like I can feel it in my bones. But, the truth of it is just out of my grasp. I've got this feeling that her and I were—are?—more like sisters than friends. The bond between us transcends friendship. Even without knowing, I can feel that.

"Oh, babes. You're not ready for that story yet. But let's just say that wherever you go, I go. You and I are connected in a way that puts your mating bond with Zander to shame," she says with a wave of her hand, effectively dismissing me. Too bad it doesn't work.

I sit up and put my book down to fully face her. "No, I want to know. I feel like it's big and maybe it'll help me."

"You sure about that?" she asks as she puts her own book down and matches my posture.

"Yes, I need to know."

"I'm not going to bore you with all the stupid, pointless details but basically, when we were pups, we got into all sorts of trouble," she begins with a chuckle. "One day, we were out in the woods, playing like pups do, when I decided that I could swing on this branch into the river. We didn't know about springtime runoff and how that makes the water a lot colder and deeper than normal."

Carmen closes her eyes for a moment, almost like she's trying to stave off the memories. She opens them, but doesn't meet my gaze as she continues, "When I went in, the cold shocked me and I wasn't the strongest swimmer. You jumped in and saved me. If it hadn't been for the fact that you were of Alpha blood, I don't think either of us would be here today. You got me out. I don't know how; I passed out almost as soon as I hit the water. From that day on, I knew I would go wherever you go. We've been together ever since. That's why when you bolted out of the room we were in and took off, it was terrifying. Because I couldn't save you like you could save me."

As she finishes, she finally meets my eyes. But I don't know what to say. I sit there, in shock. I saved her? Me? The way I feel, I don't think I could have saved anyone. But here she is, telling me just that.

"You've always been super selfless. That's why you'll make a fabulous Alpha if you still want that. Or at least the Luna of this pack." The conviction in her tone astounds me.

"Wow, okay. That was a lot. Maybe I wasn't ready for it," I try to joke.

"See! I told you. Especially since we probably should be getting you ready to meet your parents. They should be here in the next couple hours."

"Wait, *what*?" I jump up like I was shocked.

"Oh, shit. No one told you?" Carmen stands up with a look of shock on her face. I'm sure my face matches.

"What hasn't Kara been told?" Zander asks as he walks up to us. He looks between us, waiting for one of us to answer.

"That apparently my parents are coming. Today!" *Shit. Shit. Shit.* I haven't panicked in a few days, but here we go again.

"I was coming out to tell you," Zander responds sheepishly. "We weren't one hundred percent sure what day they were coming, so we hadn't said anything. We didn't even know if they would be for sure coming this week."

"Okay, yeah. I guess I should want to meet them. They are my parents, after all." Sitting back down on the lounger, I take a few deep breaths to calm my fraying nerves.

Holy hell, why didn't I think I would have to re-meet my parents? Up until this moment, I knew I had parents, but they weren't something that I put much thought into. Now, here I am, dealing with it. *Breathe, Kara. You'll be fine. You have to be fine.*

Zander moves to crouch in front of me. Resting his hands on my thighs, he draws small circles with his thumbs, grounding me. "Hey, they won't be here till around dinner time. At least five hours from now. They will message when they are on their way, and it's a solid two hours of driving. How do you feel about going for a walk to the village? Maybe grab a bite to eat?" The sincerity in Zander's voice is all I need.

I take a deep breath and smell his cinnamon and soil scent. Feeling that weird connection with him again. I realize it's not as bad as I'm making it out to be. I did want to go to the village and get the lay of the land again. Zander and I haven't really spent any time just the two of us since I got back, and I find myself wanting to be with him.

"Sure. That sounds like a good plan. I just need to go grab the right shoes," I tell him with a genuine smile.

The smile he gives me in return could light up a city, and it causes my heart to skip a beat. The butterflies in my stomach also seem to love his smile.

Without prompting, Carmen pipes up, and somehow, I completely forgot she was standing there. "I have some things I need to do, anyway. You two have fun." With a pinky wave, she flips her hair over her shoulder and walks inside.

"We will," Zander answers for the both of us. To save any more awkwardness, I head inside to change and get ready to leave.

CHAPTER TWENTY-TWO

I'll always catch you

KARA

As I REACH FOR the handle of the sliding door, I see Zander on the back lawn, pacing like some sort of caged animal. No, that's not it. *Is he nervous?* I keep forgetting how hard this whole thing is on him, too. Walking outside, Zander looks up and that nervous energy reaches his eyes for just a moment, before it's covered by the joy of him seeing me. I'll never get used to that.

"Hey," I say hesitantly. The overwhelming urge to run away is so strong, but I keep moving towards him.

"Hey, yourself. Ready?"

"Yeah." We start down the path at the far end of the lawn. Without prompting—which is a first based on the last week, honestly—I ask one of the questions that's been eating at me. "I am a bit confused as to why the pack village isn't right next to the pack house? I've been reading, and it seems like that's more common."

"Yeah, our setup is not the norm, that's for sure. When my grandparents moved the pack here over seventy-five years ago, they did so because of an attack on the pack. The main thing attacked was the pack house, so they thought to put some space between it and the village. Protection for the main pack. But the pack house is basically open to the pack at all times."

Zander's hands are in his pockets as we walk side by side, and it seems like he's trying to keep distance between us, which I appreciate, even if I don't completely want him to.

"So why haven't I seen much of the pack, then?" If the pack house is open to the whole pack, it doesn't make any sense. I've really only seen Zander, Carmen, Damien, Kai, Callum—like once—and the housekeeper and cook, Marge.

"Honestly, we didn't want to overwhelm you. We asked the pack to give us some space for the next week or so as we work through some family things. The pack is really understanding, and is giving us that. But yeah, usually it's a revolving door of a pack." He glances in my direction as he adds, "How are you? We haven't spoken much, even with you sitting in on meetings."

"I'm okay. Carmen is really helping me. She's not pushing to go immediately back to what we were, and that's helping." I realize almost instantly what that sounds like, and I rush to add, "Not that you are. If anything, I think we haven't spent enough time just talking and stuff. I think it helps to talk. Doesn't bring the memories back, but it settles something in me. Just like being around you, and others." God, I'm rambling now.

Zander smiles a knowing smile, but doesn't comment. And I'm kind of glad he doesn't. Him commenting on my awkward rush to cover up my idiocy would have probably made it so much worse. We lapse into a comfortable silence for a minute or two as we walk. I start to look around, and just breathe in the nature around me. Just like being around Zander settles something, nature settles something else. Something deeper and more primal within me. The wolf part?

I'm looking around at the different trees, plants, and flowers, not really paying attention to where I'm going when I stumble over a tree root and start to faceplant. Before I hit the ground, strong arms band around my waist and pull me back into a hard body. It sends a jolt of electricity through my entire body. I sag into Zander for a second before I realize what I'm doing, and jump away.

Zander doesn't stop me when I pull away, but when I turn to look at him, a wistful, almost forlorn, look is etched on his face before he masks it.

"Right. Umm, sorry about that," I say awkwardly. I'm really messing this up.

"Why are you sorry? You tripped, and I caught you," Zander says as we both just stand there, neither of us moving while also avoiding each other's gaze.

"Yeah, you did stop me from fully faceplanting. Thanks," I say with a smile and a little laugh.

"I'll always catch you, Kara. No need to thank me," he replies, and those simple words send those butterflies into some sort of waltz in my stomach again.

"Yeah, right. Of course," I say as I turn to head down the path again. I don't get more than two steps when I hit the same damn root, and because I'm walking at a faster pace, I fall again, but faster.

Before I connect with the ground, Zander grabs one of my flailing arms, yanking me towards him. This time, with the momentum of his yank and a spin move that just kind of happens, we come flush together for the first time since this whole mess started—was that really almost three weeks ago? We both just stand there. Him with his arms wrapped around me, and me with my hands holding his shirt like the lifeline it is. I look up and see him staring down at me.

Time seems to just freeze. Sound around us fades to nothing. All I can see is the green of his eyes. I hear the sound of his heart, and something else. It's almost like a purr, but that's not right. It's more of a rumble. *Is that his wolf?* The sound soothes me, causing my whole body to relax.

"Kara, I..." Zander's voice trails off as in the distance, we hear a howl that sounds too close—and not exactly friendly, either. Zander's head snaps up and the spell is broken.

He goes rigid. The soft, caring mountain man is gone, now replaced by something more sinister and intense. The Alpha, I realize. He puts me behind him, further away from the sound—his hands never leaving me.

"Change of plans. We're going to head back to the pack house, right now." The ice in Zander's tone is almost terrifying.

"What's going on?" I ask, the confusion and fear I'm feeling bleeding into my words.

"Rogues crossed our borders just a bit ago, and my enforcers are having trouble getting them back. Damien and Kai went to help. I'm getting you back, NOW!" He says the last word with more force than I've ever heard from him. It broaches no arguments.

We turn to head back to the pack house. I should be panicking from the threat. I've been panicking about everything else. But the way Zander continues to guard me as we walk back makes me feel safe. He grabs hold of my hand and doesn't let go.

CHAPTER TWENTY-THREE

Absolutely not, he's yours

ZANDER

OF FUCKING COURSE, THE moment our connection really sparks back to life, something interrupts it. Not just anything, either. Rogue fucking wolves on our lands. It's not out of the norm for it to happen, but to happen during the day is just odd. I was actively tuning out the pack, so the howling was the first hint that something was wrong.

Being with Kara just blocks out the world. But once that howl broke through the haze of being with her, Damien's voice slammed into my consciousness.

Where the fuck are you? Rogues just crossed the northern border, and the two enforcers we have on that side couldn't contain them. Kai and I are headed that direction. Do you have Kara with you? We didn't see her at the house when we left.

I mentally groan at the sheer insanity of it all. *Yeah, she's with me. We were headed towards the village. We're headed back to the house now. Take care of things. I've got her.*

Damien acknowledged me and let me know he would update me when he knows more.

"Why are rogues trying to get onto the pack ground?" Kara looks up at me as we move down the path. I haven't let go of her hand. I know I'm practically dragging her, but the compulsion to touch her and keep her safe is all I can think about.

"I have no idea, it's not unusual for rogues to come onto lands at night. We have more resources than they have access to. But during the day is just weird."

"Oh, do you need to go help?"

"No, Damien and Kai will take care of it. No need for all of us to go. They are more than capable," I tell her and squeeze her hand. My unsaid words hang between us. *You're more important than rogues.*

Kara stares at my outright display of affection. Before, I was basically dragging her while holding her hand, so I'm sure it felt more like *keep moving* than *I want to hold your hand*. But now, I've gentled my hold. It's the second of freezing that makes me realize what I even did. We had a moment back there. Honestly, if we wouldn't have been interrupted, I probably would have tried to kiss her. I need to kiss her again. It's a deep need to feel that level of connection with her again.

"Okay, that makes sense," she says while staring at our joined hands. I can't read her expression, but if I had to venture a guess, it would be somewhere between confusion and awe at how we just fit together. *Please be that combination.* I send up a prayer to the universe that she feels the same thing I do. I need her back.

Realizing I have been silent for longer than would be considered normal, I clear my throat and say, "Once we get back to the pack house, I'd appreciate it if you went inside and found Carmen. I'm sure there won't be any danger by the time we get back, but the rogues did cross on the north side of the pack lands. That's closer to the pack house than other borders."

"Yeah, right. Of course. That makes sense." She's still staring at our hands as we walk.

"I can let go if it makes you uncomfortable? I didn't think before I grabbed your hand. I'm sorry."

Kara finally looks up at me before she says, "No, it's fine. I think the shock of you doing it broke through something, and it actually made things feel calmer inside me. I'm not going to lie, when that howl happened, I kind of panicked

and wanted to run away. Apparently my first instinct is to run for everything."
I give her hand a light squeeze in acknowledgement.

I think about what she said for a moment before responding, and realize
something that might be critical to helping her. "Before this whole mess happened, you were the exact opposite. Throwing yourself into danger without a
second thought. It made your parents crazy when you were young, and scared
the shit out of me when I met you. I wonder if part of what happened when
your wolf was blocked or buried or whatever, was to hide that part of you, too?"

I've been scanning the woods for threats, but glance down at her to see that
she is looking up at me with almost hope in her eyes.

"That actually kind of makes sense. Carmen was telling me why we're so close,
and she said the same thing. That I didn't question it, I just saved her," she says
with a sage nod.

We make it out of the woods and break apart like there's a fire between us. I
don't think Kara's ready for the world to know there's something between us
again. Even if I have to wait the rest of my life, I'll let her take the lead on this.
I'm not losing her again.

We head up the lawn towards the house, and Carmen is standing in the
doorway, looking worried.

"Jesus Christ. When they told me rogues had come across the border and it
was relatively close to the path you two took, I kind of panicked. But Damien
told me they wouldn't get that close to you guys. But seriously, I'm tired of you
scaring me like that, Kara. My heart can't take it." She ends with a dramatic sigh
and her hand on her heart.

Kara laughs at Carmen's antics before responding, "Oh, I'm sure this big bad
shifter would have protected me." She winks up at me. Actually winks. Do not
react. DO. NOT. REACT—Dammit. Instant hard on.

Carmen looks between us with a grin on her face. "So, was the walk eventful?
Seems like it was."

Kara jumps at the words and looks anywhere but at me. "What? No. Everything's fine. Good. It's good. We're good," she sputters and adds, "I'm going to
take a shower."

I laugh at her absolutely pathetic attempt to be cool, crossing my arms and raising an eyebrow. I can't help but comment, "I said I'd make sure you got back safe, seems like making sure you get all the way to your room is necessary."

"No!" she almost shouts, but composes herself quickly. "I mean, no thank you. I can handle myself."

"You can, huh?"

"Yes—no! Wait!" she sputters again and turns a deep shade of red to match her hair. She looks between me and Carmen. Carmen, the devil, is doing everything in her power to not laugh outright, which makes Kara slap her arm. "You're not helping."

"Absolutely not, he's yours," Carmen says, losing her fight and doubling over in fits of laughter.

"That is not what I meant. Oh my God, you both are horrible. I'm going upstairs. To shower. Alone. And I'll see you both later." She punctuates her words with a shake of her finger at us and stomps upstairs.

Carmen and I are left standing in the entryway of the house. Her, leaning on a side table still laughing, and myself, shaking my head at the whole situation.

"You good?" I ask her.

Wiping tears from her eyes, she looks up at me before she says, "Yeah, I'm good. She's falling for you, and can't wrap her head around that idea, isn't she?"

I sigh and I grab the back of my neck, rubbing it. I don't want to have this conversation with anyone. But if I have to, Carmen is the one that will get it. "Yeah, I think she is. We've had a few moments where I saw the fire that was there before. But I don't want to push her. She's so skittish. It's such a switch to how she was before her mind was fucked with."

Sobering quickly, as if Carmen didn't think I would actually reply, she walks over and stands directly in front of me. She's so much shorter than Kara, the difference feels so much bigger when she's this close to me. "I get it. I've noticed the skittish thing, too. It's got to be part of what happened. She wasn't even like this before she got her wolf, but once she did get her wolf, she became a force to be reckoned with. I think if we uncover her wolf, she'll stop being so flighty and panicky."

The door to the security room opens, and Callum walks out. The look that passes between him and Carmen is a lot more heated than I'd expect. With a smile and a nod, she looks back to me before she adds, "She still loves you. She just doesn't realize it yet. Give her time. It will come back."

Without either of them saying a word, they both head towards the kitchen, and I'm left standing there wondering if they are just having fun or if we've got another mate match on our hands. Resolving that they will tell me when they are ready, I head to my office and wait for word from Damien or Kai.

Chapter Twenty-Four

Easy for you to say

ZANDER

ONCE BACK IN MY office, I sit down behind my desk and look out the big windows. I'm not a fan of being relegated to the sidelines on fights, but one thing my father always told me was that the Alpha should be the last line of defense when it comes to rogue attacks. It's not worth the Alpha's life to engage in small skirmishes. It's the big fights that the Alpha should take a larger role in. Let the enforcers do what they do best. They've trained for this.

Damien's voice breaks through my musings. *Alpha, we have a problem.*

What happened? You said it was just a couple rogues. Day's use of my title makes me sit up straighter and focus. He doesn't do that unless it's serious.

That's what we thought, but by the time Kai and I made it to the two enforcers who initially engaged the rogues, they were gone. Both our men took some pretty gnarly injuries, but will recover. But that's not the problem, Damien responds. *We're on our way back to the pack house now. I'll fill you in when we get there.*

What the hell happened? I almost scream at Damien.

They were marking the trees with sigils. It doesn't seem like they knew what they were doing. Almost like they were being forced or controlled. But we took photos of the sigils and destroyed them. We will be back in two minutes.

Make it one, I tell him, venom in my tone. This is about Kara. I know it. Shifters don't use sigils, only witches.

A minute and thirty seconds later, Damien and Kai, along with an injured but walking Marcus, enter my office. I know the other enforcer was Derrek, because those two are always together. They are twins and don't do much apart—including patrol. Their parents weren't thrilled when they found out they would be partners, but there's not much they could do to stop them.

"Where's Derrek?" I ask no one in particular. My pack members' health and safety are always my priority.

"With the healer. He will be fine, but both legs need setting before they heal wrong," Marcus responds.

Acknowledging this with a nod, I turn to Damien for a report. Knowing it's his turn to speak, he begins, "Here are the photos of the sigils we found on the trees. They had completed two before Derrek and Marcus found them. The rogues didn't seem to care that they were found until the guys actually engaged them."

Looking back over at Marcus—I always prefer to hear from the source, if possible—he picks up from there. "Once we engaged them, they shifted almost instantly and seemed feral. They fought like they had nothing to lose, and it took both of us by surprise. I called for backup, and Damien and Kai responded within a few minutes. We had them under control enough to contain them, but it took Damien and Kai to bring them to heal."

"Dead or alive?"

"Dead. There was no talking them down or forcing a submit. I don't even think *you* would have been able to. They were fighting to kill, so we killed first," Damien adds matter-of-factly.

"Good, do any of you recognize these sigils?" I ask while I scroll through the photos on Day's phone. I glance up and all three of them are shaking their heads. "Get them to Callum and have him research them. The only creatures who use sigils are witches, so this has to do with Kara. I won't let her get hurt again on my watch," I finish on a growl, practically throwing Damien's phone back at him.

Damien nods, and leaves.

"Go to the healer, Marcus." He nods and leaves behind Damien, leaving me with Kai who looks worried. "You don't usually look like that. What's up?"

Kai shifts on his feet and looks out the window before turning fully towards me. "Do you really think this was a second attack by the witch?"

"There's no other way to see it. We don't normally have interactions with witches. They're even more reclusive than shifters. You know that. But in the past month, we've had a direct encounter with a witch that ended up cursing Kara. Now we find sigils. We need to figure out what they mean, and fast." As I finish answering him, a gasp comes from the doorway, and we both look up to see Kara standing there, shock written all over her face.

"You think the witch orchestrated this attack, too?" she asks with a bit of a sway in her body.

I rush over to her and steady her with my hands on her shoulders. "We aren't sure, but that's the running theory. We'll know more once Callum identifies some things we found at the scene. Don't worry, okay?"

"Easy for you to say, but I'll do my best," she says with a half-smile. Without thinking, I pull her towards me for a hug, and when she returns it without flinching first, my knees almost buckle.

"Well, I'm going to go check on Marcus and Derrek, then write up the report. Why did we start rotating the report writing, anyway? It sucks!" Kai says from behind me with a groan.

Kara looks up as if just noticing him, and pulls away slightly, but not completely. "Are my parents still coming?"

Before I can answer, Kai gives me a two fingered salute and smiles at Kara before heading out the door.

"I haven't checked my phone, but I would assume so. They are just coming for dinner, then they have business with another pack close by. So they will leave after dinner. You still okay with them coming?"

"Yeah. Is Marge cooking dinner, or are we ordering out?"

"Marge was planning on lasagna, I think." The simplicity of the conversation isn't lost on me. I walk over to my desk, grab my phone, and see a message from David.

We will be there around 6 p.m.

I relay the message to Kara as she sits down on the sofa. The look on her face tells me she wants to ask something, but doesn't know if she can.

"You can ask me anything. You know that, right?"

She sighs before meeting my eyes. "Seriously, is everything okay?"

"As okay as they can be. But for now, we go about business as usual until we know more."

"Okay. Want any help?" she asks as she looks at the giant pile of papers on my desk that have been neglected for weeks.

Smiling, I say, "Sure. You've always been better at making heads or tails of documents, anyways. At least organizing them."

With that, we spend the next few hours trying to organize and put pack business back in some semblance of order while we wait for her parents to arrive. Again, I pray to whatever gods are out there that this meeting goes well. We need something to go right for a change.

CHAPTER TWENTY-FIVE

Soul deep

KARA

I WAKE UP, ROLL out of bed, and head to the bathroom. Standing with my hands on the counter, I look in the mirror and remember how easily last night went. Zander was insanely nervous for me to meet my parents. I guess my track record of freaking out and running lends itself to that specific fear. Mentally, I slap myself again for causing so much headache and fear when all this first happened.

But the reality is, meeting my parents was just like when I really let Zander around me again, or spent time with Carmen. Easy. Did I remember who they were? Absolutely not. Did I know deep down that they were part of my life? Yes.

Both my parents were just happy I was somewhere safe. We spent dinner talking about life—nothing formal, nothing intense. David, well Dad, did bring up what to do about the witch, sigils, and all that crap. Even without knowing the history or why it's important, I knew it was. It felt important.

After dinner, Zander and Dad, along with Damien and Dad's second, Jason, went into Zander's office for a few minutes to compare notes. Mom, Carmen, and I stayed in the dining room to help Marge clean up. It was then that Mom brought up the mate bond.

"HOW ARE YOU FEELING now that you're back with Zander?" Mom asks.

I stop what I was doing and look up at my mom. Answering as honestly as I can, I respond, "If you're talking about the pain of being separated, it's better now. I don't think I was feeling it as bad as him. Probably because I'm basically human right now."

Mom puts the dishes she was carrying down and walks around the table to stand in front of me. When she reaches me and grabs my hands in hers, she tells me, "You might feel human, but you're a powerful shifter. It may be hidden or blocked by something none of us understand, but you will get her back. Your beautiful wolf will come back when she's ready, and you will feel complete again. Until then, just because the bond you feel with Zander is different than what it was..."

I begin to shake my head, because I don't know what it was before, but Mom stops me by wrapping me in her arms and continues, "Just because it's different now, doesn't mean there isn't one. I saw you two. There's still something there. You just have to find it again. It's soul deep. it's who the universe deemed to complete us." Pulling back, she adds, "Lean on that."

With that, she walks back to pick up the dirty dishes and makes her way to the kitchen, leaving me standing there like an idiot. I look over at Carmen where she is wiping down the table, and she looks up at me with a smile.

"I haven't mated yet, but just based on what I've seen with you and Zander, and your parents and mine, it's true. You're still you after finding your mate, just more," Carmen adds.

"So basically, y'all are saying I need to just let whatever is supposed to happen between me and Zander happen?" I ask with a bit of petulance in my tone.

Carmen laughs and says, "Well, if the chemistry I saw today is any indication, you two are going to be back to being annoyingly lovey dovey VERY soon."

I roll my eyes, picking up the glasses from the table and head into the kitchen.

BLINKING BACK TO THE present, I stare at my reflection before I remember how the night ended.

After that 'touching' and rather jarring moment with my mom, I needed some alone time. So I told Carmen I was tired and was heading to my room. I messaged Zander that after the crazy day we had, I needed some sleep. I waited to say goodbye to my parents, and then went upstairs to my room. Now, it's the next morning, and I'm terrified to see Zander. Not because I don't want to, but because every single dream last night was about him.

I hate that I have no memory of us before this whole mess, but I feel so much for him. It doesn't help that he's not subtle about how he feels about me.

Sighing, I go about my morning routine until I hear my phone buzz on my bedside table.

Hey there. Sleep okay?

Pretty decent, actually. I'm sorry I kind of just abandoned everyone after dinner last night.

Don't be. After your parents left, Damien had a ton of pack business to discuss with me. I was trapped in my office till after midnight.

Yuck!

Pausing for a second, I think about what my mom, Carmen, and even my dreams have been telling me, and decide to be a bit brave.

Have you had breakfast yet?

Not yet. Want to try that walk to the village again? There's a great breakfast place I haven't been to in months.

> Oh, that sounds great. Give me twenty minutes and I'll meet you downstairs.

> **It's a date. ;)**

I catch myself smiling at my phone and spend ten minutes trying to psyche myself up for my date with Zander, because that's exactly what this is. I spend the next five throwing half my closet on my floor, trying to find something to wear, and the final five throwing on some simple makeup and my hair into a halfway decent ponytail. I decided on dark, wide-leg denim jeans, a green, off-the-shoulder sweater, and my super comfy pair of sneakers.

I take one last look at myself in the mirror and fling the door open, only to find Zander leaning on the wall across from my door, looking like perfection. Washed-out denim jeans, a gray tee that hugs his muscles in the best possible way, the same brown boots I always see him in, and a brown flannel that looks divine. My mountain man nickname is so fitting right now.

"I didn't see the need to wait for you downstairs when I was going to walk right by your door myself," Zander says nonchalantly.

"Obviously," is all I can think to say as I just stare at him. Luckily, I sound a lot less flustered than I feel.

Kicking off the wall, Zander reaches his arm out towards me and says, "Come on, it's a nice morning. We should be able to actually make it to the village. Provided some of us avoid certain roots in the path." He winks at me.

"Hey! I'll take the blame for the first one, but you're totally at fault for the second one. You got me all flustered." I take his arm like it's the most natural thing in the world.

"Did I now?" He laughs as he leads me down the stairs.

"You know what I mean." I laugh, too, because I totally walked into that one, and there's no denying his effect on me and my inability to control my reactions or words around him.

"Sure, I do. But you are super fun to tease." He winks as he holds the back door open for me, and we head out into a perfect morning.

Chapter Twenty-Six

Earth–shattering

Kara

Having successfully avoided the roots and awkward moments, we come out of the path at the edge of the village. Ironically, all I can think about is how I should have tripped so that Zander would touch me again. Because other than offering me his arm when we first went down the stairs back at the pack house, he kept himself annoyingly separate. *What the hell is wrong with me?*

Even though it's still relatively early in the morning, the village is alive with people getting their day started. It's obvious Zander hasn't ventured to the village in a while, because about every fifty feet we take, someone stops to speak to us. Well, him mostly. If they aren't stopping us, they are calling out and waving.

The closeness and comfort of the village is evident on every block. It helps settle more of my racing thoughts. Each new thing, or new-to-me thing, puts me back together. The more I explore and experience, the better I seem to feel. Slowly, I feel like I'm finding myself again, even without my memories.

The pack members speak to me like I'm one of them, as well. I do my best to play the part Zander and I had talked about on our walk. That I've been gone for a few weeks helping out my family's pack. I guess I hadn't ventured too many times to the village, so knowing names wasn't something I needed to worry about, but it was still slightly stressful.

We make it to the restaurant and walk into the place which is almost completely full, but Zander leads us to a table in the corner, like it's waiting for us.

"I might have called up and let them know we were coming." He glances back at me sheepishly. "I told them two seats at the bar would have been plenty, but here we are, table and all."

The server comes up and hands us menus. We're secluded enough I don't feel like people will hear me, so I ask, "Have I been here before? And if so, what did I order?" I feel stupid having to ask, but here we are.

"Yeah, and you got pancakes and bacon," Zander replies with zero judgement. "You loved them, and said next time you wanted waffles."

I put my menu down and just stare at him. "Seriously? You remember that?"

"We came here the day before...well, you know. I've had a lot of time to replay the last day with you. So, yeah."

"Oh." It's all I can manage as I pick my menu up and hide behind it, hoping to hide my embarrassment.

"Hey," Zander says as he lowers my menu so I'm forced to look at him. "That is just part of our past. It doesn't help to pretend it didn't happen, at least between us. I'm just glad you're here now. Let's focus on that."

I look at him, really look at him, and realize how much he cares. I mean, I knew he cared about me. But part of me thought that maybe it was the bond between us that was driving him, or him being the Alpha. But, the truth is, he cares about me. If there's one thing I've learned by watching him or speaking to others about him, it's that when he cares, he cares with his whole self.

I find myself smiling and say, "Waffles it is."

"Sounds good," he responds with a smile that lights up his whole face. God, I love that smile.

"Good morning, Alpha, Luna." The server comes back over with coffee, and I mentally cringe. The title feels weird. "Did you want anything else to drink besides coffee? Ready to order?" the server asks, completely missing my mini panic attack.

"I'm fine with coffee, Tracey, but I'm sure Kara would like a water. Yeah?" Zander replies, looking to me for confirmation.

"Yes, water is good. And I think we're ready to order," I tell Tracey.

Orders placed, I busy myself with doctoring up my coffee and doing anything in my power to not stare at Zander. Glancing up, I realize he's doing exactly what I was trying to avoid—staring. "What?"

"Sorry, it's just nice to be hanging out. Just the two of us." Zander winks at me.

"It is. Although, I feel like I'm kind of shit company. I don't really have anything great to talk about," I tell him, because it's true. Honestly, other than the physical and emotional connection I can't deny anymore, I don't have any other type of connection with him. Well, not one that seems worthy to talk about. Being around Zander is easy, and letting him in my bubble is comfortable and almost necessary, but opening up to him scares me.

"We don't have to talk about anything earth-shattering," he says, completely oblivious to the turmoil I'm feeling inside.

"Okay, umm. So what are your plans for the day?" Because I've got literally nothing else.

"Damien and Kai have been running the show for the last few weeks, so I figured they can handle it today. I thought you and I would just spend some time together. Get to know each other better," Zander says, almost too eager to blow off his duties and just be with me.

"Yeah, but don't you have a bunch of stuff to catch up on?"

"Nah, it can wait."

I know we really haven't spent a ton of time together since I've been back, but the time we have spent together, alone or with others, he seems to only want to focus on me. It's like I'm his number one priority. Nothing else matters to him. "Okay, if you're sure it won't cause any problems. I'd love to spend the day with you."

"It will be great!" Zander perks up. "I was thinking we could go to the first place I took you when you originally got here. There's this awesome spot not many pack members go to this time of year, so I think we will be there pretty much alone."

"Where?" I ask, curiosity piqued.

"It's not far." He smirks.

"You're not going to tell me, are you?"

Zander shrugs before he finally says, "Nope, but you'll love it. I promise."

An hour later, we've finished breakfast and are heading to the far edge of the village. "How long will it take us to get to this 'secret spot?'" I air quote.

"Well, in this form, about thirty minutes. But if you want, I can shift and carry you? Would cut the time down to about ten." Zander looks down at me with hope.

I scrunch my face before I say, "Yeah, I don't know if I'm ready for that quite yet."

Zander just shrugs and leads me to the edge of the forest. We take off down the path, walking at a leisurely pace, but still with purpose. Before we make it more than a few minutes down the path, Zander gets that faraway look in his eyes that I've come to realize is him communicating with someone.

After about a minute of silence, he refocuses and I look up at him closely. "What was that about?"

"Oh, just Damien informing me they found a few more sigils from yesterday that they missed. He was wanting me to meet him out where they found them. I told him I was otherwise engaged, and he could handle it." The absolute nonchalance that Zander has about it kind of confuses me, but maybe it isn't that big of a deal?

"We can hang out another time. It's not like I'm going anywhere," I tell him, because I don't want to be the reason he's not fulfilling his duties as Alpha.

"No, it's fine. You're more important. It's not something I need to deal with myself. I'll get the report later," he says as he grabs my hand and pulls me down the path.

"Okay, if you're sure," I respond and fall into step next to him. If Zander isn't worried, I won't be either. Even though, deep down, something doesn't feel right.

CHAPTER TWENTY-SEVEN

Time and companionship

KARA

THE MORNING AIR IS crisp as we step out of the wood at the edge of a lake. The lake is so still, the brilliant, blue sky is reflected perfectly on the surface. Even with the crisp temperature, I'm surprised Zander said not many come out here this time of year. All the same, he leads me over to an outcropping of rocks that sit just at the edge of the water. With grace I couldn't hope to replicate, he climbs to the top of one of the larger boulders, and reaches down to help me up.

From this vantage point, the whole lake is laid out before us, and the feeling of calm inside me spreads. I breathe in the pure air and on a breathy sigh, I say the only thing that encapsulates this feeling, "Beautiful."

"Absolutely," Zander replies, and I look at him expecting to see him looking at the same view I am, but no. He's staring directly at me. The intensity in his eyes is almost too much.

"Are you talking about me or the view?"

"You, obviously. The view is nice, too." He shrugs. "But, I've seen it since I was a pup."

There's so much I want to know, so much I still don't understand. Maybe I should just bite the bullet and ask. Stop playing with the *what ifs* and actually make progress to getting myself back. Taking another deep breath, I let the crisp air do its thing before I ask, "Can I ask you a question?"

"Of course."

"According to what I've been told, you've known me since we were teenagers?"

"Yep. As the children of Alphas, we were kept pretty sequestered within our own packs till we had our wolves, but as we became stronger, our parents started taking us places. As teenagers, we aren't given the blessing of knowing who our mates are. At that point, you were still just an ally pack's Alpha's daughter. Yeah, I was interested, but you don't fool around with Alpha kids. Then, we met officially about four months ago, and everything changed," Zander finishes as he sits down, looking out over the water.

I sit down next to him and look out, as well. This is the one topic I've been wanting to bring up since I really started believing that Zander and I are something. Picking up a small pebble, I throw it into the water and say, "Would you tell me how we met? Like when we realized we were mates."

Glancing up, I see he's staring at me with a look I can't figure out. "It's totally fine if you don't want to," I rush out. *Ugh!* I didn't want to make him uncomfortable but here we are.

Zander must see the panic on my face, because he turns slightly towards me and rests his hand on my shoulder. "No, I would love to tell you. I can't believe I haven't told you about that yet."

"Then why do you look like, well...the way you do?"

"The way I... Oh! Sorry, I just realized that I should have given you this part of our history long before now." So his weird expression was self-deprecating, noted.

"Okay, so when did we meet? As adults, I mean?"

He closes his eyes, as if remembering every detail of the moment. After a few seconds, he opens them again and begins.

"Like I said, it was about four months ago when we met again as adults. I took over my pack about two years ago when my dad was killed, and I've been dealing with a lot of that transition stuff, so this was the first time I went to a smaller ally pack meeting."

"Smaller ally pack?" I interject.

Zander shoots me a small smile and answers, "There are about fifteen packs in our region, and of those fifteen, ten are allies. The other five aren't hostile, or haven't been for a long time, but they still aren't packs we want to deal with. They cause more problems than fix them. Of the ten ally packs, there are a few different close relationships between packs. We have two allies. Shadow Creek, you parents' pack; and the pack that is relatively between ours, Silver Hollow Pack. It was at a smaller ally pack meeting that we met."

I nod my head, doing my best to follow his explanation. It's so frustrating knowing that at one point I knew all this. But now it's just...blank.

"You arrived with your father because as his named heir, you were to be the next Alpha, and he believed it was time to have you start participating in the larger world of the packs. I wasn't paying attention to who was arriving as I was speaking with Grayson, the Alpha of Silver Hollow, but my wolf perked up as soon as you walked in the door. He became almost unbearable, wanting me to find you. He knew you were there before I even clocked it. Our wolves always know. It's the wolves that form the mate bond. We just get to reap the benefits."

"So, is that how you know my wolf is still there, just hidden?"

"Yeah, our emotional and physical bond is still present, so she has to be part of you still." Zander picks up another rock and throws it into the water.

Without taking his eyes off the water, he continues. "Anyway, I turned, saw you, and almost fell to my knees. My father always told me that when I found my mate, it would be like that. Instant, uncontrollable, all consuming. And it was. Without even saying a word to Grayson, I turned and walked up to you. You were standing right there, next to your father. But I think you must have told him before I walked up, because the second I came over, he stepped away like he knew."

"What happened at the meeting?"

"No clue. We turned around and walked outside. Your dad found us two hours later, sitting on the curb outside, just talking. We spent the next two days figuring out logistics, and you were moved to my pack, Carmen in tow, within the week."

"That seems really fast." I'm sure surprise is written all over my face. We went from not really knowing each other to moving in together within less than a week?

"That's pretty typical of wolf shifters. We need our mates, and now I know that physical separation actually hurts us. But typically, mates move in together even faster. If mates are found within the same pack, they could move in together within forty-eight hours in some cases. It takes longer when mates are from separate packs."

"Wow, I hate that I don't know any of this. I feel so disconnected to what seems to be literally half of myself." I find another pebble and throw it in the water. I'm glad I know the story now, but realizing how monumental it was for him just hurts.

"Hey." Zander reaches over, tipping my chin up so I'm forced to meet his eyes. "Just because you don't remember how we met before, doesn't mean what we feel for each other isn't there. That was our story then, not now. Honestly, finding you in that bar is a much better story." He laughs, not breaking eye contact or letting go of my chin.

"Zander..." I lean towards him.

"Yeah?"

This moment is perfect. I could easily just close the distance and kiss him. Feel his lips on mine. His scent of earth mixed with a warm, spring day is everything I could ever want. It fills my senses and makes me almost lightheaded. But I'm not ready. I'm not capable of separating the overwhelming feeling of need for him with what my mind is telling me is way too fast.

The me in this form, has only known him—truly known him—for a little over a week. I can't shake off the feeling that I'm supposed to know him more before anything happens. Sighing, I snap myself out of my head and back to the moment. I pull away, not ready for what he's so clearly ready for. "Thank you for telling me."

Before I fully turn back to the lake, I see his eyes flash bright yellow. I remember seeing the same thing that day in the woods. *His wolf is that close to the surface?*

"I'm sorry," I tell him. "I know you want things back to the way they were. I'd really like that, too, if I'm being honest. I'd love to know who and what I am. I want to see you like you see me."

Zander tenses and tries to speak, but I cut him off. I need to get this out, need him to understand that I'm here, but I'm not ready for more than I can give right now. "But I'm not there yet. I hope to get there, but I can't give you more than time and companionship right now."

Zander's eyes fade back to the green I'm used to seeing, and he smiles. He's still slightly tense, but is visibly trying to relax. "I get it. Part of me keeps forgetting that you, as you are right now at least, are human. And humans need time to form connections. Shifters feel everything all at once, and we jump in head first."

He looks out over the water, a pair of ducks splashing and swimming near the shore, and finishes, "I just want you to know I'm all in for as long as it takes. I'm here and won't be going anywhere. Take the time you need, but I'm not giving up on us. On you."

CHAPTER TWENTY-EIGHT

Yeah, after...

ZANDER

On the surface, I hope I look calm but determined, because inside, I'm struggling. Not with anger or rage, but a feeling of defeat. We were so close to moving forward, but Kara pulled back. I get it—I do, but this still sucks.

My wolf is practically raging inside me. I know my eyes flashed because he's so close to the surface. I had to work to force him back and not take what Kara isn't offering. He still feels her wolf, but doesn't understand why our connection is weak. Our wolves are the most primal version of ourselves. As an Alpha, his primal drive is stronger than most. *Protect, mate, reproduce, lead.* That's what he focuses on. Right now, two of those things are in danger, and he's lashing out.

I brought Kara here to hopefully push us closer to getting back to what we had. I think it did move the dial in that direction, but not as far as I was hoping. I can tell that her body and emotions are there, but her mind isn't. I have zero experience with human mating rights and rituals. *Do they even mate?*

I meant what I said that I'm all in. I'm not giving up on us or her. This will all work out. It has to.

Collecting myself, I look back over at her, and Kara's staring at me.

"Are you sure you're good with it?" she asks. She looks into my eyes like she's trying to find something deep inside.

"Yeah." I shrug and cock my head to the side. "Not going to lie, I want to kiss you." Her face morphs from curious to a cross between shock and something more. "But, you asked me not to right now, so I won't. Right now." I punctuate my words. I'm giving her the time she's asking for, but I'm absolutely going to keep fighting for more.

Kara has become my full focus over the last few days, the whole rest of the world be damned. Just thinking about that gives me pause. A mate bond completes us, but we're still our individual selves. There's still a separation. We're two people who have distinct roles, especially within the pack. But right now, she's it. My priority. My obsession. Screw everything else.

Shit. Where did that come from?

"We probably should be getting back." Kara cuts through my spiraling thoughts as she stands. "I'm sure Damien will need to give you a report on whatever he found earlier."

Pushing the crazy thoughts from my mind, I stand and jump down to the ground. Looking back up at Kara, I reach up, and she shocks me by sitting on the edge and letting me help her down.

As I lower her down to the ground, I can't help but bring her closer to me. Flush together just feels right. Kara's eyes widen and her breath hitches as our bodies align, and I groan. We stare at each other, neither pulling away for what feels like a frozen moment of time.

"Please, just one kiss," I whisper. I know I'm begging, pushing for something she outright refused just moments ago. But the look in her eyes makes me believe it might be possible.

"Zander, I..." she starts. "I don't want to say no. I feel like I should say no..." Kara's eyes drop to my lips and hold there. The fire I know that's banked in my own eyes is blazing through hers, as well.

"*Should* is a silly word."

"It is a silly word. It won't change things." I'm not sure if she's trying to convince me or herself.

"If you still need time, you'll get it. After."

"Yeah, after..." Never breaking her stare of my lips, she adds almost so quietly I don't hear, "kiss me, please."

I dive down and claim her. It's not sweet or gentle. I can't do that right now. I haven't tasted her in weeks. I've been going crazy not having her in my bed, and if all I get is one kiss, I'm pouring every piece of my soul into it.

Kara gasps into my mouth, and I take the opportunity to take more from her. Her arms wrap around my neck, and she holds onto me like I'm her lifeline. I get it, because right now, she's mine, too. My anchor in a storm. My life is laid bare in front of me, at her feet. What almost brings me to my knees is she's pouring herself into this kiss as much as I am.

The kiss spirals into something dangerous and powerful. My wolf surges forward, and I struggle to maintain a hold on him while trying to keep myself from falling over the ledge, as well. This kiss holds so much power, the axis of my universe shifts.

"Well, I'd like to say this is a surprise, but as soon as I heard you were out here, I figured I'd get to see something good. I should have brought popcorn. Or maybe some dollar bills?"

We fly apart like we're two teenagers who just got caught by their parents. Both of us struggle to catch our breath as we turn to face not just the speaker, Carmen, but Callum as well.

Callum is leaning against a tree at the edge of the woods with a shit-eating grin, and Carmen is just out of his reach with her hands on her hips, sporting a diabolical grin. Meanwhile, I'm struggling to rein in my wolf that was already riding me hard. Now, he's almost feral with protectiveness.

I know my eyes are glowing, and a growl leaves me that is all my wolf. There's no stopping it. Callum notices almost immediately, and perks up. Taking a step forward, he stands between Carmen and myself, as if to protect her.

"Hey, man, we were just trying to find you. I ran into Carmen on her way to find Kara, and said I was looking for you. We decided to find you together. You've been ignoring our attempts to contact you through the bond, so we kind of guessed something was going on." Callum puts his hands up in submission, but also begins to lower his head and step backward.

It's that moment I realize I'm allowing my Alpha energy to seep out again, and it's starting to affect everyone around me—including Kara, who has backed away from me and is pressed against the boulder we were just on.

Holy fuck, what is wrong with me? Why am I gearing up to attack my own pack? They aren't a threat. I back down and shove my wolf as far down as I can get him to go. Staggering with the force of it all, I look at my mate, her best friend, and one of my closest friends, then shake my head.

"I'm sorry. I don't know what came over me. I guess I was just startled, and it was a bit too much," I say to each of them.

Carmen steps out from behind Callum, rolling her eyes at him before looking at Kara. "You good, girl? Caught your breath?"

Kara, in her defense, seems like she's recovering from that mind-blowing kiss faster than me. She steps around me to walk up to Carmen, and gives her a big hug before she responds, "Yeah, I'm good. Why were you looking for me?"

"Well, you disappeared after we finished clearing dinner last night, and then snuck off with this one." She hikes her thumb at me and continues, "I just wanted to make sure you were okay. You're my girl."

"I am, thanks," Kara replies with a smile. "We should all be getting back, anyway."

"Yeah, we should." I give her a heated look, and she shakes her head.

"You have pack business to deal with, and Carmen and I have a lunch date with the men from our books." She punctuates what she says by pointing at me, then swooning with Carmen.

"Exactly!" Carmen agrees, fanning herself. "Those men are perfect!"

"Hey!" Callum growls, but Carmen just laughs at him. This isn't the first time I've noticed something between them. Interesting.

"Come on," I say and reach for Kara, who eagerly grabs my hand. "Let's get you back so you can have your fictional date," I playfully growl at her.

Ten minutes later, our little group is breaking through the tree line back at the pack house. *Thank you, grandparents, for cutting that direct path from the lake back here.* Damien and Kai are sitting on the patio, waiting for us.

I told both we were on our way back through the bond, and their responses were typical for each of them.

Damien: *Not listening to the pack bond when we've had a rogue attack recently is not a good look.*

Kai: *Thank fuck Callum and Carmen found you. I was getting worried when you wouldn't reply to anyone.*

My boys. They really do keep this place running.

As we make it to the patio, I reach for Kara and settle my hand around her waist, giving her a quick hug and a kiss on the head. "You and Carmen have fun."

"Oh, we will!" Carmen answers for Kara. The girls link arms and Carmen whisks Kara out of my arms and into the house.

I turn to three of my inner circle, and before I can say anything to them, Damien is the first to speak. "Jensen and Marek are waiting for us in your office. We are having a full inner circle meeting, and you aren't getting out of this. There's too much going on for you to pass shit off on me and Kai."

His words stop me in my tracks. It's just a couple rogues and sigils? I don't understand what the big deal is. I've had them deal with bigger stuff on their own before.

"Okay, if you think that's necessary. Has there been more activity than what you've already told me?" I look directly at Damien, but he just nods and heads for the door.

His outright dismissal of me makes me rage in a way I don't even understand. "Do not turn your back on me." There's zero inflection in my voice, but my Alpha aura radiates over him so heavily that Callum and Kai are slammed to their knees. Damien doubles over, but to his credit, stays upright.

Seeing my closest friends become crumpled heaps on the ground shocks me to my core. This is the second time I've had zero control of my aura in less than an hour. *What the fuck is going on?* I drop the command almost as quickly as I launched it at him.

"Jesus fuck, Day. I don't know what the hell came over me."

"Same thing happened out at the lake, but not that strong." Callum groans as he climbs to his feet, using the door frame to support himself.

Kai struggles to his feet as well, and adds, "This, plus you've already been absolutely blowing off your duties to the pack. I think we need to talk, and talk now."

"While that wasn't my intention, I think your reaction actually proved what I think I've figured out," Damien adds as he slowly turns around. You can tell he's a bit dazed.

"Let's get to my office, before I fuck anything else up," I say, a little resigned and a lot confused.

CHAPTER TWENTY-NINE

Based on how you've been...acting...

ZANDER

I sit down at my desk and stare at the five men who make up my inner circle. Damien and Kai have been with me since I was younger. Jensen and Marek were my father's second and third. They come with knowledge that we just don't have yet. Then there's Callum. He's part of my inner circle because his tech skills are unmatched. Normally, he stays in the background and doesn't take an active role. The fact that all five men are sitting in front of me means this is bad.

The silence in the room is deafening. No one speaks. I don't plan on starting this shit show. Waiting them out was my father's favorite tactic when it came to situations, so might as well do the same here. My men glance from one to the other, waiting for someone else to take the lead. *What the hell is so bad that all of them are tucking their tails?*

If I'm being honest with myself, I don't even want to be here right now. I could be with Kara. She's currently hanging out with Carmen, but I could be part of that, too. Just being in her space calms me.

She calms me in a way nothing and no one ever has. Even more now than before she forgot everything. It's like a part of me is tied to being physically near her.

I continue to stare at my men and wait them out. I might not be known for the patience my father was known for, but I'm a stubborn asshole. One of them is going to crack. The question is, which one? At this point, I'm actually curious which one will. One by one, I make eye contact, and they dart their eyes down and away. It takes a lot longer than I would expect.

Damien and Jensen are both Alpha in strength, but not blood, so they withstand my stare the longest. Kai and Marek break eye contact slightly faster. Technically, they are both Beta in strength. So not as strong, but still carry plenty of pack power. Callum, though? He's a Gamma. He's not a fighter. It's his brain that makes him powerful. He buckles fastest.

Finally, after what feels like hours—but were most likely just a few minutes—Damien gives in and begins, "We have answers to what some of the sigils mean, and we think that's part of the reason you've been so...off...the last few days."

"Meaning?" I ask with a turn of my wrist towards him, waiting for the rest.

"Some of the sigils work in tandem to create a spell. The shifters came and drew them, but they were close enough to the border that we believe the witch came back and activated them without stepping on our land. When we went back out there today to take a better look, we found four more that were on trees within feet of the border. We missed them because the rogues were already about a hundred feet onto our lands. Our mistake was assuming they were deep into our lands before they started."

"So you only destroyed the ones they were near?"

Marek continues for Damien, "Exactly. When the men engaged them, they didn't look at the back side of the trees right by the boundary because of how far the rogues were already in."

"Now the bad part," Kai says half under his breath.

My gaze whips to Kai. "Bad part?" This is just great.

"The sigils close to the border have been activated, and we can't destroy them. We tried." Damien takes back over. "Callum figured out what some of them were, and Jensen reached out to an old contact who was able to confirm they work in tandem to create a spell."

"Who's this old contact, and are they trustworthy?" I don't want this getting out to other packs.

Jensen replies quickly, "They're known as The Fixer. They aren't aligned with any pack, and for a price, will find out just about anything. From what I understand, they work for whoever will pay. I paid them with the pack account that's still set up from when your father was Alpha." I gear up to rage, because this is something I should have known existed. "And before you ask," he continues, "your father did tell you about this, but he rarely used the resource. The last time he used it was over a year before he died. I completely forgot it was an option. And yes, I've already given Damien all the info to use."

I nod and look back to Damien who continues without missing a beat, "Based on how you've been...well...acting..."

"Watch it," I growl.

Clearing his throat, he tries again, "Based on your abrupt reactions to both Callum and myself, as well as how you seem to need to be around Kara more than before, we think the spell is directed towards you."

Kai jumps in quickly, "We think it's some sort of proximity spell. You feel normal," he throws in air quotes, "around Kara, and feel only primal urges when separated. Everything is heightened. You need to protect, mate, and be around her. It's a driving force in mates that haven't completed the bond, but with you, it's more than that."

"So you're saying my need for Kara is being warped?" I ask, skeptical, but knowing these men wouldn't be bringing this to my attention without due cause.

They look between each other again, but Damien says, "That's exactly what we think. You almost attacked me for suggesting we go somewhere away from Kara. Callum said you almost did the same thing to him at the lake. It's a pattern we need to be aware of."

I lean back in my chair, resting my elbows on the armrest as I steeple my hands. "So what does all this mean?"

"It means we need to come up with a plan to break not only Kara's curse, but the one that's been put on you, too," Jensen says with zero inflection. I can see why my father had him as his second. He's so similar to Day, it's kind of scary.

"Before we do that, I think you two need to explain to me why this witch acted like this whole thing is retribution for something that happened a long time ago." I glare at Jensen and Marek.

They look at each other for a moment. I know they're communicating, and it pisses me off. "You know I don't allow mind speak when we are in a meeting," I say with ice in every word.

They crop their heads in deference and respond in unison, "Sorry, Alpha."

It's Marek who attempts to explain. "About fifty years ago, just after your father became Alpha, a few of the regional packs created an alliance that was focused on the old ways. To keep the she-wolves under the male thumb, to put power back into the ruling class, and create full separation between humans and shifters. They attacked the allied packs, but their numbers weren't enough to truly take out the other packs, and they were pushed back."

He stops for a second, expecting me to say something, but I just nod for him to continue. "From what I remember, that's how the rock-solid alliance between Moonrise, Shadow Creek, and Silver Hollow was initially established. We were the packs that pushed off the main attack from Thorncrow and Darkridge. They are still allied. I believe Blackpine was also part of that initial alliance, but they don't currently have any alliances that we know of."

"So where does this witch come into this? You neglected to answer that." I'm still trying to figure out how the hell this all fits together.

This time, Jensen takes over the story. "We are honestly not exactly sure. There were rumors back then that Blackpine had contracted a coven of witches to help them succeed in their plans, but nothing was ever confirmed. Of the three packs, Blackpine was definitely stronger than they should have been. We never had any direct dealings with them, though."

"So it sounds like we have a starting place, and that's it." It's not a question. I don't need to ask a question, because these men know me, know what we need to do.

"We need to find a connection to the witch who is currently causing us all this grief, and that coven from fifty years ago," Damien says with a resigned scowl.

"Exactly. What are we going to do about the sigils that we can't deactivate?" I ask the room, because I have no idea who will have the answer to that one.

Kai looks at me like he has an idea, but isn't sure how I will take it. "What, Kai?" I probe.

He ducks his head and says, "We know you get aggressive at the thought of someone separating you from Kara." I growl, but he quickly continues, "But it's not your fault. You're being influenced by an outside source. So what if we keep you together? That way you can better handle what's going on inside, but also still actively participate in undoing things?"

"That's not a bad idea." Callum speaks up for the first time since we all got in here.

"You're saying basically make Kara sit in on meetings and shit?" I ask, not daring to breathe. "More than she's already been?"

"Well yeah, but also, if we need to deal with things without her or she needs time to herself, she is the one to do that. You don't seem to mind if she wants to be apart. Only if someone else wants it," Callum adds. He may not speak a lot during meetings, but you can tell he's always listening and putting things together.

I sit there and think about it for a minute. The reality is this is the best-case scenario. I get to spend unlimited time with Kara, and no one can tell me I can't. No one can get close to her. It's perfect. "Sounds like a plan. I need you five to keep working on this. Find the connections, create an action plan. Do whatever you need to in order to fix all this mess. I'm going to find my mate."

I stand without another word to them or thought, and leave my inner circle sputtering and confused. But I don't care. They told me being with Kara will keep the pack safe from me, so I'm going to be with her.

I storm into the entryway just as Kara walks in through the dining room without Carmen around. Without thinking, I bend down and sweep her into my arms, causing her to yelp and throw her arms around my neck.

"Zander! What the hell is going on?" she squeals. There's not fear or even anger in her voice. Just confusion, and I would even say happiness.

"It's been decided that I need to be around you in order to keep my temper in check, so we're going to spend some time together." I don't give her time to even think about what I said. I just head for the stairs, taking them two at a time.

"Where are we going?" Now the trepidation has entered her voice, and I can understand why, but I can't seem to care.

"My room. Well, our room," I say as I hit the first landing and continue to the next.

"Wait, what? Put me down! We're not doing that!" Kara starts trying to get down, but my grip is too strong. She's never going to get out of my hold.

"We're not going to do anything but watch a movie. I have a bigger TV and bed. Technically, it's your bed, too. We upgraded it when you originally moved in. But you *are* spending time with me," I say the last sentence on a growl that leaves no room for question.

"Promise me you're not going to try anything."

"No, I will be a gentleman—until you ask me not to be. Then all bets are off." Looking down at her, I realize she's not unaffected by being this close to me or by what I'm saying, so I add quickly, "And Kara? You will ask me soon."

Her breath hitches, but she doesn't respond. I kick my door open and set her down. "The remote is over on the side table. Put on whatever you want to watch. I'm going to get comfortable."

I walk into my closet and change into athletic shorts, forgoing a shirt. I may be keeping my hands to myself, but I can still tempt her. When I emerge from the closet, Kara hasn't moved from the spot I left her in, and I chuckle.

"Come on, sweetheart. Let's just get comfy on the bed and watch a movie."

Saying that gets her out of her head, and she replies, "Yeah, okay. Can we watch anything?"

"Whatever you want. Just pick." I lay down on the bed and pat the spot next to me. It's only now that I realize from the second it was suggested I spend time with Kara to keep my head on straight, I completely went into that with a single-minded focus. I should be worried about that. I really should.

CHAPTER THIRTY

Alone. Together.

KARA

DUMBFOUNDED. THAT'S THE ONLY word I can think of for whatever this is. Zander was with his inner circle for a little over an hour, enough time for Carmen and I to grab a quick lunch.

We had just finished cleaning up when Zander practically kidnapped me in the entryway. Now I'm standing in his room—our room—while he's lying on the bed, waiting for me to join him. The muscles of his upper body on full display for me to see.

The slope we've slid down the last two days is almost a vertical cliff at this point. It's too much to handle and yet, not enough. We went from casually hanging out in hope that doing normal activities would unlock my memories, to now being in his room.

Alone.

Together.

I'm not stupid, I know where this is headed. I could just leave. I *should* just leave. But after that kiss earlier...after igniting my whole body with the explosion of sensations that were pulled out of me from the depths of my soul. The way he controlled and worshiped my body. It remade me. My mind might not be back to what we had been before, but my body and emotions—hell, my very soul—are all fully on board with whatever the fuck this is.

With that thought, I finally move from the spot I've been rooted to for the last however long. Grabbing the remote, I find that I have a whole profile on his Netflix account. Of course I would. Clicking on it, I look through the movies and choose something I assume I should like. Now it's time for the part I am equal parts dreading and anticipating: lying next to him.

Luckily, before Carmen and I ate, we changed into comfy clothes for our outdoor reading adventure—that won't happen now, I realize. I only have to kick off my sandals and flop on the bed next to Zander. Without preamble, he grabs me and pulls me to him, so I have no other choice but to rest my head on his chest.

"Can you even see around my head?"

"Of course I can. You are in the exact right spot."

"If you're sure..." I trail off.

"I'm sure. Now, shh, we are cuddling and watching a movie." He gives me a squeeze and kisses the top of my head.

Over the next couple hours, we watch a movie in relative peace. What's most surprising is Zander doesn't make a move, other than stroking his hand up and down my back.

As the movie ends and the credits roll, I look up at Zander through my lashes, and I'm surprised to find him looking down at me. He had stopped rubbing my back, so I assumed he fell asleep. "Now what?"

"What do you want to do?" Zander answers my question with a question, and I can't help but roll my eyes.

"I'm not sure." I know what he wants me to say, but I keep that to myself.

"I know what I want to do." He surprises me by actually verbalizing it. It shouldn't surprise me. He's always been straightforward. Never hiding behind anything. The look Zander gives me could melt my clothes off my body if I'm not careful. The problem when I'm this close to him, in his arms, is I want to give him exactly what he wants.

Steeling myself, I respond, "That's good for you, but that's not on the table today." There, I said it. Look at me keeping my own boundaries in place.

The air leaves the room with the look of longing and desperation Zander gives me. But, ever the gentleman, he responds, "I figured you'd say that. But we could still kiss. I won't take things any further than that, I promise."

Am I actually considering this? Yep, I am. I'm not going to lie, that kiss we shared earlier has been carving its way through my brain. Eating away at the resolve I had thought I built up. With an internal sigh, I ask, "Do...do you swear you won't take it further than that?"

"Of course. I may desperately need to be inside you, to feel you, but if you aren't ready, I won't ever cross that line. I would never disgrace you like that."

The blush that was already starting on my cheeks spreads down to my neck. I don't need a mirror to know it's the exact color of my hair.

For the second time today, Zander reaches up and tilts my chin back up towards him, forcing me to look directly into his eyes. "Do not ever doubt that you are mine." With that, he surges down to my mouth and claims me with even more ferocity than he did by the lake.

The mix of his scent and my addled brain makes the kiss even more powerful than I could have dreamed. The earthy scent of him wraps around me, and it feels like coming home. Before I can even think about what's happening, he wraps his arms around my waist and yanks me fully on top of him.

He gives me power to pull away from him at any moment, his grip not iron-clad. Zander holds me to him by my hips, his grip bruising but not unwelcome. I know I could get off this bed at any time. But I don't. I cling to him and deepen the kiss.

As much as he wants me, I want him, too. We just fit together in a way I haven't experienced. Or maybe I have experienced it before, and it's always been him. That thought drives me deeper into the moment.

This man, this wolf, has practically put his life on hold to make sure I'm okay. He focuses on me, makes me his priority, cares about my emotional and mental health. He protects me from everything and everyone—even my own chaotic self. God, he's truly perfect.

And he's mine.

The thought rips through me like a wave of euphoria and relief. My memories aren't back. My wolf is still hidden. But I know in my bones that I'm right where I'm supposed to be. I don't know if I love him, but I *need* him. That has to be enough for now.

"Zander," I say on a breathy moan.

He takes that as his cue and flips us so he's on top. Breaking the kiss, he puts his forehead to mine, his breaths coming just as quick as mine. "There you are."

I smile but still ask, "What?"

"The way you said my name, I haven't heard that from you in weeks. It's intoxicating."

"Well, then I'll say it more." I give him an impish smile and repeat his name with a bit more flourish this time.

"God, love, you keep doing that and I'll break my promise to you. Fuck." He grinds his erection against me and it makes me gasp, so he does it again. Zander resumes kissing me, and this time it's not feverish. It's exploring and sweet.

His exploration of my mouth and my neck is paired with his gentle thrusts into me. His hands move up my sides, and he takes my breast in his hand, kneading it like it's the only thing he can focus on. I wrap my arms around his neck and pull him closer, trapping his hand between us.

We're fully clothed, but it doesn't matter. This whole moment is wrapped in tension with a pretty frustrated bow on top. I told him I wasn't ready for more. I need to keep my word to myself as much as him, but this feels like heaven.

We stay like that, just exploring each other through our clothes for what feels like an eternity and no time at all, when my phone goes off next to me. It's just enough to break the spell we're under, and I reach over to grab it.

I had told Carmen what happened earlier, so she knew what was going on. But that doesn't mean she won't still message me.

> **Hey, bitch. You still upstairs with your hunk of a man? Clothes still on?**

I laugh out loud, and Zander gives me a wicked grin. He must have seen the message, too.

"Tell her I'm being a gentleman and you got to keep all your clothes. But her rude interruption denied you an orgasm." Zander laughs again as he flops back to his back while I sit up and prop my back on the headboard.

"I'm not going to tell her that!" I balk at him.

He puts his hand under his head and replies, "Your loss."

"To which part? The response she'll give me, or the orgasm?" I give him a look dripping in sarcasm.

"Both." The impish grin he now sports makes me roll my eyes.

> We are still in his room and clothed. Not for effort on his part, though.

> Get it, girl! But seriously, you staying up there all day or are you going to come down anytime soon?

> Not sure, Zander said something about in order to keep him from killing his pack, he and I have to stay together. I'm not sure what that means?

> Sure, sure. Whatever the big man needs to say to keep you all to himself.

> I'll keep you posted.

I look back at Zander and ask, "So what is the plan? Do I just need to be around you to keep you calm? Or what?"

"Honestly, we don't really know for sure, but we know you are the focus of it. I probably should go get some work done. How about you come hang out in the office with me? You can read or whatever, just being there should be good."

"Sounds like a plan to me. Let me stop by my room and grab my book. I'll meet you down there."

"I'll get dressed in something more than shorts, and we will walk down together," he says with a kiss on my forehead before he rolls off the bed.

"You're really milking this for all it's worth, aren't you?" I cross my arms over my chest and try for a sour expression, but end up just smirking.

"Not true, I'm enjoying you getting to be with me," Zander says from his closet.

I get off the bed and head for the door. "I'm grabbing my book now, I'll see you in a second." Walking out of the room, I hear a faint growl behind me, but brush it off as nothing. I can't believe how my life has turned upside down, multiple times, in just a few weeks. Maybe things are starting to look up for me, finally.

CHAPTER THIRTY-ONE

I. Almost. Killed. Her.

ZANDER

THREE DAYS. THREE FUCKING days since I had Kara in my bed, under me, breathing my name. We've been in proximity of each other during the day, but as soon as she gets tired, no amount of convincing—really, begging—can get her to move back into my room. We both sleep alone.

We spend our days together, with the exception of the times Kara insists on being with Carmen, or doing something on her own. Because, in her words, *"I still need me time."*

But these times, like now, aren't good for anyone. I sit here at my desk, trying to focus on what Damien and Kai are saying. They had a report from some of our enforcers that have been scouting outside our borders to try and get traces of the wolves or witch. Anything that gives us some sort of clue about what happened to Kara and what is happening to me.

There's no denying it. Something is happening. Even Kara finally confessed she noticed something is different about me just this morning. She said when she's around, I seem calm, happy even. But as soon as there is a chance she will be leaving my proximity, I feel like a part of me is ripping out of my body.

"Are you even listening?" Kai asks on an exasperated sigh.

"Of course, he's not. He hasn't been listening for the last ten minutes," Damien responds to Kai without a hint of acknowledgement to me.

I growl, and my vision flashes white hot. *Who the hell do they think they are? I am the Alpha of this pack! Not them. They speak to me, not around me!*

Standing from my desk so quickly my chair topples behind me, both Damien and Kai freeze. Slowly, they turn their heads towards me as if I'm a caged animal and they've been dumped in here with me. Because I am, and they are confined in this room with me.

"Z? You good, man?" Kai asks without making direct eye contact. First good decision he's made in the last few minutes.

"I am the Alpha of this pack. You will address me as such. You speak to me when I'm here. No one else," I growl at them. Hair begins to sprout on my arms and my canines and claws slip free.

Damien stands from where he was sitting on the other side of my desk, but keeps his head lowered. Deference that he visually shows, but I know he isn't feeling. I need to make him feel it. I need them to know who is in charge. He reaches into his pocket and pulls his phone out. Looking down for a split second, he dials a number. He's calling someone now? Does he even understand that his life is on the line? Does he care?

"Kara, I need you to come to the office right now, but do not come in further than the doorway," Damien says into the phone. There's a pause, then he says, "We may need to limit the time you two spend apart, because I'm not sure he even knows who we are right now." His tone is even but stern, and it pisses me off more.

You know what, fuck it! I charge Damien, but it's Kai I collide with. I dimly hear Damien still on the phone, "Actually, no, do not come in here! Call Jensen and Marek, and go to that place we talked about. Now!"

They're hiding Kara from me? They want her for themselves. I saved her! I brought her back! "She is mine," I snarl and lunge again at Damien, but this time, he's ready and both of them charge at me. They aren't fast enough, and I evade both of them, making for the door. *I will get to Kara. I will keep her safe!*

"Zander, Alpha! You need to stop. You'll hurt her if you go to her now." Damien growls as he tackles me from behind. Kai lunges for my legs at the same time. My chin slams into the floor a few feet from the door, but the second the stars clear from my vision, I unleash hell on them.

I shift. My wolf surging forward without any restraint. Snarling and snapping my jaws at the two men in front of me. I struggle to maintain any semblance of the man I am. I'm torn between protecting them because they're my pack, and destroying them because they're keeping me from Kara. My wolf? He's 100% on board with ripping the flesh from their bones.

I smash through the office door and into the entryway. A scream comes from my right, and through the red haze of my vision, I see Kara being dragged upstairs by Callum—Carmen following close behind. *Threat.* He does not get what's mine. Turning towards the stairs, I see two more men out of my peripheral, but they don't have what's mine.

I charge, all restraint forgotten. I need to get to Kara. Before I make it to the bottom of the stairs, a set of jaws clamps onto one of my hind legs while something else body slams me to the side. I'm forced to refocus on the threats around me. Four wolves surround me. Three stand equidistant around the entryway, while the final one is between me and Kara.

I look up at Kara and she's moving slowly down the stairs. The wolves around me brace themselves for whatever is going to happen next.

"Hey, there." A soft voice from the stairs. *Kara.* "What's gotten into you, big guy?"

We don't have our pack connection, so I can't speak to her in her head. So all I can do is dip my head towards her in acknowledgement. Damien, Kai, Jensen, and Marek—the other two in the room—have been constantly screaming at me in my head, but I've been ignoring them. They're keeping me from what's mine.

"You've destroyed your office and did some damage in here, too," she says just as softly, almost like she's talking to a scared child—or a wild animal.

"Kara..." Callum warns from the stairs. "Be careful." He's not stopping her or putting his hands on her, so I might let him live.

I grumble and huff in response, but Kara just nods that she's heard him and continues forward.

"What's going on in that head of yours? No one is hurting me. I'm safe here, you've made sure of that. These men, well wolves, are here to protect me and help you. You know that," Kara continues.

"I need you to come back to me. I can't talk to you like this. I like talking to you." She reaches out towards me, and all four wolves as well as Callum tense. *What am I doing?* I'm not just scaring Kara, I'm hurting my friends, my pack, my brothers.

I force control back from my wolf, but he's still controlling the shift. Since shifting back isn't an option, I lower myself to the floor to make myself less intimidating. I realize I'm the biggest wolf here by a mile, but I don't want to scare Kara more than she already is.

Even though Kara's voice is even and she's projecting an aura of confidence, I can see her hand shaking. She keeps darting her eyes to Damien, who has taken up a spot immediately to her left. I let her reach me, and she moves her hand into the scruff on my neck, the feeling of her touch grounding me.

Kara digs her hand into my fur more, taking just as much comfort from the touch as I am. I let out a gentle rumble from deep in my chest, letting her know what she's doing is welcome. She understands and adds her other hand into my fur, hanging on like she needs me.

"Come back to me," she whispers, only for me to hear. "This isn't you. You don't hurt those you love. You protect them. That's your job, your right as the Alpha. I'm not in any danger. We will figure this out, together. You and me. You brought me back, let me bring you back, too."

I wrestle with my wolf, forcing him to the back of my mind and forcing control back from him. With a snarl, I force the shift.

For the first time in years, the shift back to my human form isn't smooth. It's painful. I feel each and every muscle and bone realign—each pull of the tendons. With a howl, I finish the shift and collapse onto my hands and knees. My breaths are ragged and shallow, and it feels like the pieces of my soul realign.

Kara falls to her knees next to me. Her hands find my face and she forces me to look her in the eyes. "Hey, hey, you're good. You're okay. I'm here."

My thoughts are racing. *What the hell happened to me?* I fling myself out of her grip, sitting back on my heels before stumbling to my feet. With wide, confused eyes, I take in the state of the entryway and my pack. My closest friends. Damien and Kai have shifted back, but Marek and Jensen are still in wolf form as a secondary layer of protection for Kara. They are there to step in if I lose it again. I know this, but the fact the plan we put in place to protect her from others was the plan they had to use for *me* destroys something in me.

I look down to where Kara hasn't moved from the floor. She's staring at me with a mix of fear, and dare I say...love? Does she love me? I breathe for her, live for her, would die for her.

And I fucking almost killed her.

I. Almost. Killed. Her.

Me. I did this. I destroyed her sense of safety. What the hell is wrong with me? "Kara, I..."

"Hey, it's fine. We're fine," she tells me again, standing and stepping towards me. But we're not, I'm not. I step back, keeping the distance between us.

Damien, I say through the bond as I keep my eyes on Kara. *Keep her safe.*

What I don't say is, *because I'm not safe.* But he understands. He looks at me with a stoic, determined look on his face, and nods once. I allowed the other males present to hear as well, and they all shift into new positions. Kai, standing on the other side of Kara now, looks broken but determined. He, too, nods and moves closer to Kara, but doesn't touch her. Not yet. Jensen and Marek take a few measured steps away from the door. I know they will be my shadows, but not now. Not yet.

"I'm sorry," is all I can bear saying to her. I can't say more. With that, I turn and run out the door. For the second time in less than a month, I take off for the woods. Running from the one person who completes me. The one person who doesn't see me as a monster.

I. Almost. Killed. Her.

It's my last thought before I shift and seed control to my wolf, as he too realizes what a completely fucked up situation this is.

CHAPTER THIRTY-TWO

All the more reason to drain it

KARA

THE SECOND ZANDER RUNS out the door, I attempt to follow, but Kai grabs me around the middle and hangs on while I thrash. "ZANDER!" I scream, but it's no use.

Jensen and Marek, who haven't shifted back, follow Zander outside like they plan to go with him. I want to go, I need him. He needs me! I was just feeling like things were getting back to a place of normalcy, and then he just leaves.

"I can't let you go with him, Kara," Kai tries to soothe me. "This was part of the plan. If he couldn't control himself, he was going to separate himself from you. The only way to do that was to shift and go."

"No!" I shake my head, unwilling to believe that the man who promised me he would help me find myself just left me. Sobbing, my knees give out, but Kai is still holding me and keeps me vertical. "Why didn't he tell me it was getting this bad? Why didn't he tell me?" My words come out broken.

Damien stands near us, still watching the door like a feral wolf might come back through and attack me. *Would he have attacked me?*

Carmen comes down the last few stairs. "Did you know? Did you know it was that bad?" I ask in a barely there whisper.

"No, sweetie, I didn't. Callum told me as it was happening, that they had decided that Zander might not be able to stay around you." As she reaches for me, I throw myself into her arms, and we crash to our knees. I hadn't even realized Kai had stopped holding me back.

"This isn't fair. He told me it would be okay as long as I was with him most of the time," I say to no one in particular, then whisper, "He said he'd be okay."

Carmen and I move to sit on the bottom of the steps while Kai and Callum join Damien, standing in the middle of the destroyed foyer. They begin to talk to each other in hushed voices.

"Stop that!" I scream at them, jumping to my feet. "This is about me, about Zander. You don't get to keep this from me! If I would have known he was this bad, I wouldn't have tried to keep some space between us." At least they all look property cowed at my vehemence.

"What in all hell set him off?" I ask the three of them.

Sighing, Damien looks at me and responds, "We're not exactly sure. He was on edge more today than he's been. Anytime you've been off doing something, he's been testy. Right before he lost it, I made a comment about him not paying attention to Kai. We've ribbed each other for years about shit like that."

"It was like a switch flipped," Kai adds. "Zander went from just being testy and broody, to attacking us. I don't think he was in control at all. His voice didn't even sound like his before he shifted. It was almost like his wolf was speaking."

"Wait, so you think his wolf took over his human form and forced this whole thing?" Carmen asks. I'm glad she did, because I am way too stunned to speak.

"That's what I'm thinking, yeah," Kai responds.

"Hang on," Callum joins the conversation. "Didn't we determine that Kara's issue is mostly with her wolf, too?"

"We did what now?" I ask, whipping my head towards him.

"Sorry, backing up, we figured out this morning that it seems like your inability to shift changed your personality."

"Personality? Excuses you!" I shouted, my anger piqued. I get in his personal space, which is laughable. All these men are at least ten inches taller than me.

Callum throws up his hands, placating me and says, "I mean, the fact that you went from being someone who charged into things to someone who ran away at first instinct. It all links to your wolf. We think your memories are tied to your wolf, too. I was doing more research into those sigils and was speaking to Alpha Grayson since he's the oldest amongst our allied packs. He said that our wolves are the parts of us that are the deepest, most primal."

"It makes sense," Damien adds in that flat, no-nonsense voice that makes me crazy half the time.

"So you guys are saying that Zander's wolf is the issue with him, like my nonexistent wolf is the issue with me?" I ask, dumbfounded.

"Yeah, we think so," Damien says.

Sitting down hard on the steps again, I put my head in my hands and say, "I need a drink."

"I think we all could use one," Damien says and adds, "I'll call some people to clean this up and get an update from Jensen and Marek. They are following Zander and will hopefully bring him around soon."

Kai reaches down and offers me a helping hand. I take it with a smile. These people—shifters—really are great. I just wish I remembered more than what I've seen since I've been back.

We all head to the entertainment room where Callum heads to the bar and pours us all a drink of some sort of whiskey. I don't even care what kind it is right now. But I shoot it back and ask for more.

Chuckling, he refills my glass but says, "Careful, this is Zander's good stuff."

"All the more reason to drain it. 'Cause I'm mad at him right now." I smirk and take my refill, heading for the couch where Carmen is already sitting.

The five of us sit there in silence for a few minutes. It's not awkward; we're all just processing the last hour and trying to figure it out for ourselves. Sighing, I break the silence and ask, "What's our next step? Who do we need to speak to about breaking both these curses?"

Damien and Kai share a look I don't like, but Damien answers me, "We're not sure who we need to speak to, but we think the first step is dealing with Zander. He's the wild card here. You can't shift and don't have your memories, but you're not on the verge of murdering everyone."

"That's true," I huff. "I want him back."

"We will get him back, honey." Carmen puts an arm around me and squeezes while I rest my head on her shoulder. "We just need a plan."

"Well, get going, Mr. Pack First!" I tell Damien, who whips his face to mine with a look of shock on his face.

Kai, Callum, and Carmen all outright laugh, and I look at each of them with confusion. Kai is the first to recover and says, "You used to call him that all the time."

"*Seriously*?" My gaze jumps between each of them.

"Yep, I wonder if you're slowly starting to remember small things?" Kai laughs again.

"I'll take whatever I can get at this point," I respond and look back to Damien. "Well, get planning."

CHAPTER THIRTY-THREE

Cheese is life

KARA

"Ugh, what else do we need to figure out?" I ask, exasperated.

"It's been forever!" Carmen groans as she flops back down on the couch.

"It's been four hours," I tell her, but sit back down on the couch with a huff.

Over the last four hours, we've talked, planned, and strategized until our eyes crossed. We've even contacted this 'Fixer' person who apparently can find info about anything for a price. Not having Zander here makes this so much harder. Since I haven't completed the bond with him, my power in the pack is kind of stunted.

"Why don't you ladies take a break? We have a solid plan to help Zander, and the rest is just figuring out who is doing what. We can take care of that," Damien says with a surprising amount of care.

Carmen jumps to her feet, turning around to pull me up, too. "Don't have to tell me twice, I'm starving anyway."

Rolling my eyes at her, I say, "Are you sure you guys don't need our help?"

"We're good," Kai says. "This is the boring part. Plus, nothing really starts till we get word from Jensen and Marek that Zander is calmed down enough to come back."

"That's what I'm afraid of," I tell him. "Will he be calm enough?"

"He will. Alphas normally run on primal emotions first, then everything else second. Once he gets a handle on that, he will be fine," Damien reassures me.

"Unless he seeded control to his wolf," Callum says under his breath, rubbing the back of his neck.

"Unless he...what?" I start.

"Nothing, it will be fine," Callum says quickly.

"Unless he what, Callum?" I don't even have the energy to be mad so I go for ice.

Sighing, he repeats himself, "Unless he seeded control to his wolf. Then it will be a lot harder for him to calm down and let those primal emotions stop controlling him."

"What the hell does that mean? Do you forget I know none of this? Tell me like I'm five."

"If Zander lets his wolf take control, and his wolf is currently calling the shots, it's going to be a lot harder for him to find himself again. Our wolves are our emotional center. Because he's an Alpha, his wolf is a lot more powerful than the rest of us," Callum tells me.

"So, what you're saying is that Zander may or may not be able to come back today?"

"When you first left, he seeded control to his wolf for over a week," Damien says.

"Are you fucking kidding me? None of you thought to tell me that? This is all because of me." I drop into the closest chair. Everything keeps coming back to me.

My fault. It's all my fault. If I hadn't bolted, he wouldn't have struggled so bad that he had to leave his pack for a week. He wouldn't have had to come find me. He spent four days trying to get me to come back with him, then another four days trying to get me to see him as his mate. Now he's struggling with control because of me.

"None of this is your fault. You didn't ask for this." Carmen kneels in front of me.

"But my reactions to everything have caused a lot of this. The past month, everything about this pack has been in a tailspin, and it's all centered around *me*." I can't meet her eyes. Staring at the floor, I try to hold back the tears that threaten to break through.

"Your reactions may have not been the best, but you did what you thought you had to at the time. No one is blaming you for any of this. Now come on, you need some comfort food. Let the boys figure out what to do next. You and I will help Marge get dinner ready." Carmen pulls me to my feet again, and ushers me out the door despite my protesting.

Heading to the kitchen, I turn around and notice Callum following after us. "What are you doing?"

"Where you go, one of us goes. Right now, it's me," Callum tells me with a shrug.

I throw my hands up, exasperated. "Oh, absolutely not! I do *not* need a babysitter. I don't need to be guarded."

"This isn't something that's up for debate. Zander told us to protect you. We will. So let's get to the kitchen." Callum says as he ushers us in that direction, ignoring my continued protests.

I dig my heels in, but it's no use. I'm outnumbered and outpowered. Even Carmen is stronger than me. I hate this power imbalance. Yet again, this just shows me how out of my depth I really am.

"You will be fine. It will all be alright," Carmen reassures me.

I sigh defeated, because apparently, that's my new normal. I follow after her while Callum follows behind. *Hey, at least I'm not panicking every time something happens anymore.* I chuckle to myself, but it sounds a bit manic.

Carmen reaches back and loops our arms together. "I promise."

"Dinner better have something covered in cheese, because I need to feel love." I sigh wistfully.

Callum responds with a hefty dose of confusion. "Food covered in cheese makes you feel love?"

"Obviously. Cheese is life," Carmen replies flippantly.

I glance back at Callum to catch him rolling his eyes, but his stare is glued to Carmen. As we enter the kitchen, Marge is already putting food out, and nothing has cheese on it. Story of my life.

We sit and eat, talking about nothing substantial. After a bit, Kai and Damien join us and fill their plates. Digging in, they talk about what they've figured out, but I tone it all out. We've made plans, but they just want to wait till Zander comes back to himself. I'm not willing to wait that long.

This all started with me. Zander freaked out because of *me*. So while they keep planning their *let's wait and see* bullshit, I'm making my own plans. I'm going to get him back myself. It's time to stop being scared and worried. I'm bringing my mate back.

And I'm doing it tonight.

CHAPTER THIRTY-FOUR

Unstable

ZANDER

ZANDER! ALPHA!

I've been running for hours. Somehow, even though my wolf hasn't given me back control, I'm able to hear someone calling me. It's faint, like they're far away, but it's there.

The words are enough to give me pause. I'm still running, but I know someone is following me—two someones? They're keeping their distance, but are close enough for the pack bond to work.

Alpha, let us help you. Marek. Of course, it's Marek. Now I remember. This was all part of the plan. Damien, Kai, and Callum were to stay with Kara and protect her. Marek and Jensen were to follow me and attempt to bring me back to myself.

Tough shit. It's better if I'm alone. *I'm not coming back,* I tell both of them.

That's fine, but let us catch up. Jensen is speaking now.

Why would I do that?

We're part of your inner circle, our job is to work with and for our Alpha. That's you, so slow the fuck down and talk to us, Marek bellows through the bond, and that's what does it. They're only doing what I asked them to. What we decided as a group.

I slow down, and within thirty seconds, they catch up before we just run. The three of us. We haven't run as a pack in any way for weeks, but just running with them in this form brings me a bit of the peace I've been missing.

After a while, Marek must feel a shift in my aura, because he speaks to me again. *You ready to talk about it?*

I slow down to a stop, but don't shift back. I couldn't even if I wanted to. My wolf may have given me back my mind, but he won't be giving my human form back to me anytime soon.

I take in my surroundings. The only birds I can hear are the crows—the rest have gone silent. They know a predator is near. I smell the earth, the trees, my pack. I feel the soil beneath my paws. Each sense helps ground me.

So why won't you come back with us? Marek begins the conversation I know we need to have, but I don't want to.

Why would I? Just being around Kara heightens my instincts. All I want to do is protect her. But this far out, this much separation, gives me back some semblance of control. My next words sting, but I need to say them. To tell him how I really feel about all this. *I'm being a terrible Alpha.*

You're being an Alpha that hasn't completed the mate bond, Jensen tells me. *Your father was the same way with your mother.* He shakes out his deep brown coat to release some of the tension he's been holding.

My father was this...unstable? I find that hard to believe.

Marek ducks his head as he replies. *Well, you're definitely beating him in that category. But he struggled to control his wolf when he and your mom first got together. I even struggled with controlling mine when I first met Bianca.*

I look away from both of them. I know they want me to understand that it's natural. Normal to struggle at this point in the mating process. But this isn't normal. My mate was stolen from me, and my focus has been pinned on her. I don't even have a desire to see my pack. I've never been like this.

You actually think my outbursts are mating issues? Have you missed that part where I tried to kill everyone, including her? I was going to grab her and abscond with her. WITH MY TEETH! I growl at them. They don't get it, or they do and they are just trying to get me back.

You wouldn't have hurt her, Jensen says with confidence, but I see the touch of fear behind his eyes. They do get it, and they just want me back. Too bad I'm not going with them.

You can stay and run with me for a while, or you can go. But I'm not going back, not tonight. My wolf won't let me shift right now, anyway.

If that's what you want, Marek says, resignation dripping from every word.

Let's get moving then. Without another word, I take off through the woods, Marek and Jensen running with me. The three of us hit the edge of the pack lands, and we start making the loop we've made a thousand times before. With all the issues we've had lately, I decide to re-mark the border. It will help keep Kara safe so my wolf is on board.

An hour of running later, we've made a complete lap, and I'm finally tired enough to stop. I head to the lake and decide this is where I'm staying tonight. The same rock that Kara and I spent a wonderful morning not that long ago.

If you want to head back, you can. I'm staying here tonight.

Do you want us to stay? Marek asks. I can tell he is torn between staying and going.

No, go back to your families. Kara is safe with the guys. I'll stay out here.

If you're sure? Jensen asks, but neither of them make a move to leave. They're going to make me force them, aren't they?

Obviously, I'm sure. Now go. I turn away from them because while it was nice that they came and ran with me, I need to be alone again.

I hear both of them slowly move away and head back down the path. I jump up on the rock outcropping and settle in to watch the lake and the stars. Part of me actually thought they would stop a good distance away, but to my surprise, they keep going. I'm no fool—they most likely went just far enough away to make contact with the rest of the inner circle back at the pack house. But I'll take what I can get.

The night air is cool, but in this form, the temperature doesn't bother me. As much as I hate what I'm becoming, I can at least enjoy the little things. Part of me wants to fight to shift back to my human form. I can tell my wolf is slowly seeding control back to me, but the shift would still be a struggle. Besides, there's no reason to shift back right now. I don't even have clothes with me.

Laying down, I take a deep breath and breathe in the clean air. Questions bombard me. *Has it really only been a few days? Why can't I control my wolf? Why am I struggling so much with all this? Maybe I should just slip away and let Damien and Kai run things. Become a lone wolf.*

Ha! An Alpha abandoning his pack, all because he can't control himself around his mate. A mate who doesn't even know him. Sure, things have been great, but let's be honest: she doesn't want to move past what we are now. Kara and I won't ever be on the same page. Even if she did want me the way I want her, she most likely can't complete the bond. At least, that's the going theory.

"It would be helpful if you shifted back, 'cause I could use a hand up?"

CHAPTER THIRTY-FIVE

Mine

ZANDER

I ROCKET BACK TO my feet and stare at Kara. She's standing there on the outcropping of rocks, holding a bag and looking at me like this is the most normal thing in the world. I dig in and fight my wolf for the last bit of control, and force him to the back of my mind.

Once I get full control back, I shift. Just like earlier today, the shift is painful. I feel like a pup that just started shifting again, but I manage to control my expression. I don't want to add to Kara's worry.

"What the hell are you doing out here? ALONE!" I put way too much force into the last word, and Kara flinches. "Sorry, love. What are you doing here?"

Kara recovers and smirks up at me. "Help me up and I'll tell you."

Reaching down, I grab her outstretched hand and pull her up onto the rock. Kara hands me the bag she's holding. Taking it and looking inside, I realize she's packed clothes for me and food for us.

"This whole thing has been because of me, so I knew I needed to try to fix some part of it. That meant coming to find you," Kara tells me as I pull on pants.

"How did you get out here without anyone noticing? Because I knew Damien and Kai wouldn't have left you alone."

She smirks and sits down to unpack the rest of her bag. "I mean, I slipped away from Kai before."

I grunt and glare down at her.

"What? Too soon?" Kara casts me a wicked grin over her shoulder, looking up at me.

"It will forever be too soon," I grumble and sit down next to her, now fully clothed. "Seriously, Jensen and Marek didn't leave me that long ago. You would have had to pass them on the path."

"They got back about two hours ago, and I 'went to bed' early." She air quotes.

"Two hours?" I really wasn't paying attention to time. I could have sworn they just left.

"Anyway, I think you and I need to talk. Everyone else is trying to figure out the curse shit I have on me, and apparently you, too. But you and I need to figure us out."

The look Kara gives me leaves no room for argument. I wasn't expecting to have a relationship talk tonight, but I also wasn't expecting to go off the fucking deep end earlier either, so here we are.

Kara looks out over the lake, holding one of the sandwiches she brought. I sit and wait. For whatever reason, I feel like there is something she needs to say, and if I say anything, she won't.

Without taking her eyes off the lake, Kara says, "I think we need to finish the mate bond."

I sputter on the water I was in the process of drinking. *Did she really just say what I think she did?* I'm dreaming, I have to be dreaming. I fell asleep and this is absolutely my dream self making up my perfect scenario.

She looks at me with confusion and pats me on the back. "You okay?"

"Yeah, fine. I'm fine. Just went down the wrong pipe," I wheeze. "You think we should complete the mate bond?"

"I've been thinking about it, and I think it might help you. Everyone keeps saying Alphas have a hard time controlling their wolf and temper once they find their mate, but before they complete the bond. So, I think that if we take that factor out of the equation, it might help."

"So, you're agreeing to this purely because it will help me?" There's no way. This is wild.

"No, I may not remember anything from before, but I know one thing for certain—you are mine. I feel it in my bones. I'm happier when I'm around you. I figure the rest will come eventually."

"Completing the bond isn't as simple as accepting it. There's the ceremony, the marking, and mating. All three things need to happen for the bond to be fully in place." I need to give her an out. I want this more than my next breath, but I will not do anything unless she knows every detail. I'd kill myself before I do anything without her consent.

"I know. I've been doing my own research. Asking questions. I know what has to happen, and I'm telling you I'm ready for all of it." Kara pauses, and I can see it in her eyes. She has more she wants to say, but she's scared.

"What is it?" I take her face in my hands and force her to look at me. "I can see there's something else. What else?"

"It's nothing."

"Kara, love, what is it?"

Her eyes dart to the side, but I lightly squeeze my hands on her face and she looks back at me. "I'm scared I'll never be able to fully complete the bond with you if I can't find my wolf."

"If all I ever get with you is a ceremony and mate marks, I'll be happy," I tell her. Because it's true. If all I ever had with her is a human marriage, I would still be devoted to her just as I would if I was fully mated.

She holds herself a little straighter and says something I never thought I'd hear from her again. "I love you, Zander." Then she laughs and adds, "It's weird knowing my body and heart love you, even if my mind hasn't caught up, but I do love you."

I think I just stop breathing. I can't believe that we've reached this point. "You, Kara, are my everything. For as long as I live, you will be my focus and my heart. Even if we never fully mate, it will be you and me, always."

I lean forward and kiss her. Slow and sweet, then I push all my love into it. I'm not trying for more right now. This moment is about us promising that no matter what, it will be the two of us. But in the next moment, it's Kara who pushes the kiss from sweet to something more volatile.

Kara grabs onto my shirt and pulls me closer. Groaning, I move my hands from her face and grab her hips. In one swift motion, I pull her onto my lap and she takes control of the kiss. My entire world shifts, focusing on her.

She sighs, and I take the opening for what it is and shove my tongue past her lips, and we battle for dominance. This kiss is all tongue and teeth, both of us struggling to maintain control.

My grip on her hips increases as I kiss my way from her jaw to her ear, then down her neck. Sucking on the spot just above her collarbone, the moan Kara lets out causes my canines to extend unbidden. They scrape across her skin, and she moans again.

"Zander," she breathes, "more. Please, more."

I groan and pull back from her, squeezing her hips just enough to get her to open her eyes. "Tell me you want this. Tell me you don't want me to stop." I need to hear the words. I wasn't planning on this to happen, but I'll give her whatever she wants.

"This...us...move...please! God, please!" she practically begs, and that's all the encouragement I need.

In response, I growl and I grind my impossibly hard cock up into her, and she presses down just as hard into me. Rolling her hips, I know she's trying to ease the ache just as I am. *Damn it, why did I put clothes back on*? Removing my hands from her hips, I grab the hem of her shirt and tug it up. She lets go of mine just in time for me to whisk hers over her head. I grab mine and do the same.

Pulling back, I see her perfect breasts set in a sinful, black, lace bra. Her nipples are two hard buds, and I bend down to pull one of them into my mouth. The moan she lets out makes me suck just a bit harder.

I let go and lean back. Kara has her head thrown back, her eyes closed, the picture of feminine perfection. I growl one word before I dive back down onto her.

"Mine."

CHAPTER THIRTY-SIX

It's not that pretty little mouth

KARA

OH. MY GOD.

"Mine," Zander growls just as he takes my nipple into his mouth again. One of his arms band around my waist while his other hand digs into my hip with so much force, I know I'll be bruised in the morning. My hands tangle in his hair, holding him to me.

I didn't originally come out here for this to happen. I really did want to talk. We have so much we need to figure out. So much has been going on around us. I knew it needed to be me who initiated any and all conversations, because he's been so volatile. The pack has almost written him off, but I can't—won't—write him off. But the way he held my face, told me no matter what happens it would be us, kissed me so sweetly—it undid me.

My body craves this man, this wolf. I need him like I need my next breath. *Is this the mate bond?* The past few days, while I've been hovering around Zander to help keep him calm and in control, I've been doing my own research.

Everything I've read says that mate bonds are soul-deep. Not just a decision, but a feeling that without the other person, you won't ever be the same.

That's who Zander is to me. I made the decision this evening while I was waiting for the right time to sneak out that I would help him the only way I could. The one way no one else can. By going through the mating ceremony and becoming his Luna. Am I completely out of my depth? Absolutely. But you know what? Fuck it. The past month has been one moment of upending my life after another. Might as well do it one more time. But this time, this isn't a rash *maybe this will help* decision.

Now here, in this moment, I fully understand what having a mate means. It means no matter what happens, it's the two of us. Together. And I can't imagine it any other way.

"Zander, please!" I plead. "I need more."

Zander bites lightly one more time at my nipple before licking the sting away. Coming back up, he claims my mouth in a searing kiss that takes the breath from my lungs.

As carefully as he can manage, he turns us and lays me down on our discarded shirts, and kneels between my legs. I thank whatever god is out there that this rock is massive, because falling into the water would really kill the mood right now.

The sight of Zander looming over me makes my toes curl. Before he has time to do anything, I undo the center clasp of my bra, freeing my breasts, and he stills.

Zander grabs my shorts and panties, and rips them down my legs in one motion, leaving me completely exposed to him. I should feel embarrassed being out in the open like this, but with him, I just can't find it in me to care. "You are fucking perfect," he groans before leaning forward and kissing his way down my body.

He scoots himself back so he can drop between my thighs, and uses his shoulders to push my legs further apart. Just the thought of what Zander is about to do makes me moan. In one motion, his tongue connects with my center while he spears me with one of his fingers. The dual sensations cause my back to arch of the rock and moan his name again.

With that, he gets to work, sucking on my clit and pumping his finger in and out of me. He adds a second finger, stretching me and making me cry out. I roll my hips again, chasing the feel of his tongue on me. I need more friction. My hands tangle in his hair, trying to pull him to me. As I get closer and closer to falling over the edge, he continues to work me.

Just as I think I can't take any more, Zander adds a third finger, and curves them up to hit the exact right spot, making me scream. Stars blink across my vision, and my orgasm rips through me like a tidal wave, but he doesn't let up.

Finally, I go boneless under his ministrations as he pulls his fingers out of me, lapping up the evidence of my release. I can't even string two words together, but the look he gives me makes me realize this is only the beginning.

Climbing back up my body, he takes my mouth in a kiss full of promise and desperation. I taste myself on him, and it's everything.

"I'm not done with you, love. This is only the beginning." Zander's words cause me to whimper, but I know he's not just talking about tonight, this moment. He's talking about the future. Forever.

Zander sits up and unfastens his jeans, freeing his cock in one swift motion. I've seen it before, but this is the first time I've seen it like this. Fully erect and ready for me.

I try to sit up to return the favor, but Zander places his hand on the center of my chest, pressing me back against the rock. "Not this time, baby. I don't have the patience or strength to let you do anything to me. This..." he grabs the base of his erection, "is only going in one hole tonight, and it's not that pretty little mouth."

I whimper again as Zander lines the tip of his cock with my entrance. I can't help my moan when he slowly enters me. I know just based on conversations that we've done this before, but it still feels new, different, exhilarating.

After what feels like minutes, Zander stops moving, fully seated inside me. We both groan at the bliss of it all. "Move," I whine. "God, please move."

As if my words rung a starting bell, he pulls back and slams into me. My. World. Shatters. He folds over me, pinning me beneath him while he pistons his hips again and again. Reaching up for him, I yank him down for another searing kiss, and we lose ourselves in the rhythm of each other.

Moaning, I struggle to breathe as Zander changes angles and somehow drives deeper. Our mouths break apart on a gasp, and before I have time to process what's happening, Zander lowers his head to my neck to nip and suck on the spot where my neck and shoulder meet.

"Zander...God, please," is all I can manage to say between gasps and moans. With a growl, I feel his canines extend and scrap along my collarbone. The sting is the perfect amount of pain.

Without any warning, Zander sinks his canines into my flesh, and I stop breathing. The orgasm that rips through me erases any last semblance of who I was, and I'm remade. As if my reaction is all he was waiting on, Zander removes his canines and picks up pace, beginning to lose his own rhythm. With a roar that I'm sure can be heard for miles, he stills and fills me with his release.

We lay there, him still inside me, both of us struggling to catch our breath. The absolute bliss of this moment overshadows whatever chaos was still in my mind. Zander lowers his head one last time to kiss the top of mine before he lathes over the bite mark he left with his tongue, sealing it.

CHAPTER THIRTY-SEVEN

I thought we were over the panicking?

KARA

AFTER WHAT FEELS LIKE seconds, minutes, and hours rolled into one, Zander pulls out of me and rolls onto his back. I follow him and roll to drape myself over his chest. We lay there, just breathing each other in. Time turns into an abstract moment of communion and peace in his arms.

"You okay?" Zander breaks the comfortable silence with a kiss to the top of my head.

I sigh. "Yeah, I am. You?"

"Better than. Although I fear we're both going to freeze if we lay here for much longer," he says with a chuckle.

It's only then that I remember we're laying out in the wide open, on a giant ass rock in the middle of the night. I can't help but tease him when I respond, "You're a furnace, I'll be fine. You, though?" I shrug noncommittally. Zander squeezes me gently, sitting us both up.

"Seriously though, we probably should talk about that," I say deftly, waving at where he marked me.

His face falls, and he looks like he's genuinely upset he did it. "I'm sorry. You didn't verbally say you wanted me to. My wolf was riding me hard, and I couldn't stop myself even if I wanted to."

"No! That's not it at all. I'm glad you did. But what I wanted to say is I wish I could reciprocate," I rush out. I don't want him thinking I'm upset by it. Honestly, it's the truth. I hate that I can't mark him properly.

"Hey," Zander cups my face, "just because you can't mark me yet doesn't make me any less yours. I'm yours, today, tomorrow, and every day from now till my last breath. And probably beyond. I'll get one of those rings that humans wear if it makes you feel better," he adds with a chuckle.

"I love you, Zander Holt."

"And I you, Kara Lancaster." He pecks my lips before he adds, "Although, I would really prefer it if it was Kara Holt." He smirks.

I laugh. "Remind me to tell you about using your last name the entire time I was gone."

Zander, to his credit, doesn't fully freeze, but he does stop mid-pull of his pants and says, "I'm sorry, you what?"

"Yeah, that first morning in the diner. It just came out. Like it felt like the name I should use, but I knew in my mind it technically wasn't right."

Shaking his head, he finishes putting his pants on, then comments, "You still ran." I snap my eyes to him to defend myself before he quickly adds, "I get it, though. I'm just glad you felt like it was right." He pulls his shirt over his head before he turns to me, pausing for a moment.

"Seems like they discovered you snuck out. They've been looking for you."

"I said I was able to get away, not that they wouldn't figure it out at some point." I shrug and finish dressing.

I find the bag I brought with me just as Zander jumps down off the rock. Turning around, he reaches up for me to jump to him. This time I have no hesitation about the contact like the last time he helped me down, and I jump into his waiting arms. Placing another quick kiss on my forehead, he says, "Come on. If they are close enough for them to communicate via the pack bond, we'll probably meet up with them quickly."

He turns towards the trail and starts walking, but I'm rooted in place. "Oh my God, Zander!"

"What? What is it? What happened?" Zander turns around and scans the area for threats.

"Do you think they heard us?" I whisper-squeak, horrified.

Zander laughs. Laughs!

"Seriously! You said they were close enough to communicate through the bond. Were they close enough to *hear us*?" I punctuate the last words, but still whisper-yell at him.

"No, love. They just got into range. If anything, they might have heard me at the very end, but they didn't hear you, I promise." He wraps me in a hug, kisses the top of my head, and pulls me towards the path back to the pack house.

"I swear to God, Zander, if they say anything about hearing us, I will die." I'm completely mortified. I just had sex out in the open on a rock where anyone could have seen. I mean I knew this, I even thought about it before, but it's just hitting me what we actually did. *What the hell was I thinking?* I wasn't, that's what. *Pull yourself together, Kara.* You will be seeing other people soon, and you can't look like you just had the best sex of your life.

Fuck. Me.

"Love, you okay?"

"No, I am not okay. I mean, I am okay. Better than okay. But I look like I just had mind-blowing sex, and we have to see people," I screech at him.

"You're panicking. I thought we were over the panicking?" How the hell is Zander this calm about everything? "But it was mind-blowing?" He raises an eyebrow and smirks. Damn him.

"Of course, I'm panicking. And yes, you know it was," I practically growl.

"Babe, we are fine. Everyone knows we are mates. Shifters are very physical creatures. Sex is a major part of our lives. Especially once mated. No one will care." He shrugs then adds, "They might never climb on those rocks again if they find out, but that's fine.

"Oh my God!" I slap him on the arm, but he just laughs and continues to maneuver us down the path, just as we hear voices coming towards us.

Up ahead, two figures come around the bend in the trail. Even though they're too far away to make out their features, Zander leans down and whispers, "It's Damien and Kai." I breathe a sigh of relief that I at least know them and it's not random enforcers, but it still worries me they'll know what we were doing. As if reading my thoughts, he adds, "They wouldn't have heard us, but they will be able to smell what we were doing."

I gasp and slap Zander again. "You said..."

"I said they wouldn't have heard us. You didn't ask about smell."

"I'm going to kill you." Zander just laughs and calls out to his men.

"Apparently, Kara's escape skills have bested you twice, Kai."

"Hey! I wasn't on *watch Kara duty*. That was Day," Kai exclaims, and Damien just shakes his head.

"How the hell did you slip out of the pack house without anyone noticing you? And how did you know where Zander was?" Damien looks at me with clear frustration.

"I heard you two talking to Jensen and Marek when they got back, and Zander already took me here once, so I knew the way. The other part, I'm not telling you." I know I'm being a bit petulant, but I don't care.

"It's a breach of security that someone can leave or return without our knowledge. For your safety, I need to know," Damien growls.

Zander takes a menacing step forward, putting himself between me and the guys and growls, "Watch it, Day. You may be right on the how, but the tone needs improvement." But his eyes are shockingly his own. He's still in full control. Part of me was certain we'd have another *she's mine* moment.

"Sorry, Alpha." Damien turns to me and says, "If you could get out without someone noticing, that means someone can get in. With the threat to both of you not mitigated, we need to take precautions."

"Fine." I roll my eyes but continue, "The door in the kitchen to the back patio's alarm is disabled. I thought I'd have to do it myself, but it was already done."

All three men stare at me, then glance at each other. "That's...a problem." Kai rubs the back of his neck.

"Have Callum reset the whole system and reinstall all the door alarms in the morning," Zander says. "Let's head back to the house and get some sleep."

The four of us make our way back to the pack house, Zander's arm never leaving my waist. The weird charge we always felt when we touched before is now a happy little zing that keeps me content and calm. There's so much comfort in his embrace, my mind is able to drift off. I'm surprised when we make it back to the pack house so quickly.

As we break through the trees, Zander looks down at me and says, "You're sleeping in our room tonight. Tomorrow, we're moving your shit back."

I give him a jaunty salute. "Yes, Alpha."

He growls back at me playfully. Without preamble, he scoops me up and carries me the rest of the way back to our bedroom.

Chapter Thirty-Eight

This feels off

ZANDER

Sunlight streams through the crack in the curtains. I may have stayed awake the entire night, too worried that if I fell asleep, Kara would vanish, but I'm more rested than I've been in weeks. Glancing down to where Kara's head is resting on my chest, her even breathing is a balm to my soul. I can't help but smile.

I have her back. It's been damn near a month of terror, pain, loss, confusion and any number of other emotions, but she's here with me, in our bed. It feels like I could take over the world.

Last night wasn't supposed to happen. I was content to just stay in the woods, away from everyone. Then Kara found me, told me she thought we should complete the bond, and we made love. Soul shattering, mind-bending sex.

We've had sex before all this chaos, but this was new. Different. Better. I have zero clue why this time was so much better, but I'm looking forward to it again.

But what about the bombshell she dropped about the disabled alarm system? Kara said she intended to disable the door alarm in the kitchen, but didn't have to because it was already disabled. The moment she said that, both Damien and Kai said the same thing in my head.

What the fuck!

I agreed. Now we have to deal with that fall out, too.

With a sigh and a stretch like a pinup doll—damn, that back arch is sinful—Kara stirs from sleep. Reaching my head down, I kiss the top of her head. "Morning, love. Sleep well?"

"Mmm? Oh, yeah. I think I slept better last night than I have in a while. I don't know if it was you holding me or the mind-blowing sex." She smirks.

"So either way, I'm the reason you slept well?"

Rolling her eyes, Kara replies, "Yeah, true. I guess you were the common denominator in that one." Pausing, she adds, "So what's the plan for today?"

"I don't have one. Damien will put Callum on the security system and get that back running right. I'm sure I should help fix the office since I was the one who destroyed it."

"Yeah, you did go all alphahole on the whole of the main level. But Kai already got some of the pack working on that yesterday while we planned how to get you back and deal with all the other bullshit that's happening."

"You helped with plans?"

Kara rolls her eyes, but answers, "So did Carmen. You forget, apparently, I was supposed to be an Alpha in my own right, and Carmen was going to be part of my inner circle. I may not remember shit, but I can help in my own way."

"You're right, I'm sorry. Did you guys figure anything out? Next steps for your memory, your wolf, or my inability to function as a normal shifter?" I kiss her head again because it's become a habit I don't want to break.

Her face falls. "No. Although, Damien did say something about reaching out to Alpha Grayson. I guess while you were gone dealing with me, Grayson was a big help in research and such. He seemed to be really willing to step in and offer guidance and help."

Kara rolls from her side to sit up and straddle me. I thank whatever god is watching that she is only wearing a thin sleep dress, because the view is perfect. Grabbing her hips to hold her in place, I arch into her. Moaning, she throws her head back before refocusing. "We probably should be getting up."

"Or, we stay right here and enjoy each other." I thrust up into her again, and growl when she shifts herself so her sex is perfectly aligned with my straining cock. *Damn these boxers.*

"Z, that feels so good." Kara almost gasps out as her hands find my chest. Her blunted nails scrape me. So I do it again as she falls forward, crashing her mouth to mine in a hungry meeting of teeth and tongue.

It's like whatever decision she made in her head yesterday about us opened up a dam. The physicality of our relationship was stunted, but not anymore. She rubs herself on me, creating the most devilish friction. Sinful in all the right ways.

Ring.

"What the fuck..." I growl.

Ring.

Kara leans up and over to the side table, grabbing my phone, because of course it's mine. She hands it to me, and begrudgingly, I answer it without even looking at the caller.

"This is Zander."

"I have some information on Kara's condition you may be interested in."

I pull my phone away from my ear to see who the hell is calling me this damn early, specifically about Kara. *Alpha Grayson.* Bringing the phone back to my ear, I growl into the phone, "Okay, what do you know?"

Kara climbs off the bed, heading to the bathroom.

"This is something we should talk about in person. I think we should meet at the meeting house on the neutral land we use for meetings."

"Why do we need to meet somewhere neutral?" This feels off, especially when Kara just said Grayson was more than willing to give info not even a few weeks ago. But I need to know what he knows, even at the risk of a false trail.

Grayson growls, "Trust me, you need this information, and being in a neutral place is safe for everyone involved."

"Fine. When?"

"1:00 p.m. Bring your second if you feel you need to."

"You know I don't go into any meeting without him. You do the same. I'll see you at one." Hanging up, I drop my phone next to me on the bed. I groan and close my eyes, digging the heels of my palms into my eyes to alleviate the growing pain there.

"Everything okay?" Kara calls from the bathroom.

"Grayson says he has info on your condition, but refused to tell me on the phone. He wants to meet in person at the meeting house at one." I open my eyes and look towards the bathroom.

"Well, that's good, isn't it? He knows something." She comes to lean on the door frame, crossing her arms and looking at me.

"Yeah, it's good he knows something, but not wanting to say it over the phone is concerning. He's been one of this pack's closest allies for years. Longer than I've been alive. But being secretive isn't ever a good thing." Kara moves to the foot of the bed with a look of concern on her face.

"So we go, find out what he wants, and keep our guard up," she says with finality.

I sit up and look directly at her. *She is not going to like this.* "I don't want you going. This situation isn't the safest, and there's too many unknowns."

"Oh no. You don't get to decide what I get to know about my own problems. Don't even think about it." The ice in Kara's words is surprising.

I stare at her and sigh. "If you insist on going, Damien and Kai will both be with us. Damien would be going anyway as my second, but Kai will be coming specifically as your guard."

"I can come as long as someone is babysitting me? Got it." Kara rolls her eyes and heads for the door.

"Where the hell are you going?" I jump out of bed and cut her off at the door. I spin her around, grabbing her shoulders and holding her in place.

"My clothes are still in the other room. I figured I'd shower over there and change. We have time before we need to leave, so I'll start moving my clothes and stuff beforehand."

"That...makes sense." I let her go, realizing I yet again overreacted. Then I pause and look at what she's wearing. "Wait a damn minute."

"Hun, cool it. It's early, no one is awake yet. No one will see me. Besides, I thought shifters were used to seeing each other naked? It kind of goes with the territory."

"Yeah, but I don't want anyone seeing what's mine."

Rolling her eyes, she reaches for the door handle. Damien reaches out through the bond.

Zander, are you guys awake? We need to talk.

Yeah, we are. I'll meet you in my office in ten minutes.

Okay, see you in ten.

In the time it takes me to finish speaking with Damien over the bond, Kara has slipped out and made it to her room, so I turn around and get myself ready. As I head down to my office, I remember the state I left it in and mentally kick myself for destroying it twice in one month. When I hit the bottom of the stairs, both Damien and Kai are waiting for me.

"Your office isn't really up for having any sort of meeting, so we figured the lounge would work. That's where we've been camping out since yesterday," Damien says without prompting.

"That's fine," I respond and lead the way into the common space we use when we aren't in need of complete privacy.

I take my seat in one of the high-backed chairs near the fireplace. Kai takes the chair across from me, but Damien remains standing. With a huff, he starts pacing—and I know whatever he plans to say, isn't good. The male only paces when things aren't just bad, they're fucked. Resting my elbows on my knees, I lean forward and track his movements. He'll talk when he's ready.

After a few minutes, Damien abruptly stops in front of me and drops a bombshell. "We think the curse put on Kara and the sigils that have fucked you up were put on you by a witch who was paid by another pack. Maybe multiple packs."

I close my eyes and fight the surge of anger that my wolf will use to take over again. I can't afford to let him. The fact they bring this to my attention at the same time Grayson calls with 'info' is odd, to say the least. "How did you come by this information?" I ask with measured, even words.

"Callum has been digging into pack relations because we had nothing else to go on, and he found a connection with some of the packs and payments to a coven or maybe a solitary witch within our region, we can't actually tell." Damien says as he finally deigns to look at me.

"That makes the call I received from Alpha Grayson less than half an hour ago a lot more interesting. He said he had info on Kara's condition, and refused to tell me over the phone. Wants to meet today at the meeting house to talk about it." Both Kai and Damien just stare at me. I know they are processing, but their silence grates on me.

"Kara has made the decision to come with, so you both will be attending as well. Damien, you as my second per usual. Kai, you'll be Kara's bodyguard. I expect you to do your job much better than the last time."

Kai flinches, but Damien questions as he resumes pacing, "Are you sure Kara coming to the meeting is a good idea?" I don't like Kara going, but I also don't want her doing anything rash like following us.

"She is capable, and will have all of us around her. Kai won't be leaving her side. Nothing will happen. Grayson and his pack are allies of our pack, and have been for longer than any of us have been alive." I pause, choosing my next words carefully. "I admit, I find the timing of these things concerning. As well as Grayson's insistence to only meeting in person. But we don't have much else at the moment."

Damien stops pacing and looks directly at me. "If you believe we should go and Kara should come, then I will make arrangements." With that, Damien takes his leave and Kai stands to join him.

"Did you need anything from me?"

"No, go help Damien plan the little outing," I tell him.

With a nod, he turns to head out the door and I sit in silence hoping this biting feeling of *wrong* is just a feeling, and not something more.

CHAPTER THIRTY-NINE

What. The. Fuck?

KARA

AFTER LAST NIGHT AND this morning, the ease of us being around each other has increased even more than before. But there's a tightness to Zander. Grayson's caginess and insistence for an in-person meeting has him really shook up.

Damien and Kai worked out a plan for the whole meeting, knowing I made it clear I would be attending. This is about me, after all. Kai will be with me from the second I exit the truck, till the second I'm back in it and we're heading home. Zander wanted to be the one guarding me, but we know he needs to be actively participating in the meeting, and Damien, as his second, needs to focus on what's happening and his role.

"How much further is it to the meeting house?" I reach down and wrap my hand around Zander's hand as it rests on my thigh. We left the safety of the pack lands about twenty minutes ago. Zander and I in his truck, while Damien and Kai are ahead of us in Kai's. Behind us is a black SUV with what I would assume are extra enforcers.

"Not much longer. The meeting house is used by all the packs in the region as a neutral place to hold meetings. Usually, this is where we hold multi-pack Alpha meetings.' Knowing I would actually like more clarification, Zander continues, "We will get there in about fifteen minutes. We're lucky 'cause we're one of the closer packs to the meeting house. Grayson is about an hour. Your parents' pack is about two."

He glances over with a smirk and adds, "This is the place we met."

"Wait, seriously?"

"Yeah, it was the first and last time you ever went to a meeting there as part of Shadow Creek Pack." Smug pride flows off him, and I roll my eyes.

"Okay then. I know Kai will be with me once we get there, but what's the plan? We just hear him out?" I ask, trying to get this conversation back on track.

"Hopefully, that's exactly what happens. But I don't think we'll get that lucky. Damien agrees this could be some sort of trap, but Grayson has been one of our closest allies for years. His father and mine were allies long before any of us were born."

"So this could be that he is worried what he needs to say could be overheard, and wants to say it somewhere that feels more secure?" To me, that's the most logical conclusion. Why would an ally that close to us want anything but to help us?

"Exactly, but all the weirdness lately has me on edge." Zander brings our hands to his lips and places a gentle kiss on the back of mine. The simple gesture eases that little niggle of doubt I have.

I can't lie that I'm a bit scared I'll mess this up. It's the first time Zander and I will be out in public and around non-pack shifters as mates. Even though everyone keeps reassuring me it will be fine, part of me doubts that.

Just like Zander said, fifteen minutes later, we arrive at a nondescript cabin in the woods. It's not tiny, but nowhere near the size of our pack house. As we pull into the lot in front, I have to ask the one question that's been plaguing me since I heard what we're doing. "Who takes care of it since it's not always occupied?"

"Each pack pays into a fund that pays for a caretaker to live and work on the property. That person maintains everything," Zander says with a laugh. "I was wondering when you were going to ask."

"It's a valid question. And it's not like I know, anyway." I shrug, but Zander flinches. "Too soon?"

"It will always be too soon to joke about you not being whole." Zander leans over the center console, grabs my face in both hands, and kisses me deeply. It's a kiss full of all the pain and promise he can show me. I moan into his mouth, and he deepens the kiss.

Before we can get too carried away, a knock on the window startles us apart, and we both look over at Damien rolling his eyes. "Guess we should get this party started," Zander says with what I think was supposed to be humor, but it comes off more like a strangled groan.

"Let's hear what he has to say, then we can go back and have as much fun as we want." I wink and open the passenger door. Kai is right there to help me down, and takes up position next to me, my guard. Looking up at him, I can't help but tease him a little. "I promise I won't give you the slip this time."

"Do I have to handcuff you to me? 'Cause I will." He winks, but there's hurt in his eyes, too.

"Hey, I'm sorry. I didn't mean to make it weird."

"I know, I just still feel really bad about the whole thing. I should have realized something more was going on than you just being spooked."

"Meh, it's all good now. We just move forward," I tell him. I want to hug him, but the last time I got anywhere close to hugging or even shaking hands with another male, Zander lost it. So I just nod in acknowledgement instead.

We fall into step with Zander, with Damien close behind. With the other vehicles already in the parking lot, we know that Grayson and whoever else he invited are already inside. For a moment, I worry this whole thing is a trap until Grayson himself opens the main door ahead of us.

"Thank you for meeting with me," he says as Zander places his hand on the small of my back. He ushers me up the stairs onto the porch, then past Grayson into the large meeting room.

A large table, big enough to fit at least twenty people, sits in the center of the room. The curtains are all drawn closed, so the only light is from the overhead lights and the crackling fire that gives off the right amount of heat.

Two other men are in the room as we walk in, and they stand from their spots on the far side of the table closest to the fire. I can only assume they are Grayson's second and third. From what I understand about pack dynamics, rarely does an Alpha meet anyone outside the pack without at least one or both of their top pack members.

That theory is crushed the way Zander, Damien, and Kai all stiffen at the sight of them. I look to Zander, but he's staring at the men with almost hatred in his eyes. Turning to Kai, I attempt to ask him something, but he just shakes his head and steps in front of me.

What. The. Fuck?

"Why are they here?" The growl that laces Zander's tone is downright terrifying.

"Just come in and sit. We can talk and all this will make sense." Grayson's tone drips with something akin to false bravado and ire. The tension in the room goes from uncomfortable to dangerous in a single breath.

That flight instinct is coming on hard and fast again. Zander turns to me, and his eyes flash gold, letting me know his wolf is just below the surface. "You need to go with Kai. He will take you home." There's no room in his tone to question, but I need to know what the hell is going on here.

"Let her stay, Zander. This involves her, too," Grayson says to Zander, and it makes my skin crawl.

"It will be fine. I'll stay close to Kai," I tell him, but I'm far from comfortable with whatever this is.

Grayson walks with purpose to the far side of the table and takes the seat to the right of the two men who sit down as well. I follow Zander and Damien, staying between them and Kai. Zander sits, Damien standing behind him. I take the seat next to Zander and reach out to rest my hand on his leg.

That little moment of connection seems to ground him, and he visibly relaxes a fraction. Anything is better than nothing. I wish I could speak in their heads. I need to know who these people are. The menace they both exude is almost suffocating.

"It's nice to see you again after so long, Zander," the man on the far left says without a hint of kindness.

"I can't say the same, Varek. I don't even know the last time we even spoke," Zander says with a surprisingly even tone. "Last I heard, your pack was limping along, still trying to correct the wrongs of the past.

"The rumors of our demise were greatly exaggerated." *What a stupid, evil villain line.* "Grayson here has been a big help in keeping the old ways alive." Varek has zero emotion when he speaks. His dead eyes make me queasy.

Varek is a big man. If Zander is a mountain, this guy is the whole fucking range. The aura he has is dark, almost evil. This is the kind of person I thought I was running from. The physical effort to not cringe or get up and just bolt is almost too much.

"Interesting. What has Grayson been so kind to help you with?"

"Numbers, in exchange for a sizable monetary contribution to his coffers." Varek shrugs like this is old news.

For the first time, I notice another man standing by the far wall. Kai leans down and whispers in my ear, "That's Grayson's second, and by the looks of it, he has no idea what these guys are talking about."

I straighten at that, and realize we are in deep shit. If fight or flight is going to come into play, I'm choosing flight—and soon.

"So explain it to me. What did you want us here for? This isn't just a little meeting to gloat about your numbers improving and Grayson making easy money." Zander's carefully controlled rage is impressive.

The second man leans forward and rests his elbows on the table, steepling his hands to rest his chin on them. "It's all about power and who's in control." He looks directly at Zander and continues, "You and your pack have been top of the heap for too long. Your father destroyed any chance of other packs gaining the much-needed land and resources, and it's all because we aligned ourselves with witches."

"I'm sorry, what the what now?" I say out loud before I can stop myself. Zander squeezes my leg, and I close my mouth, realizing what I did.

"Ah yes," Number Two looks pointedly at me. "The she-wolf who would be Alpha, but instead found herself in a bit of a pickle."

"What's that supposed to mean?" I ask him with what I hope is disdain and not fear.

"When the Alpha of one of the strongest packs in the region finds his mate in a would-be Alpha of another strong pack, something must be done to stop it. One of you is bad enough, but both of you? No, we won't stand for that. Especially a she-wolf."

I glance at Zander, confused because they just admitted that they had something to do with what happened to me. The look in his eyes is terrifying, and I'm not sure what to do. I want to know—need to know—but I don't think Zander can handle this. I glance the other way at Kai, and he has the same look in his eyes that I feel: confusion and a hefty dose of *we need to get the fuck out of here.*

"Come now, Zander, the solution is easy," Varek says with a casual edge. *Creepy fucker.*

"And that is?" Zander responds.

"Step down as Alpha, submit to the way things have been run for centuries, and we let you all leave and live in peace."

CHAPTER FORTY

You want my honest answer?

ZANDER

"COME NOW, ZANDER, THE solution is easy." This has got to be some sort of sick joke. I've only met Varek in person maybe twice in my life, but my father hated the man. He's been a thorn in the side of most packs since he became Alpha, but his family has been just as bad for generations. Until today, we had no idea that Black Pine was back in play.

"And that is?" My temper is hanging on by a thread. My wolf is chomping at the bit to tear him in two, especially since the reality of Grayson's betrayal is so obvious.

"Step down as Alpha, submit to the way things have been run for centuries, and we let you all leave and live in peace," Varek says simply.

The way things have been run for centuries? Is he insane? Of course he is. He's asking me to give up my heritage in order for someone to turn my pack into something out of a fucked-up history book.

When I give the signal, get Kara out of here. I don't care what you have to do to make sure she leaves. Do it. I tell Kai, but let Damien and the men outside listen.

We've had an open line of communication between us since we got here. I only wish Kara was able to participate. This would be a lot easier if she could.

I could just force a shift and make mincemeat of them? my wolf offers me, and I internally cringe. He would, too. He's become a lot more brazen and bold in the past few weeks. There was a time I couldn't communicate with him like others can with their wolves. It came in stages. When I became Alpha, we started communicating randomly—usually with heightened emotions—but it grew. Once Kara came into our lives, it was like the dam broke. Impressions still tend to be normal, but words flow freely now. Well, on his schedule, not mine.

I will keep her safe, Kai responds to me, not knowing the internal battle I'm having with not only my wolf, but my need to kill the man responsible for my grandfather's death. He might not have ripped his throat out himself, but he gave the order.

"How about we don't go back to the time when shifters had to hide and Alphas ruled their packs like their own personal slaves," I say, going for calm and confident, but I know it's coming off as forced.

"The fact you even brought your little she-wolf pet tells me all I need to know. Tell me," Varek looks directly at Kara now, "how is it being around so much power when you're nothing more than human?"

Without missing a beat, Kara responds, "Surprisingly easy. I'm no one's servant, and I'm sure I'll be back to full capacity soon." If I wasn't in love with her already, I am now. Damn.

Silas, Varek's second who has never acted like a second and more like an equal, has a surprised look on his face for all of half a second before he schools his features. He looks at me and says, "You should really keep your bitch in line. She shouldn't even be here, let alone be speaking." Kara goes to get up, but I grab her leg, holding her in place. She has a warrior heart, but is currently as weak as a human. Outright attacking three powerful shifters will get her killed.

"I'm not interested in what you think I should or should not do. You do not threaten my mate," I snarl.

"You honestly think you have any room to tell us what we should be doing?" Silas practically snarls.

This is devolving faster than I could have predicted. But the one person who hasn't said a word since we walked in just sits there, saying nothing. I look directly at Grayson when I say, "No." Simple, to the point.

"No?" Varek actually sounds shocked by my answer.

"No," I repeat, but this time add, "no to submitting. No to telling my mate to stand down. No to this whole charade of a meeting." I stand quickly, pulling Kara to her feet while simultaneously pushing her towards Kai. We're going to have to fight our way out of here, and I need him to get her as far away as possible.

"Zander, what the hell?" Kara asks, but I know Kai has wrapped her in a bear hug and is dragging her out of the room. *Mine!* my wolf snarls, and I respond to him quickly, *she's being protected. We need to focus to make sure they can get away.* With a growl, my wolf refocuses on the males in front of us. No one has shifted, but the energy has.

Damien steps up to my side and says, *Derrek and Marcus are outside. Do we need them in here?*

Without taking my eyes off the men in front of us, I tell him, *not yet. We're going to try to get out of here without anyone shifting.* To the men outside I say, *be ready, but don't enter. We've already been betrayed once today. I'm sure others are nearby.*

Kara and Kai are gone, Marcus tells me, and I sigh in relief at the same time my wolf loses his shit.

Focus the rage on the men in front of us. We're going to have to fight our way out, I tell my wolf.

"You know, we came peacefully. Gave you a choice," Grayson finally speaks up.

"You sold your pack for what? Money? Sorry if I don't believe a word out of your mouth. But answer me one question." I look directly at Grayson, because above all else, I need to know. "Why have you been helping us with Kara's issues?"

"What makes you think I have? I've been feeding you just enough to stay up to date on where things stand." He shrugs with a smug grin. The bastard.

I stiffen, and Damien does the same next to me. *We need to go, now.* Damien's slightly panicked words break through the haze of whatever the hell is going on here. Damien nervous and panicky is enough to sober me from the bulk of my rage.

"That's what I figured." To the other two, I say, "So you assume I'm just going to roll over and take this? I sent my mate away because there's no way I'd expose her to any more of your vitriol."

Grayson's second, who has been leaning against the wall, slowly moves around the table. Not quite behind us yet, but closer to the door than we were. That's fine. The other men, the ones who are actual threats, are further. And if we haul ass, we will get outside before they reach us.

Varek just smiles when he says, "We let her leave. She's useless as she is, anyway. Pathetic, weak, nothing more than a human."

His words hit their mark but Damien is the one to respond. "Being human doesn't automatically equal weakness. Especially when you're speaking of the Alpha's mate. A mate to an Alpha is just as strong, if not stronger."

The laugh that leaves both Varek and Silas is chilling, but it's Grayson who seems uncomfortable. That smug grin he was sporting slips. He's definitely a pawn in this whole thing, but his alliance with this pack has put him on the outs with the rest of the region.

Marcus, get my truck started and do the same with your vehicle. We're making a quick exit.

On it, is his only response, and it's enough to put me at ease. I trust my men more than I trust myself on a good day. If he says he's on it, it will be done and better than I could.

On my signal, I tell Damien. The only sign that he even heard me is the slightest tensing of his hands. That minute movement is his one tell, and I only see it from years of training with him. We've fought together, bled together, buried our families together. Our movements are aligned with a bond deeper than blood or pack.

"Well, gentlemen. I wish I could say it's been a great chat, but that would be a lie. We'll be leaving now," I say, and Damien, knowing that's the only signal I'll give, turns and bolts. I follow right behind him.

The crash behind us lets us know that not only are the three men coming after us, but at least one has shifted. This is going to be close. *Be ready, we're on our way and have company.*

We burst outside and see that both my truck and the SUV have been turned towards the lot exit, and the doors are wide open. Marcus is on the porch in human form while Derrek has shifted and is standing at the bottom of the stairs, facing the door to the building.

Damien and I sprint past him while he surges forward, going low and biting the wolf less than three feet behind me. Damien turns and shifts in the same instant. Derrek makes sure I get to the truck. They don't stay in place long, but bolt towards the vehicles. Marcus has already jumped into the SUV. I make it to the truck, happy that it's not lifted to the damn sky like Kai's, slam the door closed, and wait for a sign from either Damien or Derrek that they're in the bed.

Go! Derrek and I will head for the woods and jump in the bed a mile or so down the road. They are both already sprinting as fast as their paws will carry them. Marcus and I peel out of the lot. Thankfully, Marcus had the thought that at least one of us would be shifting, and didn't open our passenger doors.

We make it to the main road without incident, and that's when I realize they let us go. This whole mess is far from over.

A mile or so down the road, both Damien and Derrek appear out of the woods and shift back. We pull over to let them climb in, but not before they get into the emergency clothes we always keep in our vehicles.

"What the fuck was that?" Damien growls as he jumps in the passenger seat.

"You want my honest answer?" I ask him as I take off down the road.

"That you have no fucking clue and now we've lost one of our closest allies."

I grip the steering wheel so hard that it starts to creak under the strain. "I don't fucking know what that was. But we need to get a hold of David and let him know what happened."

"You're remarkably calm for being separated from Kara," Damien regards me with suspicion.

"I think it has something to do with marking Kara. We've been making steps towards completely the bond, and I think that's helping me settle. Or at least giving me more control over my wolf. But I'm not doing well. I need her back in my arms. Soon."

The only response Damien gives me is taking out my phone from the center console and dialing David's number. *This is not going to be a fun conversation.*

"Zander." David's voice comes through the Bluetooth of the truck. "What happened with the meeting?" I had texted him and let him know Grayson wanted to meet about Kara, and he told me to keep him informed.

"Grayson is working with Varek," I say the words through gritted teeth. The silence on the other end of the phone stretches longer than I would have guessed.

"I'm sorry. Our ally—Grayson of Silver Hollow Pack—is working with Varek of Black Pine? The same Varek who tried to destroy the packs as we know them fifty years ago?"

"Well, not working with. I think he's been giving Varek pack members in exchange for funds for I don't know what."

"Yeah, that doesn't make it better. Where are you? Where's Kara?"

"Kara is safe, Kai got her out before anything went down. Thing is, I think they let us go. Which makes me more nervous. They want me to submit and step down as Alpha. I think they want me to hand the pack over to them," I tell him and the growl we hear through the speakers is the same one filling my head.

"I'm coming out and bringing some of my best enforcers for you." It's the only thing David says before the line goes dead.

"Great, in the past hour, we've lost an ally, found out Varek is back in play, and had our pack and specifically our Alpha threatened," Damien rattles off the key points with a hefty amount of sarcasm.

I just stare at the road, willing the truck to go faster even when the winding turns of these woods don't allow it. I need to get back to Kara.

CHAPTER FORTY-ONE

We've got work to do

KARA

THIS WAS A WHOLE big pile of shit. The drive back to our pack is just about as tense as when I was running. The irony of being with Kai in his truck isn't lost on me.

Staring out the window watching the trees blur by, the pit that's settled in my stomach only grows. Looking at Kai, I see the same tightness I'm feeling written all over his face. "Do you think they're okay?"

"We'd know if something happened to Zander," is the only response I get, and it doesn't answer anything. Kai has been practically silent since we fled the meeting house, other than relaying that getting me out was his priority. Now, he's white knuckling the steering wheel and doing his best to get us back as fast as possible.

"What do you mean?" I ask Kai, because I need this conversation to keep going. I need to stay out of my head.

"Zander, he's the Alpha. We'd know if he was killed. We'd feel it." Pausing, he glances my direction, but focuses quickly back on the road. "Well, I'd know. I have no idea if you would. The bond would sever."

"What about Damien, Marek, and Derrek?" We wouldn't have any clue about them. Knowing about Zander makes me feel a little better, but not knowing about the rest of them sucks.

Sighing, he says, "Until we hear from them, we won't know."

I reach for my bag, intending to grab my phone and call Zander, but Kai stops me with one word. "Don't."

"What? Why?"

"We don't know if they were right behind us or if they're still there. They didn't take their phones into the meeting house, so they might not even be able to answer."

I throw my head back against the headrest and close my eyes. He's right, I know he is. But this whole thing sucks. We drive through town just outside the pack lands, so I know we're close to home. I will us to get there along with everyone else.

As we pull into the drive, my phone rings. I almost accidentally launch it when I dig it out of my bag. Recovering quickly, I answer before I even look at the screen. "Zander?"

"Hey, love. We're about twenty minutes behind you, but we're all on our way.

"Thank fuck! What the hell happened?"

"Long story. We'll talk when we all get there. Your dad and a few of his enforcers are on their way there, as well. They'll get there in about an hour, I'd guess."

My mind races. My dad is coming? I already knew this was bad, but this is even worse than I thought. Grayson was a close ally of both our packs. Him aligning with someone like Varek, I assume, is as bad as it gets. Knowing my role in all this is to support, I say, "Okay, I'll make sure everything is ready." I don't know what the hell I need to get ready, but I have Carmen and Kai. I'll figure it out.

"Thanks, love. See you soon."

"See you." I hang up and look at Kai, who's parked and is waiting for me to get out. "My dad is coming, and he's bringing some enforcers to boost our numbers."

"So we have some work to do." Kai immediately goes into work mode. The fun and carefree version, even the guard version, has been put aside, and his position as Zander's third takes center stage. "I'll let the rest of the inner circle know to get here. You let Marge know we'll be needing an easy dinner. I'll also confirm we have room in the barracks for the enforcers." Pausing to think, Kai drums his fingers on the dash and asks, "Did Zander say how many your dad was bringing?"

"No, I wouldn't think he'd bring too many. Why would he want to put his own pack in danger?"

"His pack is twice the size of ours. We're physically and financially stronger, but he's got the shifters." With that, he jumps out of the truck and looks up at me. "Come on, we've got work to do."

By the time Zander, Damien, and the rest pull up to the pack house, Kai, Carmen, and I have rearranged and set up the lounge to accommodate the upcoming meeting as the rest of the inner circle make an appearance.

The truck barely comes to a stop when Zander throws his door open and begins stalking towards me. If I didn't know that I'm the only person safe from him, the look he has would absolutely make me pee myself. I jump up from my spot on the front steps at the same time he bends down and scoops me into his arms.

My feet leave the ground as Zander buries his face in my neck, inhaling my scent. I wrap my legs around his waist, clinging to him. I remember thinking I wanted to climb him like a tree, well here we are. *Kara, meet your own personal tree.*

I pull back just as he does, and our foreheads meet in what is the most grounding thing I've ever experienced. I close my eyes and just take in everything that is Zander. His love, his strength. His power and protectiveness. This man is truly the only thing I could ever need.

"I was so scared," I whisper as a tear I didn't know I was holding back makes it through my lashes. "I have no idea what the hell all happened, but I know it wasn't good."

"Everything we thought about our alliance is a lie. Grayson has been playing us for weeks, but most likely months or years." The rage that pours out of Zander is almost terrifying. "Letting Kai take you away from me was the hardest thing I've ever had to do. But I had to keep you safe, and getting you away from that was the only way."

"You did everything right. Kai kept me safe. You and all your men came home safe. We're safe."

I feel him tense as he holds me, and I pull back to look into his bottomless, green eyes. "What?"

"I think they let us leave," he says as he sets me down. "We had to fight our way out, but they didn't really put up much resistance." Before I can respond to that, Zander grabs my hand and pulls me towards the house. I stumble over my own feet, but keep up. Damien and the rest have already made it inside.

CHAPTER FORTY-TWO

So something big is coming

KARA

THE REALITY OF THE actual shitstorm we're in doesn't fully hit me until we go through the entryway. The whole of the inner circle is there, plus Marcus and Derrek. On top of that, a few other enforcers and other shifters are milling about, but I don't know their names. Carmen is hovering by the stairs, close enough to be included, but not too close to be in the way. I pull out of Zander's hand and head to her.

"This is crazy. I feel like we're gearing up for some sort of attack." She wrings her hands and looks up at me as I approach. We hadn't had much time to speak before Z and Day got back. Carmen had been helping Marge in the kitchen while Kai and I set up the lounge.

This whole thing has shaken everyone. The normally jovial Kai looks like someone stole his favorite toy. Carmen has zero sassy quips. Damien is pacing—I've never seen him pace. The others are all shifting on their feet nervously. Then there's Zander. He looks like he's ready to murder everyone and do it with a smile. But once his eyes land on me and he realizes I'm staying nearby, just out of the way, he does calm slightly.

"Yeah, I don't know the details or even who those men were, but the energy in that meeting room was..." I shudder. "Zander looks like he's ready to kill someone, and Damien looks shaken."

Carmen blows out a breath and says, "So something big is coming." It's not a question; it's a statement of fact. A fact that seeps into my bones and freaks me the fuck out more than I already was.

"Yeah, especially since my dad's coming." I go for nonchalance, but it comes off like I tried to eat a lemon whole.

"Fuck me." Carmen gapes at me, but I just shrug and tilt my head to look at her. "So what do we do? What can we do to help?"

Hell, what do we do? I have zero memory of pack life, and I can't even shift. Carmen is my best friend who can shift, but she's working towards being a healer now that I'm most likely not taking over my parents' pack. Taking a deep breath, I look her in the eyes and repeat what I told myself in the truck, "We support. 'Cause I don't know what else to do."

Carmen nods once and focuses back on the males in the center of the entry-way. I turn as well, my eyes drawn to Zander like gravity. He must feel my eyes on him, because he turns and looks up. He gives me a tight smile and raises his hand towards me, beckoning me forward.

While I want to go to him, I feel so out of place that a part of me wants to hide in the shadows. Or run. Yeah, panic and run sounds good right now. But instead, I take a deep breath and walk to him. When I reach him, he wraps me in his arms, pulling me to his side. Immediately, a feeling of peace and comfort washes over me. Safe. I feel safe.

When I left his side at the meeting, my anxiety shot through the roof. I figured that was adrenaline. Even in the truck, I wasn't really calm. I was probably giving Kai an aneurism with my twitching. When Zander got back, we were so wrapped up in making sure the other was whole that I didn't even process this feeling then, either. Now? It's all I can think about.

Zander stiffens a fraction, but relaxes quickly and looks at Damien. "Go meet David to bring him here. Have his enforcers rendezvous with Marcus and Derrek at the barracks while we meet."

With a nod, Damien heads for the front door and disappears outside. *How the hell did he know?* Enforcers telling him? Zander must notice my confused look, because he responds to my questions without me having to actually voice them. "Any time an Alpha from another pack crosses the borders, I sense it. That, and my enforcers watching the road alerted me." He shrugs. Okay, that makes sense. "How are you doing?" It takes me a moment to realize he's speaking to me.

"Oh, umm. I guess fine. I'd be happier if I knew what the hell is happening. I mean, I know what's happening, but I don't know the background. There's obviously background to all of this." I'm babbling now, but I can't help it. The not knowing is ratcheting up my anxiety.

Putting a finger to my lips, Zander just chuckles and says, "We will talk about it. While we're in the meeting, you ask any questions you want. Honestly, I don't know a ton about Varek because the whole shifter war happened before I was born. But your dad knows a lot. So ask away."

Knowing that I'm not the only one who feels out of sorts at the lack of information is oddly comforting. So I just squeeze his middle, and he reciprocates.

The door opens, and my father walks in along with Damien. I break away from Zander, knowing instinctively the hug my father will give me will fix every problem, or at least feel like it will. I walk into his open arms, and his scent washes over me like a wave. "There's my firefly," he says with so much love I almost cry.

"Hi, Dad. How's Mom?"

"Pissed I wouldn't let her come. Worried about you. Other than that, she's great." He chuckles into my hair.

"Why couldn't she come?" I pull back a little to see his face.

"With Varek in play, we don't need her around for that. I don't even like you being involved, but I can't stop that now, can I?" He smiles down at me, but raises an eyebrow.

"Nope, I'm involved, and I'll be involved till the end."

"That's what I get for having an Alpha for a daughter." Dad chuckles and shakes his head as he releases me to shake Zander's hand. "Zander, we have much to discuss."

"Yes, we do. Let's head into the lounge and we can discuss everything." Zander releases my dad's hand and turns his back to stride into the lounge. Even I know that's a power move, one my father lets slide—but barely.

CHAPTER FORTY-THREE

That's barbaric!

ZANDER

I WALK INTO THE lounge ahead of everyone. I probably shouldn't have turned my back on David. He could easily take me down. Yes, he's older, but he's also stronger. An Alpha's strength is directly tied to their pack. The stronger the pack, the stronger the Alpha. The lounge has been rearranged into a meeting space, no doubt by Kara and Kai. There's even a table in the corner with a bit of a food spread on it.

I turn back and beckon Kara over. Without hesitation, she leaves her father's side and comes to mine. I lean down and whisper in her ear low enough so no one else can hear, "Remember, you belong here. Ask questions. Give opinions. You are my mate. But you are also an Alpha."

She stiffens for a fraction before settling, and nods once that she heard and understood. So I lead her to the chair next to the one I plan to take. Taking a deep breath, I turn to the rest of the room, taking in the group assembled—my inner circle, David, his second, and Carmen who is hovering by the door. Normally, I wouldn't want her here, but Kara needs support right now, and Carmen can give it when I can't. It will also keep my wolf contained knowing she's with a female and not another male.

Having her around Kai for so long without me was a lot. My wolf hated every second of it. Somehow though, since I've marked her, I'm not on edge as much, and neither is he. I think marking Kara helped my wolf as much as it helped me.

I motion around the room. "Please, sit. We need to get started." I sit in my chair at the same time David sits down across from me. Kara looks around the room like she's trying to figure out if she belongs, but I lightly grab her hand and pull her into her chair.

Without missing a beat—probably because he's used to running these meetings—David begins, "How involved is Grayson with Varek?"

"As involved as you can be. He's been supplying Varek with what we assume are enforcers and possibly she-wolves, but we haven't confirmed that. We know Varek has paid him a shit ton for whatever he's supplied. What we don't know is how much Grayson has told his pack. His second seemed genuinely shocked."

"So we can safely assume that Grayson has broken our alliance." David leans back in his chair, resting his ankle on his opposite knee.

"There's no assumption, it's a fact. But also, it seemed there's no alliance between Varek and Grayson. It's more of a power play. Varek is pulling the strings," Damien adds from where he took up position behind me.

"Exactly. Varek and Silas are the ones in control."

"Fuck me, that bastard Silas is still alive?" David seems genuinely annoyed. I glance at Kara, curious how she's doing, but she's the picture of patience and calm.

"Yeah, my dad would have been shocked, too," I say before continuing. "Grayson seems like he wants a bigger role, and that makes him unpredictable." I look right at David. He has a history with Varek and Grayson, and I have to come to terms with the fact I'm way out of my depth.

"Varek has been a thorn in most of the regional packs' sides for years. Before he was Alpha, his father was just as bad. That pack has never been on the good side of any conflict," David begins with a sigh, and I don't think I'm going to like anything he says. "Your father was the key component in stopping Black Pine when they attempted to take over multiple packs. His leadership rallied the other alphas of the packs that usually don't get involved in interpack politics."

Surprisingly, I'm not that shaken by his revelations. I knew my father was important to the last pack wars. "That makes a lot of sense since they wanted me to submit and step down as Alpha, handing the pack to Grayson."

David leans forward with his elbows on his knees and looks directly at me. The intensity he exudes would knock a weaker wolf on their ass. "What exactly did he say?"

"That I should submit and step down as Alpha so they could usher in the old ways."

"Fuck," is the only thing David replies with, and that is what shakes me. David basically kept his shit together for the most part when Kara ran off, but this is messing with him. On a scale of one to *damn it all to hell*, I think we've passed damn it.

"What did he mean, *the old ways*?" Kai steps forward from my other side.

"Where it was numbers that made a pack strong. She-wolves were only good for breeders and basically slaves. Packs rarely interacted with anyone outside their own packs. Humans were looked at as something less than she-wolves."

The gasp Kara lets out mirrors the horror I'm feeling. I know for a fact that my father never ran the pack like that. But did my grandfather? His? What the absolute fuck?

"That's barbaric!" Kara finds her voice, saying the exact thing we're all thinking.

"That's why a lot of those 'traditions,'" David air quotes, "were outlawed at least seventy-five years ago. I remember the pack meetings that made them law. I wasn't Alpha yet, but I was old enough to attend. The sentiment had changed in most packs many years before, but the Alphas found it necessary to make it official."

"And Black Pine rebelled at that idea," I piece together. It's the next logical part of this insane story.

"Yes, Black Pine, Thorn Crow, and Dark Ridge didn't want the change. They were the only Alphas to push back against making it illegal to threaten she-wolves as less. When it still passed, they didn't take it lying down. They also didn't start an all-out war for another twenty-five-ish years. It took time. But when they did attack the other packs, your father rallied the alphas and was seen as the reason the attackers failed."

"So this is all about revenge?" Kara asks. I've been listening to David, but my attention has been focused on her. As her father relayed more and more of the story, she grew more tense.

Reaching over, I rest my hand on her thigh and use my thumb to draw small circles there. I wish we could communicate through the bond. It would make this so much easier. Since we only have the nonverbal right now, I push whatever energy I can into my touch.

"It would seem so," David says, leaning back and giving his daughter a sad smile. Turning back to me, he adds, "You said they let you go. What did you mean?"

"Just that. We got Kara out with Kai. Which, thinking about it, was really easy, as well. But we geared up to fight our way out. Grayson's second was in our way as we left, but let us pass without any real resistance."

Damien takes over and says, "We did have some resistance on the front porch and had to hold one wolf back while Zander got to his truck. I believe it was Silas. Derrek and I shifted to hold them back while the rest left with the vehicles. We escaped through the forest and weren't intercepted at all. The whole thing seemed planned. Like they knew we would balk at their offer and outright refuse."

"I'm sure it was. No one would willingly submit and give up their pack." David hums in agreement. "Now the real question is, what do we do from here?"

With that, we begin to formulate a plan. Which, in all regards, boils down to waiting. We wait for their next move. We don't have anything other than knowing Varek is back in play and Grayson is a fucking asshat traitor.

We get word that the enforcers David brought are settled into the barracks and have joined rotations. Each of them are well-trained and perfect for patrol. Thanks to David, they will help bolster our numbers and give us the eyes we need at the borders.

We may not have much, but we at least aren't completely out of our depth now.

CHAPTER FORTY-FOUR

Good thing I'm not typical

ZANDER

As EVENING GIVES WAY to night, David announces he and his second will be heading back. Kara, being the caring person she always is, insists they stay, but he declines. As they pull out of the drive, Kara leans back into me and I wrap my arms around her. The stress of the day hits hard. I can feel her losing her will to stay upright.

"Come on, let's head to bed. You're exhausted." I wrap my arms around her tighter, and she looks up at me.

"Yeah, I think bed sounds good." Her smile is wanton and wicked, sending arousal straight to my cock. *This woman.* Doesn't matter if we only ever can mate like humans, she's mine. Without another word, I swoop down and pick her up bridal style. She shrieks and throws her arms around my neck.

Turning, I carry her through the front door and head for the stairs while Carmen and some of the guys are coming out of the kitchen. They hoot and holler, but it's Carmen's voice that's louder than the rest. "That's it! Get it girl!" Kara buries her head in my shoulder, embarrassed by the whole scene.

Not one to be outdone, I murmur directly into her ear, "Oh yes, you will be getting it. Right in that perfect pussy."

"Zander!" she squeals and hits my chest, but I just laugh and head upstairs.

I slam the bedroom door closed with a swift kick behind me, and head straight to the bathroom. I've been dying to get this woman naked, and we both need showers. So, two birds and all.

I set her down on the counter, caging her with my body. Her caramel eyes look up at me, wide and unsure. *Why unsure?* It's not like this is our first time. Even this go-around. I reach up and take the clip out of her hair, letting those scarlet locks fall over her shoulders and back. God, I love her hair. It was the first thing I saw when my wolf realized our mate was there, followed closely by her ass.

"Wha.. What are we doing?" Kara stutters, and I put my hands back on the counter on either side of her.

"Showering. We both need to take one, and I figure this will speed the process along," I say the last words with a lot more levity than I feel. This girl has me on a knife's edge.

"Don't we need to be naked to shower?" She arches an eyebrow at me, and I realize then she's not nervous, she just wasn't sure if we were on the same page. Time to rectify that.

"Let me be real honest with you, love. We are showering, but getting clean is not necessarily my priority here." I pause to bend down and nuzzle her neck. The moan she lets out makes my wolf and I growl. *I know, buddy.* "Before we leave that shower, you will come. *At least twice.*" I emphasize the last words like the vow they are.

"Zander..." Kara says with another moan. Without another word, I crash my mouth to hers and force my tongue past her lips. After the day we've had and the shitstorm that's brewing on the horizon, being with her feels like the only safe harbor in a sea of confusion.

Kara's hands find the waist of my jeans, and before I can process what's happening, she has them undone and is yanking them over my hips. *Naughty mate.* Not to be outdone, I rip her shirt from her body and unclasp her bra, freeing those perfect breasts I love so much.

I break the kiss and make my way down her neck to her breast. I suck one of her nipples into my mouth while my hand kneads her other breast. The sounds Kara makes only drive my need higher, and I almost come right there when she reaches down and squeezes my length.

Rubbing her thumb over the tip, I growl around her breast and bite down. Not hard, but hard enough that she jolts. Lathing the sting away, I scoop her into my arms and turn towards the shower.

We're both still partially clothed, so I reluctantly set her down and shove my pants to my ankles, kicking my boots off in the process. Kara stands in front of me, not even trying to hide the hunger in her eyes as she watches me reach for the collar of my shirt behind my head, pulling it forward and off.

"Your turn, love." I growl. I'm sure I look like a predator and she's my prey, but I can't seem to find a part of me that cares right now. That startles her out of her head, and she grabs the band of her pants. She brings them down over her ass and peels them off her legs.

Before Kara has a chance to stand fully, I swoop back in. This kiss is even more feral than the last. I push her backward into the expansive shower, the steam swirling around us. I angle myself so she doesn't get blasted by the water straight away and push her up against the wall.

The squeal she lets out when the cold tile hits her back makes me chuckle into her mouth. "Z! That's...cold..." Kara says between kisses, but doesn't actually try to move. She couldn't if she wanted to. I have her right where I want her.

She pulls her head away and asks, "I thought we were going to shower?"

Nipping at her nose, I laugh again and say, "I said we were going to get *in* the shower. Getting clean isn't high on the priority list." I snake my hand down her body, the other one on the wall next to her. Without any warning, I bend to sink my fingers through her center. It's not the water that's made her this wet.

"Oh," Kara says on a gasp. "Yes, please, more." She's already so close to coming apart, so I do the one thing I know will push her over the edge: I drop to my knees.

I look up into Kara's eyes, and her face is a mixture of confusion and desperation. "How's this going to work?" There's a hint of sarcasm mixed in, too.

Okay, I get it, our height difference doesn't really lend itself to this working in the typical fashion.

Good thing I'm not typical.

I grab her behind the thighs and lift her, settling her legs on my shoulders and placing her core right at my mouth. Between my shoulders and the wall, she's fully supported, and the buffet is open for business.

I bury my face between her thighs, licking a path back to front and sucking on her clit like it's my favorite candy. Her hands fly down to my head and she moans my name—gasping and beginning to thrash already. I bring my hand around and push two fingers inside her, turning and twisting them until I find that place that makes her scream.

And scream she does. She breaks apart faster than I expect, and I revel in the knowledge that I made that happen. Working Kara through the last of her orgasm, I only stop when she seems to go boneless in my grasp.

Carefully lowering her down off my shoulders, I keep her in my hold as I rise. "When I'm done with you, you won't know how to walk anymore." The look on her face as I align my cock with her entrance is one part reverence and one part feral need.

Kara's head falls to my shoulder where her hands have already found a hold. Breathing hard, she gasps into my shoulder, "Please, Z. I need you." That's the only push I need, and I give her exactly what she asked for.

I shove inside her in one hard thrust, and don't give her time to adjust. I set a pace that's maddening, even for me. But I couldn't slow down if I wanted to. After the day we had and the absolute terror I felt knowing Kara was in danger, I thrust into her with all the pent up emotions I'm feeling. It's hard, rough, desperate, and she's right there with me. Meeting me thrust for thrust, hanging on for the ride we both need.

Just as I think I'm not going to hold out any longer, Kara throws her head back and screams as another orgasm rips through her. I follow her over the edge with only a few more jerky thrusts before I bury deep and give her all I have.

We stay like that for a moment, both panting and trying to come back down to earth. The way she feels in my arms, I know there's no way she will be able to walk, so I pull out and keep her in my arms.

I reach over, turn the water off, and carry her out of the stall and straight to bed. We don't dry off, just lay down tangled in each other's arms.

Kara cracks open her eyes and says, "Love you," with a sleepy sigh.

Those two words fill me with such hope, joy, and exhilaration. I don't think I'll ever tire of hearing them.

I kiss the top of her head and say, "I love you, too. Now go to sleep." Before I even finish speaking, she's out, with me following closely behind her.

Chapter Forty-Five

Nothing more than a human

Kara

THE PAST THREE DAYS have been a blur of meetings and utter chaos. The only time Zander and I spend time alone is at night when we crawl into bed, utterly exhausted. Chased kisses, quick touches, short hugs. That's all we seem to have time—or energy—for.

But this morning, he went into a meeting with his inner circle to work on a strategy for when something happens. It's been eerily quiet. No phone calls or messages making demands. We haven't had any rogues crossing the borders. It's making me—and everyone else—antsy. So Carmen and I decided to head to the village to get lunch.

We might have snuck away, but it was the best couple of hours we could have had. No one breathing down our necks trying to keep us safe. Just two girls enjoying each other's company and talking about our favorite things—books, boys, and bitches.

We walk slowly down the path back to the pack house, knowing our quiet, male-free time is rapidly coming to an end. The wind blowing through the trees creates a beautiful background noise to our easy conversation.

"So you all in with Zander? I know he marked you and everything, but how is that going to work? Your wolf hasn't made herself known again, right?" Carmen kicks a rock off into the woods.

I shouldn't take offense to her words, but she's right. I'm no better than a human and can't really mate properly. But I don't voice that concern. Instead, I opt to complain about the lack of time together. "Honestly, I have no idea. We haven't really had time to talk about it. With the constant threat of attacks and Zander being on edge constantly, it's a lot."

"Have you guys spent any time together? Just the two of you?"

I shrug. "Does sleeping count?"

"Is that all you're doing?"

"Sadly." I glance over at Carmen who is looking right at me with sympathy.

Looping her arm through mine, Carmen leans into me and says, "Well, maybe you need to force him to spend some time with just the two of you. You've been doing so much for him. Being in so many of those meetings and such. He hasn't blown up again, so that's got to mean something, right?"

"Yeah. Honestly, he relaxed a lot once we started having sex."

"Nice! Magic pussy!" Carmen fist pumps the sky.

I roll my eyes and continue without a comment on that. "Hasn't needed me around twenty-four seven which is nice. But I liked being needed."

"He still needs you, just not in his space as much. It's obvious he's a better Alpha with you by his side."

"Well, obviously," I say with a fluff of my hair, and we both freeze. Me because that felt right to say, her because...well, I'm not sure.

"You haven't done that since...before." Carmen looks shocked and elated all at once. Turning to face me, she grabs my hands and adds, "Quick, feel inside. Do you feel your wolf? Are you getting your memories back?"

She starts vibrating with excitement at the thought of me gaining part of my old self. But, inside it still feels like a hole in my chest. The hole isn't nearly as big as it was before. I don't know if that's because I'm regaining what I lost, or filling that void with the new me. Maybe both? I hope both.

"I don't think so. Sometimes I get feelings and glimpses of my old self, but I think that this is just kind of me now. Part old, a lot new," I say with a wistful tone I almost don't recognize as my own.

Before Carmen can reply, a crashing sound ahead of us makes us both jump. Putting herself between me and the threat, Carmen braces for whatever is coming straight for us. The sound is too close to run, hide, or really do anything. So we stand there, stupid and scared.

Between one breath and the next, a giant wolf comes barreling through the woods directly in front of us. For a second, I think it's a rogue that broke through the line and is on a rampage, but then I realize the truth. It's Zander. Frothing at the mount, angry as hell, Zander.

"What the fuck!" I fly around Carmen because I know I'm the only one who's fully safe from him. I think. God, I hope I'm safe. He didn't kill me when he almost went feral last week. Was that only last week? So much has happened.

Zander comes to a screeching halt, digging his claws into the dirt to slow himself down and not slam into us. But the menace he's throwing makes both Carmen and I take a step back. From behind Zander, two more wolves break through the tree line. Giving Zander a wide berth, they each circle and come to stand to the side of Zander, but closer to us than him. Even if I didn't recognize them, I'd know it was Kai and Damien just from their presence.

"What the fuck are you doing?" I repeat, because why is he acting like a fucking maniac?

Zander's shift comes hard and fast. He stands and takes a menacing step towards me. His eyes have yet to return to the green I love, and his canines are still elongated. His wolf may have let the shift happen, but he didn't fully let control go. Even completely naked, that menace he's projecting doesn't abate at all.

Growling, Zander looks directly at me. I don't look away, don't submit. It may be foolish given what I've learned about shifter culture and rules, but right now, I don't care. Carmen has dropped her head in submission and is fighting to stay standing. I know why. His Alpha aura is oozing off of him, and it's making my skin crawl. Surprisingly, it's not enough to make me feel the need to drop.

"What are you doing out here?" Zander continues to growl, but at least he's speaking now.

"We went and got lunch in the village," I say with zero inflection. I may be annoyed at his alphahole attitude, but I'm not giving into this display, either.

"Let me rephrase. What are you doing out here? Alone. Without a guard." Okay, maybe that Alpha energy is going to put me on my ass. Nope. Not giving him that satisfaction.

"You all were in a meeting, and we needed food and alone time. So we went, and now we're on our way back. We could have been even closer to the pack house by now if you didn't barrel up on us like some crazed lunatic." The look he gives me when I'm done with my little speech makes me regret it. Only a little. I'm not below him.

"Are you fucking kidding me?" He doesn't even raise his voice. It stays even, eerily calm, and absolutely *shit your pants* scary. "With all the bullshit we're dealing with, you two thought it was okay to just wander off on your own? Carmen might have been training for your inner circle in your old pack, but she's just a Gamma. You are nothing more than a human right now, and can't protect yourself. You don't even realize how absolutely fucked we are if anything happens to either of you."

By the end of his tirade, his calm has evaporated and his anger slams to the forefront. But that pales in comparison to what I'm feeling. He fucking didn't just call me a human. The one person who has maintained that my status as wolfless doesn't matter. Now he throws it in my face.

I hadn't even realized both Kai and Damien have shifted back and have inched closer to Carmen and myself. It's probably a good thing because one of them is going to have to get Carmen out of the firing line. 'Cause I'm pissed.

"How dare you throw my failings in my face like that?" I scream at him. "I know I'm 'nothing more than a human,'" I throw up air quotes, "but I also know that without me around you, you become unbearable. I also know that I don't give a flying fuck about war plans or what we need to do to secure our borders. That's not my job. Not anymore. I wanted to have some time away from all that."

Damien and Kai stiffen, and Carmen squeezes my arm like I need to shut up. I don't. I'm tired of all this bullshit, and if Zander gets to be a jerk to me, then I can be a bitch to him. I pull out of Carmen's hold and take a step towards Zander. He doesn't move towards or away from me, and I don't even care.

"I lost my fucking memories, apparently a whole other side to myself, and the only way I could deal with it was by being alone for a while. I come back here because you said it would be safer and you could help me find myself again. We get back and all hell breaks loose. You lose your shit when I'm not with you. I finally realize I do want to be with you, and then you basically put me under house arrest!" I'm absolutely losing it, but I don't care.

"You don't even know the half of what we're dealing with! Keeping you safe in the pack house is more important than anything else. And yes, partially because you're basically human. You don't have the strength, speed, or anything that would help you protect yourself. Then you go and sneak out to go to lunch. No one knew where you were. We thought someone kidnapped you!" Zander is pacing now, refusing to make eye contact with anyone. His aura is pouring off of him, and I'm the only one who hasn't succumbed to it.

I throw my hands up and say, "Oh! So I am no better than a prisoner? I'm a human fucking prisoner," I raise my hand and start counting off on my fingers the idiocy of it all, "I'm not allowed to leave the pack house. I have to have a guard if I step outside."

"Kara, you have to—"

"But I actually just need to be with you all the damn time so you don't lose your fucking mind. Oh, and I forgot the most important part—I'm a fucking waste of shifter space!"

Zander stops and just stares at me for a moment before saying the absolute most horrible thing he could. "Calm down, you're not thinking of the bigger picture here."

I don't even respond. I completely dismiss him, and that was probably a dumb thing to do with him being this agitated, but I don't care.

I look at Damien, because Kai looks like he's going to be sick. Honestly, Damien doesn't look much better, and Carmen has slunk away, practically hiding behind a tree. "Since I can't go anywhere without a guard, you're it, buddy. I want to go back to *my* room." I throw the last two words at Zander over my shoulder like a whip, then refocus on Damien.

"Let's go!" I march right past Zander, and for the first time since this whole encounter—fight?—started, I realize all three men are buck-ass naked. I would think it's funny if I wasn't so pissed.

Zander reaches for me, but I lunge out of his reach and keep walking. Damien, to his credit, is close on my heels. Carmen gives Zander a wide berth, but also follows. Kai, well, I have no idea what the hell he's doing, but that's not my problem.

The walk back to the pack house is cloaked in oppressive silence. I can only assume no one's speaking because there really isn't anything to say. Getting some separation from Zander made me realize I might have overreacted, just slightly. He's still a fucking asshole. His complete disregard for my feelings really hurt.

"You know he really did freak out when he thought something happened to you," Damien says into the quiet of the walk. *Would you look at that, someone does have something to say.*

"He's got a funny way of showing it." Sarcasm is apparently my new default setting. We break through the trees into the yard, and I keep motoring on.

"I know you don't remember, but protection is practically hardwired into Alphas. It's why they do so well leading packs. Protecting those who are in the pack is essential." Damien comes to stand in front of me, forcing me to stop or plow into him. "You're more than just a part of the pack. You're his mate. That means whatever it takes, no matter who he hurts, he has to protect you."

Carmen comes to stand at my side and adds, "In his twisted way, telling you that you are weak wasn't a slight to you. It was him telling you that no matter what, he will protect you."

"I thought you were on my side," I scowl at her.

"Oh I am, he fucked up. But he was also right. He just did it in a dumb-as-shit way," she says flippantly.

"And you?" I look up at Damien.

"What she said. Also, Z is currently yelling at me to keep you safe. So there's that." He shrugs. "He only let me go with you because he needed space to cool off, and didn't want you alone."

"Well, you're not joining me in my room. He would probably really lose his shit if that happened. I don't want you dead. But that's where I'm going." I skirt around both of them and march up the steps of the back patio and into the house.

Heading upstairs, I walk right into our shared room, Carmen and Damien trailing me. I block the door so neither of them can enter. "You might as well tell Zander he can find somewhere else to sleep for the time being. I like this room. I'm keeping it."

I slam the door in their faces and turn, sliding down the back side of the door. Pulling my knees to my chest, I stare at the room that's become our haven. Now it feels like a prison.

CHAPTER FORTY-SIX

Rogues!

ZANDER

WHAT THE FUCK IS she upset about? She's the one who took off on her own without anyone protecting her, and she's mad at me? I pace and growl as Kai stands a respectful distance away, avoiding eye contact like the plague. How does Kara not know the danger we're in—that she's in?

Protect our mate, my wolf growls in my head. I think the only reason he allowed us to shift back was because he knew we couldn't speak to her in wolf form.

I know! What do you think I'm doing? I continue to pace while fur sprouts on my arms and my fingers grow claws. I'm fighting with everything I have not to shift, but I'm losing ground. I don't even know if I can speak normally right now. My canines have elongated and sharpened, cutting into my lower lip. Am I growling or is it my wolf? I can't even tell.

Over the last week, Kara went from my mate to etching herself on my soul. Between her going all in on us, sleeping next to her every night, fucking her, and talking to her, my wolf has been much more relaxed. Then this happened, and I feel like I am back to square one with my control.

You let her go with him. She is with him!

Who? Damien? She's safe with him, nothing will happen. Right? Fuck! Now I'm picturing him with her! No! She may be mad, but that's not even a thing for shifters.

She's no better than a human, shifters' mates do not matter.

Fuck me! This is crazy.

"Umm, Zander? You good, man? Need to go for a run? Want to talk about it?" Kai's words cut through the haze of insanity that's taken over my mind. I look over at him where he's standing slightly behind a tree, as if he can use it as a shield if need be. His hands are up, attempting to show as little aggression as possible.

"Run." The word comes out gruff and clipped. I'm barely holding back my shift, and I'm over it. I let the shift take over without another word.

Kai's shift isn't as quick, but he falls into step next to me as we take off through the woods. Sometimes the only thing that actually calms a shifter is the woods. The feel of running without a destination, the dirt on your paws, the smell of the forest around—it all creates the perfect environment.

I've always needed it more than most. My mother died when I was young, and my father was Alpha first. He loved me, cared for me, but I was raised to take over the pack. That was my priority. Running became the thing that kept me sane. We really need to bring pack runs back. Since Kara left, we haven't had one.

For the next twenty minutes, we don't speak. Our paws hitting the dirt, the breath leaving our lungs, the birds overhead, and the breeze through the trees are the only sounds around us. Finally, Kai's words cut through my thoughts. *You ready to tell me why you lost your shit on your mate?*

I stop so fast he skids to a halt twenty feet ahead of me, then turns back to me. He's right—I know he's right—but I'm still so angry with her for being reckless. That's it. That's the whole reason I'm upset. She didn't think about her safety, and it scared the fuck out of me.

I shake my whole body, relieving the tension as I tell him, *I thought she was taken. It scared the shit out of me. Then I find her waltzing through the woods without a care in the world, and it pissed me off.*

I can see that. But you probably shouldn't have railed on her like you did. Damien told me she's locked herself in your room and barred everyone from coming in. Including you.

That freezes me. I cock my head to the side and stare at him like he's crazy. *Why didn't Damien tell me?*

You have to ask? Even in this form, the sarcasm drips from his words. I can literally feel his eye roll.

Damien thought I went broody and wouldn't listen.

Damien thought you went alphahole and tried to go feral. Luckily, he was wrong, but yeah. You probably should let him know you're not going to make him take over for the third time in less than six weeks.

Fuck, Kai is right. I'm making an absolute shit show out of being the pack's Alpha, and here I am, getting pissy because one thing doesn't go my way. *Let's head back to the pack house.*

Rogues! The call echoes through the pack bond to every enforcer, inner circle member, and me. Marcus seems panicked, and it flips me into high alert. *They broke through the south line and took out Kade. He's alive, but injured. Six rogues are heading directly to the village.*

Kai and I turn in unison and head in the direction of the village. We're on the west side of the lands, but close enough to the village that we will make it in a few minutes. *Damien, is Kara safe?* Was that panicked tone me? Damn.

Yes, Alpha. I can tell he's running with how broken and choppy his words are. *Jensen is guarding her. She's still in her room. We told her the danger and she agreed to stay up. Carmen is in there with her.*

I breathe a quick sigh of relief before I refocus on what we're running towards. Without a full report, I can only imagine—and it's not pretty. Two minutes later, we break through the trees, and it's worse than I thought. Absolute chaos greets us. Some wolves have shifted, but many of my pack are running in human form. The young and pregnant or nursing can't shift, adolescents who can shift don't think to. The elders—who technically can shift—haven't in so long that they don't even try knowing it probably won't happen. But my enforcers and those who are able to are in wolf form and doing everything they can.

Houses have broken windows and doors. Vehicles are destroyed. People are screaming. Shit, there's even at least one of my pack members on the ground.

We both pull up short. How the hell have only six rogues caused this much damage? Then I see one. *What the actual hell?*

Are they feral? Kai's voice drifts through my head with a lot of trepidation. This is the first time since I took the pack over that we've had an outright attack, and I fight the urge to freeze.

I think so, I tell Kai, and to the whole of the pack, because I can't tell through the chaos if it's only enforcers fighting. *Kill them, but attempt to leave one alive for interrogation.* With a howl, I dive into the fray.

I charge forward, heading directly for one of the rogues. I'm not the one who will be keeping anything alive. They've hurt my pack, and they will die. I lunge for the hind end of one of the rogues, a sickeningly gray wolf with a snarling muzzle and blood dripping from his mouth.

Throwing my full weight into the move, I grab hold and fling him as hard as I can. Kai is right there to go for the throat. With one swift movement, he rips the throat, blood and gore spraying. The wolf stops moving. Good, at least one down.

How many left? I call through the bond.

Damien responds, *with your kill, there's two left. We have one cornered inside the corner store and the other is near the restaurant.*

Good, capture the one you've got cornered. We'll deal with the other.

Turning towards the restaurant, most of the pack have found shelter, and it gives me a bit of relief. That is until we get to the restaurant and see a rogue take out one of the elders. The howl from her mate draws the attention of the rogue, and he turns to stalk towards him. The brown of his coat is marred with blood, like he's taken numerous hits already.

Rage like I've not experienced boils through me, and I charge. I can feel Kai on my flank and another shifter on the opposite flank—Marcus. With the distraction of trying to take out another member of my pack, the rogue doesn't realize we're on him till he's thrown to the ground.

I don't even bother tossing him. Going directly for the neck, I lunge and clamp down. The rogue thrashes until he goes limp in my jaws. I launch him to the side where Marcus makes sure he's truly dead.

Looking up, I see Richard Johnson, one of the oldest in the pack who's well into his second century, stumble over to his mate and collapse at her side. Shifting back, I walk up to him and put my hand on his shoulder. With a shaking, watery gaze, he looks up at me. Richard doesn't need to say it. I know. I am responsible for this.

"She will be honored in the stars, I am sorry." It's the traditional acknowledgement, but it feels hollow. If I was there even thirty seconds earlier, I would have stopped this.

"It's not your fault, Alpha. Maureen was trying to shift to protect the pups inside. She hasn't...hadn't shifted in so long, her wolf was weak. I tried to pull her inside, but once an enforcer, always one." He just lost his mate, and he's comforting me?

"I will find answers and will avenge her death," I tell him.

Richard stands and looks directly at me. "You are a good and kind Alpha. You will do what you must." We grip forearms; he's still surprisingly strong for his age.

"Thank you." Nodding, he goes back to his wife's body, and I watch as he and his son—who just arrived—lift her and take her to their home.

Turning to Kai and Marcus, I say, "I need answers, now." Growling, I head to the town office where we keep spare clothes and throw on the first pair of shorts that fits. Damien walks in to do the same, and without preamble, I ask, "Do we have someone to interrogate?"

"Yes, Alpha. He's knocked out, but we can get answers when he wakes up."

"Good, take him back to the pack house and lock him in a basement cell. We'll deal with him once we take stock of what happened here. How many?" I know my aura is rolling off of me. I'm angry—no, I'm furious. *My pack* was attacked. We've lost members and need to repair all this damage.

I don't need to finish that sentence, Damien knows what I need. "Four, all elders." He looks at me with something akin to pity. I get it. This is the first outright attack on our pack since I took over, and we know this has to be Varek and Black Pine's doing. But these were rogues. They didn't smell like Black Pine.

"Stop that. I'm fine. We need to focus on what we can, and learn from it. We need answers," I growl at him.

"Whatever you say," he throws at me before he adds, "the pack will do what it always does. Repair and heal. Figure out what to do next."

"Right, let's head to the pack house and regroup."

CHAPTER FORTY-SEVEN

Tell me how you really feel

ZANDER

BACK AT THE PACK house, the chaos of the village has spilled here. My inner circle is doing what they do best. Jensen and Marek are handling the village, Callum is doing whatever the hell he does with those damn computers, Damien is down in the basement with Marcus making our guest comfortable, and Kai has taken over as Kara's guard since she still wants nothing to do with me. Me? I'm standing in my cobbled-together office that still hasn't been fully fixed from my last tirade.

When I first made it back here, I went right to my bedroom, but true to her word, Kara had locked the door and refused to open it. I could have broken in, but I've already fucked up once today. I don't need a repeat. Carmen is with her, and Kai checked on her. He's staying close, so I can't be too upset. So why do I feel like I'm ready to break apart?

My phone rings, and before I look at the screen, I just know who it is. David. I can't deal with him right now. So I let it go to voicemail and tell Damien to call him when he has a second.

Moving to the shelf I keep my liquor on, I reach for the most expensive liquor I have—this feels like an expensive liquor day. I grab a glass, but shrug and end up with a bottle of 18-year Macallan. Will I regret drinking half the bottle of my good stuff in one sitting? Probably. Do I care? Not in the slightest.

Taking one more good pull from the bottle, I cork it and place it back on the shelf. I head downstairs for some fun.

I lean against the far wall of the basement. Interrogation—well, torture—isn't my forte. Damien though? The man can make a brick wall sing. I don't know if it's some innate ability he's always had or if he learned how to do this from his dad. Either way, he gets the answers I want, and seems to enjoy the process.

Currently, Damien has a syringe of wolfsbane and is slowly injecting it directly into this poor fucker's arm. What's surprising is he still hasn't broken. His legs have each been broken three times, his fingers are all separated from the joints, and I have no idea what else. I'm assuming we've upped the game to wolfsbane because he's healing faster than we can pry answers from him.

Wolfsbane, while not deadly, will absolutely fuck a shifter up. It slows our healing down to that of a human's, so snail's pace. It also gives us the worst side effects. Headaches for days, a rash that won't quit; it negates strength and stops us from shifting while it's in our system.

Throwing the syringe in the sharps container, Damien saunters over to where I'm posted up at the wall and shakes his head. "Still nothing?" I raise an eyebrow at him.

He exhales a long breath and replies, "I don't think this guy actually knows anything. It seems like he was spelled or something. I've never seen a shifter go so feral, but then turn into a sniveling, sobbing, pathetic little shit immediately after."

I snort. "Tell me how you really feel."

He leans on the wall next to me, crossing his legs at the ankles and his arms over his chest in a mimic of my pose. "Seriously, Z, even with shifter healing, we don't like it when bones are broken. That usually gets most talking, not him. The only thing he keeps saying is to let him go back to his pack."

"So he's not a rogue? But he doesn't smell like any pack."

"I don't think so. I'm hoping the wolfsbane will counteract whatever's in his body, masking his scent. Once we forced him to shift back, it was like he lost the strength and crazy."

A moan comes from the other side of the room where the aforementioned shifter is chained to a chair. Poor guy, the wolfsbane is fully affecting him now. His shaggy, brown hair is matted to his face, and the black eye he's sporting is a stark contrast to his olive skin.

I take a step forward, but Day grabs my arm to hold me back. "Wait, I know the wolfsbane is in his system, but I really don't want you that close to a shifter that was just acting that feral."

Shrugging him off, I walk forward, making sure to keep to the shadows and out of the light we have above the shifter. Is it a bit Hollywood? Probably. But I kind of love theatrics. "Who sent you?" I'm sure Damien has asked this already, but I don't care.

Instead of the groans Damien has been getting for the last five or six hours—I don't even know how long we've actually been down here—we get the first meaningful words he's spoken since Damien brought him down here. "I don't know how I ended up on your pack lands. I was in my barracks at breakfast, and the next thing I knew, I was being dragged down here. Please, let me go, kill me. Just please stop this."

Well, that was not what I thought I would hear. I look to Damien, because he can decipher truth much better than I can. He looks as puzzled as I am, which makes things a tad more complicated.

I put myself directly in front of the shifter and take a big sniff. That's when I catch it. The hint of a pack recollection hits me, and I realize why it's been covered. Silver Hollow, Grayson's pack, but also Black Pine. This is one of the 'bought' pack members. It still doesn't explain why he attacked our pack.

Damien puts the pieces together faster than I can. "The witch, the coven. This is another spell, or curse, or whatever the hell it is."

I stumble back with the realization of how much worse this whole situation is. The witch and her coven must have just been hired guns in this whole mess. It's actually Varek that's been pulling all the strings. Stepping back to stand next to Damien, we give each other a look that speaks volumes. Our tight bond makes it so we can be on the same page without a word. But this time, I tell him through the bond, *get rid of him. He doesn't actually know anything, but he's a liability.*

Day nods once, and I turn and head back upstairs. I don't need to stick around. He will take care of everything.

CHAPTER FORTY-EIGHT

This is a bit anticlimactic

ZANDER

REACHING INTO MY POCKET, I pull out my phone and realize it's actually been closer to seven hours and is approaching midnight. No wonder I'm exhausted.

I head upstairs to my room, but pause at the door. Is Kara still mad? I know I'm still frustrated, but not mad. I reach for the handle, and it's still locked. *Are you fucking kidding me?* The guys said Kara was pissed and no one was allowed in the room, but I didn't realize the door was actually locked.

Reaching out to Kai, hoping he's still awake, I ask, *hey, man. I know it's late, but I need to know, is Kara still in her room?* I wait for a moment without a response and think to reach out to Carmen. It's not as easy as she's not fully been made a pack member, but she's allowed me to speak to her before, so maybe she will this time.

Before I try that avenue, Kai's tired response comes. *Yeah, she's been in her room all night. I think Carmen is with her. Definitely don't try to go in. She's still pretty mad at you. I'd sleep in the room next door if you value your life.* He's trying to make light of the situation, but it rattles me. Is she really that mad? Did I fuck up so bad that we won't get past this? No. No way. We haven't even had time to deal with it. That's all. Come tomorrow, we will discuss things and figure out a way forward.

I sigh and head towards the room Kara used until she moved back into our room. *Thanks for the heads up. Get some sleep, sorry to wake you. We'll have an inner circle meeting tomorrow morning to discuss what Day and I got out of the shifter.*

*Sounds good. See you then. And Alpha...*I stiffen, Kai only uses my title when he wants me to take whatever he says seriously. *Maybe fix things with Kara sooner than later. She was really hurt today, and then the attack freaked her out.*

I knew both things already, but hearing it from Kai emphasizes the importance. *Thanks, I'll do that.*

Inside this bedroom feels lonely, but I'm too tired to focus on that. I take a quick shower before falling into bed. Marge has changed the sheets so this just feels like it's some spare bed in someone else's house. I'll have to think of it that way, because if I think too hard about it being Kara's old room, I'll rage.

The anger I was feeling completely evaporated when Kai reminded me that this isn't just about me and my feelings. Kara is dealing with more than any of us. Tomorrow, we need to talk this out. No waiting. No hiding from it. We're stronger together.

Sleep comes, but it's unsettled and feels like before she was back in my life. Separation from her destroys me. I didn't know it was only her holding me together.

I wake up the next morning to a pounding on my door. "Zander, you're ignoring the pack bond again. It's past breakfast and we're all waiting in your office." Damien. Of course, it's Damien. The asshole.

I groan as I roll over, and realize I have no clothes in here. Fuck it. I'm getting back into my own room, even if it's just to get something to wear, not just random clothes.

I climb out of bed, wrap a towel around myself, and march with purpose out into the hall straight up to my door—that's wide open. Okay, this is a bit anticlimactic, but I'll take it. Kara is nowhere to be found, so our chat to patch things up will have to wait.

Changing quickly, I head down to my office, meeting Damien in the entryway where he practically throws a cup of coffee at me. Together, we make our way into the office where Marek, Jensen, Kai, and Callum wait, already seated. There's a massive pile of breakfast sandwiches—courtesy of Marge, I'm sure.

I sit behind my desk and look at the five men in front of me. Sparing a moment to take each of them in helps me find my own center. Marek is stoic as always. Jensen seems worried. Kai is surprisingly subdued, and I don't like it. Callum looks like he's itching to be anywhere than here. Damien is the calm to my chaos. Closing my eyes for a moment, I take a breath and say, "Well, we've got a lot to deal with and even more to figure out. So let's get this shit show started."

CHAPTER FORTY-NINE

I waited four hours

KARA

IF YOU WOULD HAVE asked me yesterday morning what the next twenty-four hours would have included, I would have told you lunch, great conversation with Carmen, maybe hanging out with Zander for a while, dinner with everyone, and wild sex before I passed the fuck out. I'm currently sitting at a 40% success rate, and that's being generous.

What the fuck was Zander on, coming at me like I'm just some shifter in his pack he can push around? Did he actually think he could make me submit? He flew up, got in my face, and told me I'm nothing but a useless human. It wasn't that he called me useless or even human—let's be honest, I basically am. But his delivery was absolute shit.

The only positive thing that came from it is that everyone seems to think my wolf must be closer to the surface than before, because I didn't even flinch when his aura juice threatened to put everyone on their ass. I mean, I felt it, but I definitely didn't get pinned by it. Okay, so maybe I'll give myself a solid 50% for yesterday.

Now, here I am, hiding in the kitchen while Zander has his debrief with his men. I want to talk to him—need to talk to him. But I have no idea how to start.

It was one hell of a fight, and it feels like it's not something we've really done, even before. Fine, I'm not really mad at him anymore. Frustrated? Sure. He was a jerk, and I think he realizes it. We need to talk this out sooner rather than later. Until then, I'm going to enjoy Marge's amazing breakfast sandwiches.

The attack yesterday really freaked me out. I was sitting on my bed sulking and planning my revenge when Carmen burst through the door with Jensen hot on her heels. I sprang to my feet with a feeling that I needed to do something, but before I could even speak, Jensen said, "There's a group of rogues actively attacking the village. We don't know if there's more or if they'll try to come here. But you two are staying in this room. I will be just outside the door. No one will get to you."

I was gearing up to argue with him when I saw the look in his eyes. He was dead serious. Carmen seemed spooked, too. My first thought? Not *is the pack, okay*? Nope. It was Zander.

"Zander..." I squeaked.

"Is heading to the village with Kai. Damien will meet them there. During situations like this, the pack bond is basically an open book. I'm monitoring what's happening. If anything happens to him, we will know." Jensen nodded once, then turned and headed to stand at the door.

Collapsing on the bed with Carmen next to me, only then I processed what Jensen had said, the same thing Kai had told me in the truck—was that only a few days ago? "*We will know if anything happens to Zander.*" I felt sick.

"Come on, we need to get your mind to stop racing. Let's oh, I don't know, watch a movie."

"You're fucking kidding, right? How the hell am I supposed to focus when we're under attack?"

"Okay—no movie. Pacing and worrying it is." Carmen stood and started doing just that.

We kept our pacing up until we heard the battle was over, but the loss stung. Four pack members, all older who couldn't or wouldn't get to shelter. It was so much—too much.

Marge walks back into the kitchen carrying an empty tray, pulling me from my thoughts, and smiles. "You okay, hun?"

"Define okay. Am I physically okay? I can't shift, but otherwise I'm healthy. Am I struggling with the aftermath of the attack yesterday? Absolutely. Am I worried that my fight with Zander yesterday will ruin any progress we've made? Also yes." I drop my head to the counter in front of me and groan.

"You and Zander will be completely fine. When I picked this tray up, he looked like he was hoping it was you that opened the door. Give him time to get through this debrief, and I know you two will talk it out." She comes over and puts her hand on my back, making small circles. I lean into the touch, the comfort in it.

"I'm going to take your word on that." I sigh, sitting up to finish my sandwich. I head to the entryway and park myself down on the steps to wait for the meeting to be over. Hopefully, I won't be waiting all day.

I waited four hours.

During that time, I counted the tiles on the floor (one hundred and seventy-six), sat in every possible place there was to sit (there were seven), laid down in the middle of the entryway where anyone and everyone would have to step around me, and I even went back to the kitchen for another sandwich. But finally, the door to the office opens with Marek and Jensen filing out, followed closely by Callum.

Standing, I practically knock them over to get into the office where the three men are huddled around the desk, looking at what I can assume is a map. All three heads turn when I get closer, but all wear very different expressions. Kai has his usual cocky grin in place while Damien is serious as a heart attack. Then there's Zander. He carries an almost apathetic mask. But I know it's just because his eyes are boring into me. There's heat and regret banked there. Maybe this will be okay.

Zander and I just stare at each other, not saying a word. "And that's our cue to come back later." Kai laughs.

"I need to check on the village, anyway." Damien adds. Still, neither Zander nor I move or speak.

As Kai passes me, he leans over and whispers, "Go easy on him. He's been struggling all morning and needs his girl." I raise an eyebrow, and the growl that comes from Zander makes my toes curl in the best way possible.

Throwing his hands up and backing towards the door, Kai can't help but add, "Just giving a little insight. Y'all have fun now."

Damien rolls his eyes before he shoves Kai out the door, shutting it with a snick that makes me jump.

Now that it's just the two of us, I have no idea what to say or do. I rehearsed this whole conversation, but now it feels like it doesn't matter. Taking a deep breath, I look back at Zander and say, "Look, I'm sorry," at the exact same time he says, "Love, I'm sorry."

We both stop and stare at each other for a moment before we both break into peals of laughter.

Zander comes around the desk to lean on it in front of me. pulling me towards him. He wraps his arms around me and rests his head on mine. I wrap my arms around him and bury my face into his chest, breathing in his scent. "I know I handled the whole thing yesterday wrong. I was so scared something happened to you, I didn't think about the how."

I snuggle closer, realizing that he is exactly what I needed to feel better about the fight. "I didn't mean to push you like that. I see why what Carmen and I did was a problem. I guess we both aren't really that great at confronting difficult situations, huh?"

"I guess not. But I don't want to fight with you about this. We need to talk about it, though."

Leaning back so I can see his face, I say the one thing I've needed to say since yesterday. "I'm fucking scared, Z. After our fight, when I was in our room, I wanted to be mad, and I was. But I wasn't mad about what you said, it was more how you went about it. Honestly, I didn't believe it was really that dangerous here on our lands. Then when Carmen and Jensen came flying and the whole attack happened, that was fucking terrifying."

"Come here." Zander tucks my head back into his chest and lets out a breath before he says, "I know, I'm scared, too. Scared that something will happen, and

I'll lose you again. Losing you once was more than I could handle. Again, it would destroy me. But yeah, you going off when it's so up in the air wasn't the move, love." He chuckles at that, making sure I know he wants me to understand the danger, but he's not upset anymore.

"So where do we go from here? What do we do?"

Raising an eyebrow, he answers, "With us, or the shitstorm around us?"

"Both?"

"Well, for us, I think we try not to rip into each other when we get pissed. Which for us, I know will be hard to stop. We're both Alpha by blood. We kind of run hotheaded."

"I've noticed." Sarcasm drips from my words. "And the shitstorm?"

"Well, we have a basic plan. We know there will be more attacks, so we're doubling patrols. We have retired enforcers that are still in good physical health patrolling the town. Our pack has a lot of pups and elders right now, so that's a lot to protect." Zander releases me and heads to the sofa nearby, sitting down. He beckons me to him, and when I'm at arm's length, he pulls me onto his lap.

"I'm guessing I'm not going anywhere alone?"

"Please don't. For two reasons. One, you don't have the strength to fend off a rogue, and two, you are too important. Not only to me, but the whole pack. I know you don't want to hear it, but you are my mate, the pack's Luna. We need you healthy and whole."

"Yeah, whole..." I scoff. I'm beginning to hate my current status. It wasn't that big of a deal when it was just the people here at the pack house, but now there are real world issues.

"Love, I get it. This isn't fun for you, but please do this for me." He bends down, moving my hair off my neck to nuzzle where his mark sits. He kisses it, and my whole body jolts like electricity passed through. I stiffen and pull back. Looking up with confusion, Zander asks, "What?"

"I felt something like an electrical jolt when you kissed the mark. What the hell was that?"

Zander almost dumps me off his lap in his shock. "Shit! Sorry!" He scoops me tighter to him and continues, "You feeling something when I kiss the mark is actually a good thing."

"I'm...not following."

"The mate mark becomes a sensual zone for mates. It is an intimate thing to kiss the mark, because it heightens sensation."

"Okay? That means what for me?" I think I'm following, but don't dare hope this means what I think it means.

"I'm not sure exactly, but I think you may be slowly bringing your wolf back to the surface. Our bond is strengthening, and that's what might bring everything back for you." The grin he sports sets me on fire. His happiness is contagious, and I can't help but also be a bit giddy.

With that, I bend down and kiss him hard. I was still pissed at him this morning and now, well, I'm wondering how secure his office door is.

"Mmmm, love, I know exactly what you're thinking. Unfortunately, I have a phone call with your dad to update him in..." he looks at the wall clock and groans, "five minutes ago..."

I slump in his lap, but he doesn't let me get in my head too much. "Hey, this was more important. The leaders of this pack need to be good. We needed to work through our first real fight to be better for the rest of this. Go, I'm sure there's something you can help with while I'm dealing with your father. I'll find you when I'm done." He stands, forcing me to stand as well. Swatting my ass and shooing me to the door, I smile as he pulls out his phone.

Now to find one of the guys and bug them till they give me a job.

I wander into the lounge and find Kai and Callum going over something on Callum's tablet. "Hey, I need a job. Zander said you have to give me one." He didn't, but I'm going to assume this is what he meant by finding something to do.

"He did, did he?" Kai raises an eyebrow, and his cocky grin comes out to play. "You two make up?"

"We talked through what happened, and we're good."

"I bet you did." He laughs.

"All we did was talk!" I put my hand on my hip like a petulant child. "And figure out I'm having more shifter-esque things happen to me."

"Wait, seriously? Now that's awesome!" Kai almost bounces.

"So seriously, I need something to do." I look at Callum, because Kai is currently useless.

Callum looks up from his tablet for the first time and says, "The only thing you could help with is researching anything we can find on Black Pine. They are the enigma we need to solve, and fast."

"Okay, show me where to set up and I'll see what I can find." Happy to have something useful to do and not be some princess locked in a tower, I rub my hands together in anticipation.

"Grab that laptop over there and see what you can search up." Callum points to the far wall where a laptop sits, waiting to be used. I run over, plop myself down, and get to work digging up any and every fact I can find on the pack trying to destroy our lives.

CHAPTER FIFTY

Overly aggressive and basically feral

ZANDER

BREACH! NORTHWEST CORNER. I freeze mid-step on the stairs. I was headed towards my bedroom. After the call with David, Damien, Kai, and I spent the afternoon dealing with logistics and the restructuring of our border security. Kara has been working in the lounge, but I was told she went upstairs for a while. I was going to find her and blow off some energy with her.

Who and how many? I respond, more irritated than necessary, but dammit, I just wanted to fuck my mate. Is that too much to ask? Turning around, I head back down the stairs, yanking my shirt over my head and throwing it and my phone on the table against the wall.

This time, Marcus's voice floods my head. *Three rogues. One is already dispatched, the other two are heading directly to the pack house.*

Good thing I'm already here. *Kai, guard Kara. Damien, meet me out back. We're the last line of defense this time.* Their words of assent flow through me, and I burst through the back door to find Damien already there, shirtless and ready for whatever is headed our way.

"Twice in just twenty-four hours, this is planned," I say as I scan the tree line towards the northwest.

"Most likely, these wolves are the same we dealt with yesterday. Spelled or whatever you want to call it, to attack and get themselves captured or killed. The question is, what's the point?" He scans the tree line as well, feet braced apart, ready for an attack.

"That's easy. To wear us down and make it difficult for us to recover." He nods and doesn't respond, but I know he thinks the same. *One rogue left.* Marcus's update comes clipped but focused. *Kill or capture?*

Are they acting like the ones yesterday?

Almost exactly the same, overly aggressive and basically feral. Intent on their goal, whatever the fuck that is, and nothing else.

Then kill. I'm not dealing with interrogating another useless shifter. I hate the needless death. These are someone's pack members, even if we keep lumping them in as rogues. But there's really no other choice. At least not that I can see.

"Think they will dispatch the rogue before he makes it here?" Damien asks, not really wanting an answer, but I answer anyway.

"Most likely." I cross my arms and relax my stance slightly. My wolf is trying to take over and make me go after this threat, but I'm not in the mood.

Noticing my attempt to physically relax and failing, Damien drops the *I'm the second in command* bullshit and switches to best friend mode. "How's *that* going?"

I don't have to question what he means, he's asking about the control issue. My inability to maintain myself. I glance at him sideways before I sigh and respond, "Could be better. I can maintain control, but I have to consciously do it. The human side isn't the dominant side. It's like it's 50/50 right now."

"You'll get there. You may lose control, but you come back faster each time."

I don't deign that with a response. What is there to say? *All threats neutralized,* comes through the bond, and I turn back towards the house. "I'll leave you to make sure clean-up is done. I have better things to be doing."

Back inside, I grab my shirt and phone, then make my way back up the stairs. I pass Kai at the top. "She's safe, didn't even know anything was happening. I think she's sleeping." Seeing my eyes flash, he raises his hands and backs towards the stairs. "I didn't actually go in, but I didn't hear anything other than the low sound of music. I'm just guessing here."

I release a breath I didn't know I was holding, and nod. "Thank you for keeping her safe." The words are as much for myself and my wolf as him. My men will do anything to keep her safe, and I know it. It's just convincing my wolf of that is going to take a lot more time than any of us have.

Kai heads down the stairs with a nod, and I head towards my bedroom. I reach for the door and open it slowly, in case Kai's guess was right and she's sleeping. Standing at the threshold, I see her beautiful sleeping form, and decide a nap sounds perfect. I wanted more, but I'm not going to wake her for that. Maybe after we sleep for a bit, though.

I close the door and shed the rest of my clothes before climbing into bed next to her. After the up and down of the last couple days, I fall asleep surprisingly easily. I have no idea how long I'm out before I'm pulled from sleep by my whole body stiffening.

The first thing I notice is Kara isn't next to me. I panic for a split second before I notice there are no covers. Then I notice what actually woke me up. Kara is between my legs, licking my dick like it's her favorite lollypop. Holy shit.

"There you are. I didn't think you'd ever wake up. Didn't want to go too far without you knowing what's going on."

"Love, get up here." I reach down for her, but she pulls back and out of my grasp. "What are you doing?"

"What does it look like? You've had a rough few days. I thought you needed some relief." The look Kara gives me is absolutely sinful.

Fuck, this woman is going to kill me. I'll die fucking happy, but I'm going to die nonetheless. "If you're sure. Continue." I wave my hand like a king giving a command, and she just laughs and lowers her head.

Her lips go around my girth, and Kara proceeds to suck my soul out of my dick. Holy. Hell. Kara spends time exploring every inch of my length, bringing her hands up to cup my balls, and I force myself to stay still. The urge to thrust up and fuck her mouth is overwhelming. But we've never done that, not even before. I don't want to assume it's something she wants.

I alternate between gripping the sheets and running my hands through her hair. The whole time she keeps working me, and it's the most exquisite head I've ever received. Minutes—hours?—tick by, and I struggle to keep still as my whole body clenches.

My balls start to tighten, my fingers dig into Kara's hair, and I know I'm close. "Kara...love. I'm going to..." I gasp through pants. Instead of pulling off, she sucks harder, her teeth grazing my shaft, and that's all it takes. My seed is ripped out of me, and she takes every drop.

Once I'm spent, I reach down and drag her up my body, sealing my mouth to hers and holding her like she's the most important thing in the world. Because she is. Pulling back, I look into her eyes and see nothing but love and devotion.

"We need to figure out the mating ceremony thing, soon." Fuck, that's the first thing I say? Not thank you? Not that was the best fucking head I've ever received?

Laughing, she snuggles into my side. "That good, huh? You still want to mate me?"

"Love, I'll marry you as the humans do with a wedding if that's what it takes." I kiss the top of her head and hold onto her.

"Well, I guess I have more research, then. I spent most of the afternoon researching Black Pine."

"Find anything useful?" Callum let me know he gave her a task that would keep her occupied, but not in danger.

"Only that Varek's dad was the real mastermind of the last war. Also, his dad took the Alpha title from his grandfather, just like Varek did to his father. It wasn't passed down from a natural or war death. But in an Alpha Challenge that resulted in death."

"Not surprising. There's a reason Black Pine has always been a problem for the regional packs. It's all about power for them." I stop for a moment and think about what I'm going to say next. I don't want to scare her more than she already is. Although, I don't think she's actually scared, more of worried. "There was another breach of the border today. Three rogues came through the northwest border and were headed towards the pack house. They didn't make it that far. Patrols were able to stop them."

Kara stiffens slightly, but that's it. "So it's ramping up like we thought it would." Of course, she would be pragmatic about it.

"Yeah, but you'll be safe," I vow, not just to her, but to myself. I kiss her head again and say, "As much as I'd love to lounge here for the rest of the day, I have to get some work done. Go hang out with Carmen and enjoy your evening. Just stay inside, please."

Kara rolls her eyes, but agrees. She stretches like a cat, but then sits up and I do the same.

Getting up to find my clothes, I head back downstairs to my office. *Report*, I say to my inner circle.

Border seems secure at the moment, Marek says.

Restructure of enforcers is nearly complete, and the new rotations begin at midnight, Damien adds.

The house is still secure. All security measures are in working order. Also beefing up cameras in the village, Callum chimes in.

Village repairs are coming along, and families are heeding the new curfew, Jensen relays.

I've coordinated with a few other Alphas, and they are willing to send back up if we need it, Kai informs.

This is why I love my inner circle. They get shit down when I'm unable to. Lately, that's about all the damn time. I don't know how to divide my time without something giving. I'm the only one who can help Kara, so that's where my focus needs to be. I just hope I'm not making a mistake.

CHAPTER FIFTY-ONE

Sandwich?

KARA

THE LAST TWO DAYS have been a lot of the same. Rogue attacks happen frequently, but luckily only amount in chaos and no death. Minor injuries heal quickly for the enforcers that sustain them, but that's it. Zander is pulled into meetings with at least one person from his inner circle almost constantly. What doesn't happen often? Zander and I sneaking off together any time we can.

At night, we sleep in the same room, but his anger and frustration with everything makes things difficult. The only thing that seems to bring him slightly under control is sex. So we have that going for us, I guess.

But times like now, when I'm sitting in the lounge doing a fuck ton of research on whatever the fuck I'm told, make me crazy. Honestly, I can't figure out if what they have me research is actually needed or it's just keeping me occupied at this point. I know that I'm not a prisoner, but I still feel trapped. The pack house is basically on lockdown. Almost every room is occupied. All the inner circle have moved in, along with other key enforcers. Even Marge moved into a spare room so that she can continue to cook and clean for us.

There's a massive commotion outside the door to the lounge, and I look up in time to see Kai burst through the door. This routine has become something we're all familiar with, but I hate it all the same. "Let me guess, another fucking attack. How many this time?"

"Five, southwest corner towards the village again." He turns and puts himself between me and the now closed door. I hate that I've genuinely stopped caring. Last night, a rogue breached the tree line near the pack house. But that's the closest that one has made it. Zander tore his throat out before anything substantial happened.

"Want a sandwich? Marge made some amazing chicken salad." I don't actually look at Kai or the sandwich in question, but continue to browse the current Wiki I've found on regional pack histories.

"A what?" Kai's confused tone cuts through my thoughts, and I glance up.

"Sandwich. It's almost lunch time, so Marge brought food." The look on Kai's face is something akin to dumbfounded confusion. "I mean, if you don't want one, it's fine. But they were here, so I thought I'd offer you one."

"You know, why the fuck not? Sure." I reach forward and grab a sandwich for him. Without turning around, I hand it behind me. After a pause, where I'm assuming he took a bite, Kai adds, "These attacks are becoming more frequent. There were two at once this morning. If I had to guess, the big one is coming. We need to keep our guard up." I hear the exasperation in his voice at my nonchalance.

"I know we do, and I am. But I'm in the middle of the house, behind at least three doors, and you're here, too. If they make it all the way to me, they deserve to gut me." I shrug and grab my own sandwich.

I glance back at Kai again, just in time to see him get that glazed look in his eyes. He's speaking to someone. I wait for him to refocus and ask, "So?"

He walks around the sofa as he fills me in. "Seems like the village attack didn't amount to much of anything. The new protocols we've put in place for the pack made it a lot harder for rogues to really do anything." With that, he slumps into the chair across from me, and I see how weary he is. Having to run from wherever he's at in the house to be by my side and not see any action has got to be shitty.

"Are you okay?" I ask, but I'm not sure he even hears me.

I lean forward to get his attention more directly, but before I can repeat myself, he responds, "What? Oh, yeah. Just tired. The constant attacks are bringing the whole pack down. It's getting old. That's why I think the big one is coming soon. It's ramping up. None of the attacks have been relatively vicious like the first one. They are definitely meant to wear us down—and it's working." He leans forward to grab a second sandwich, just as Zander and Damien walk into the room.

Damien bends down to grab his own sandwich before he takes up his typical position in the chair facing the door. Z, on the other hand, grabs the laptop off my lap and places it on the coffee table, before scooping me up and sitting with me on his lap.

Zander nuzzles my hair, breathing deeply to ground himself. It's become almost a ritual for both of us. The tension he's carrying lightens a little, but the weight of everything going on still hangs over his head like a guillotine, ready to take him out.

"No debrief?" I ask no one in particular. They all look ready to collapse.

"That's what we're doing. Just waiting for Marek and Jensen." Zander nuzzles me again, but I reach forward and grab him a sandwich.

"Eat. Even if you are mentally stressed, you need to keep your physical strength up. What about Callum?"

He takes it from me and I slide down so my legs are draped over his thighs and he has room to eat. The bite and subsequent groan of contentment tells me all I need to know. He skipped breakfast again. "Callum?" I repeat.

"He's holed up in his command room." Damien lets me know as he takes his second sandwich.

"Y'all need to eat actual meals, not random bites when you can," I scold them all.

"Sounds like our Luna is taking her role back as mother seriously," Marek says as he enters the lounge. There's a joking edge to his words but the beaten-down look in his eyes mirrors the rest of the guys. They can't keep this up.

I choose to ignore the statement and ask the question I know will get this party started. "Was the attack just another attack to keep us occupied?"

"Seems like it." Zander takes over the conversation. "From what we understand, they didn't even bother trying to attack the village itself this time. It's almost like these wolves were just sent to keep us busy. Which is why we've stopped pulling patrols when attacks happen. They need to keep their guard up. This morning was a double attack. I'm shocked this latest one wasn't as well."

"I don't think there's much to learn from the latest attack other than they aren't as organized as they have been. Which I think is meant to throw us off. So we need to stay vigilant," Day says in his big bad leader voice.

"If there isn't anything else pressing, the early morning and late-night attacks have made it impossible to sleep, so I think everyone should try to get a bit of sleep while we can. Pair off and sleep in two to three-hour shifts. That way, at least two of you are awake at all times. I'm going to nap myself." Looking down at me, Zander adds, "Join me?"

"Only if you're actually sleeping. I know how little you get. I'll stay awake so if something happens, I can rouse you from your unconscious bliss," I tell him with a half-hearted attempt at a stern look.

"Sounds good to me." Both Zander and I stand to head out. Damien and Marek follow, having won the *who sleeps first* game.

Within a minute of hitting the pillow, Zander is out cold. So, I grab the book I've been reading, curl up in the chair in the corner, and keep watch. The whole time, praying he gets at least a few hours of uninterrupted rest.

CHAPTER FIFTY-TWO

Don't be stupid, be smart

KARA

FOR THE FIRST TIME in days, Zander sleeps for a full four hours uninterrupted. At some point during those hours, I decide to move in the bed next to him. As he begins to stir, I lean over and give him a kiss. "Morning, sleepyhead."

He jolts and shoots up to a sitting position, looking around wide-eyed. "Fuck! It's morning?"

"Whoa there! It's not. It's been about four hours, and I just thought it was cute. Sorry, I didn't mean to panic you." I pet his back, helping the muscles there unknot.

Slumping forward slightly, Zander looks at me over his shoulder. "Everything stay calm?"

"I would have woken you if something happened. As it stands, all is quiet. Although, Damien asked me to tell you that you have a phone meeting with my dad in about an hour. I was going to wake you soon so you could shower and eat first."

I climb out of bed and head to the bathroom to start the shower for him. It's not much, but he always takes care of me, and I want to return the favor.

Calling from the bathroom, I add, "I also messaged Marge, and she's going to have a decent meal set out for you guys shortly."

Zander comes waltzing into the bathroom having shucked the last of his clothes. The sight sends a jolt through me. *How the fuck did I bag someone so fucking perfect?* I clench my thighs together to stave off the instant ache that seeing him gives me.

The knowing look Zander flashes me lets me know he absolutely noticed my train of thought, and approves. But I stop that train before it has a chance to leave the station. "We don't have time. Shower, then eat." I reach up on my tip toes and give him a quick kiss, then leave the bathroom, shutting the door behind me.

I hear Zander mutter, "Not fair," before he gets in the shower. Changing back into my day clothes, I head downstairs to see if Marge needs any help. I'm not in the kitchen for even a minute when all hell breaks loose.

At first, I don't understand what's happening, but then Damien and Kai burst into the kitchen, looking like the world is imploding around us. It's Kai who is able to get words out first, "The big thing, Kara. It's happening."

Fuck! Fuck! Fuck, fuck, fuck! What do we do? If this is the big thing, they all need to fight. How many? What happened? Where? So many questions, and I have no idea where to start.

Zander comes flying into the kitchen, grabbing me and spinning me by the shoulders. "I need you to go to the basement and stay there. It's the only place that's reinforced."

"Zander! What the fuck is happening?" Was that my voice? Why is it that squeaky and high?

"I need Kai and Damien with me on this one. So you have to stay safe."

"But what's happening!" I practically scream. I'm panicking, I know I am, but I need to know.

Zander growls in frustration, but answers me, "There's been a breach of at least four separate points on the border. We're being overrun with wolves. Right now, I need..." Zander's eyes glaze over mid-speech, and when he refocuses, his eyes are glowing. His wolf is right at the surface. With menace in every word, he snarls, "Grayson is here."

The weird calm that takes over him scares the fuck out of me. With another snarl, he looks at me one last time. "Hide, now!" To Damien and Kai, he adds, "With me!"

Zander turns and heads out the door, shifting as soon as he clears it.

I sprint for the door, but Damien pulls me back, practically tossing me towards the door to the hall. "Basement. NOW!" he barks, then takes off after Zander.

"Please, Kara, this is bad. Go hide. Take Marge and Carmen, and hide!" Kai pleads with me, but also follows out the door. I'm left standing there, confused and helpless.

Carmen comes flying into the kitchen. "Kara! We need to hide!"

I look at her and whatever look is on my face makes her stop short. No! I'm not helpless. I'm not weak. Zander isn't alone in this! Looking over at Marge—who has moved to stand next to Carmen—her eyes tell me she already knows what I'm going to do. "Don't be stupid, be smart. Be the badass Alpha you were born to be."

Carmen nods as well, knowing what I'm about to do. "Be strong." I nod once to them, and without another word, head into the night. I follow the path Zander took. I'm coming. I will not let him fail.

This is going to hurt

KARA

RUNNING DOWN THE PATH, my head is spinning. What the hell was he thinking? Who am I kidding? He wasn't. Ever since the meeting with Grayson and the constant rogue attacks, Zander has been running on a healthy mix of alpha energy and confusion. But that?

His wolf has been sitting just below the surface for days. Each rogue attack has been wearing everyone down, and it's causing him to lose the little piece of control he has.

The woods pass by me in a blur as I run faster than I even knew I could. My eyesight seems sharper, and I'm not stumbling like I did before. I'm not sure what all this means, but I'm not going to let Zander try to fight this on his own.

Since the breach came from multiple points, the enforcers will be spread thin. Zander, the idiot, went after Grayson. Yes, Damien and Kai followed, but they aren't Alphas. What will they be able to do? He felt Grayson cross into our lands, and like a switch was flipped, his focus went singular.

Some howling in the distance makes me slow down. It's coming from more than one direction, and I can't tell which way Zander went. Fuck! My senses are more attuned than they've been, but why can't I hear through the pack bond yet? I'm getting shifter abilities back at an alarming rate, but not the one thing that will make this a lot easier.

Five minutes of running through the woods, listening for any indication that I recognize a howl, a growl, something, and finally, I hear a growl that feels like it's part of my soul. I stop and listen for a half of a second, then I leave the trail and head directly towards it. The undergrowth is thicker in this part of the woods, and as I push through the brambles and thorns, I do my best to make no noise.

I can't afford to distract Zander. He sounds like he's already engaged with someone. He may be an idiot, but I don't want him hurt. I'm not going to make it worse by announcing my presence.

Breaking through the trees, the sight that greets me makes me freeze in my tracks. Zander isn't just fighting a couple of rogues. This is a whole damn pack. At least twenty wolves circle and attack, seemingly at random.

The rich brown of his coat is caked with blood, and I have no clue if it's his or the wolves around him. But he's holding his own, thank fuck. Zander grabs one wolf by the tail, flinging it to one side just as another lunges for one of his front legs. Luckily, Zander sees it coming and is able to dodge just in time, but not quick enough to avoid another wolf coming for his hind leg.

This is not going to end well, but I have zero clue how to help. What the hell was I thinking? I can't shift, and I thought I could help? Just as panic begins to set in, two new wolves burst through the trees on the far side of the clearing. Damien and Kai. The relief I feel when they rip through the wolves surrounding Zander is monumental.

"Zander!" I scream, and he and just about every other wolf in the clearing turns in my direction. Fuck me! That was not the move. With a speed I've never seen from him, Zander launches himself in my direction, putting himself between me and the other wolves. Damien and Kai take up positions on either side of him, pushing the wolves back.

As if it's a choreographed routine, the wolves attack as a mass. A flurry of limbs, teeth, and growls fill the clearing, and I stand there like an idiot. I mean, what am I supposed to do?

Just when I think the boys have the upper hand, a massive wolf that rivals Zander in size breaches the edge of the clearing. The absolute menace he radiates makes the hair on the back of my neck prickle and fear ripple through my body.

He takes one look at Zander, and charges. No warning. No prowling or circling. Zander must know who it is, because he too charges. The two meet in the center of the clearing, and the fight that ensues makes the last ten minutes look like pups play fighting. *Wait, where did that thought come from?*

Oh fuck! The realization of who these wolves are hits me like a battering ram. This is an actual pack, and this is their leader.

Kai keeps directly in front of me, playing my shield, but I lunge around him. I need to see—need to know. Just as my line of sight to Zander resumes, I see it. The moment I was hoping wouldn't come. Zander falters and gets pinned by the other wolf by the throat.

No! No, no, no, no. This isn't happening. Rage like I've never experienced explodes out of me. My vision, which was watery with unshed tears, turns a mottled shade of amber. Pain like I've never experienced washes over me like a tidal wave. What the fuck is happening?

Let me handle this.

What. The. Hell? That was in my head. A voice was in my head! No, not just any voice. My wolf. She's here! Her beautiful presence fills my head as a wave of relief washes over me. Then the reality of the situation slams into me a second later.

How? is all I'm able to get out, even in my own head. This can't be happening. It's been weeks of silence.

You broke the wall between us. Now give in and let me handle this.

I have zero clue what she means, but I just stop. Stop fighting. Stop thinking. Stop. Everything.

I'm sorry, but this is going to hurt. It's the last thing I hear before my world tips on its axis.

Beginning in my core, a white-hot light explodes out of me. My limbs shake so violently, I fear they will rip right off my torso. Collapsing to all fours, my breaths become ragged at the same time my vision goes dark. My canines extend and my fingers—no, claws—dig into the earth. For a moment, the pain ebbs and I can breathe normally. But it's short lived.

My whole body spasms, and in the next instant, everything and nothing hurts at once. My wolf explodes out of me, and I look through her eyes for the first time in weeks.

She charges forward, not caring who or what is in her way. Her only goal: get to Zander and save him. I'm right there with her.

I finally understand what people meant when they told me I'm an Alpha in my own right. My wolf is vicious. She fights with so much ferocity that it would scare me if I didn't know instinctively that this is right. I'm also not small like most she-wolves.

We, because it really is both of us as one, barrel into the wolf at Zander's throat, dislodging him. He stumbles to the side and regroups quickly, but Zander is back on his feet, and I try something I haven't even thought to try till this moment.

We'll do this together. I shove the words at him with as much willpower as I can muster.

Zander pauses as if stunned just for a moment, but then says, *there's my girl.* The love he has for me radiates through the bond. *Take right, I'll go left. Do NOT aim for his throat. He'll expect that. He won't expect a double back leg strike. If we get him down, I'll finish him.*

Who is this? I ask.

Grayson, the fucking traitor.

I pause for a second before I regain composure. We both begin circling, knowing Damien and Kai will keep the rest at bay. This is now an Alpha fight.

Without another word between us, we attack. I clamp down on his right leg with every ounce of strength I have. Thank God my wolf knows what the hell is happening.

Ripping both legs out from under Grayson, I hear a snap of bone and realize Zander sapped Grayson's other leg. Grayson howls, and in the next instant, Zander has him by the throat. He's clamped down with every ounce of his strength.

As I dislodge from Grayson's leg, I realize Zander wasn't going for a kill before, just submission. But now? Zander is going to kill him.

Zander squeezes just a bit more, and the sound of bone snapping ripples through the clearing again. This time, it's much louder, and Grayson's whole body stills. A howl rings out across the clearing. I glance around and see that every other wolf that was held back by Damien and Kai realize their Alpha was just killed. To my shock, Zander doesn't release Grayson's limp body. He keeps tearing and biting, ripping his head completely off.

This close, my stomach does flips, but my wolf just watches. A knowing calmness washes through me. Her calmness and knowing. This is how it has to be. It's not necessary for a wolf to lose their head. If a shifter dies in wolf form, they will shift back to human form within the hour. However, by removing the head, Zander stopped that process and is sending a message to other packs. We are strong. Attacking another pack unprovoked will not be taken lightly.

With that thought, something else takes root. Hope. My memories. They can come back. If my shifter side is unlocked, I'll get them back.

I'm sorry. I don't have all your memories. I have a lot, but not all. None from before we were joined, unless you shared them with me. I'll give you anything I have. But they will be from my perspective.

So, I may never remember everything.

I don't know. I've been locked behind a wall for weeks. Over the last week, the wall has been cracking, and I've been able to slowly give you back what you lost. It was your pain at the possibility of losing Zander that broke it down completely.

I'm glad you're back. I missed you.

I was always here, just hidden. I could feel you. Influence some actions when you were having big feelings, but that's it.

While I was conversing with my wolf, something I didn't realize I missed, the wolves around the clearing leave. Most likely back over the border. Damien and Kai followed them into the woods, but are making their way back to us.

I turn my eyes back to Zander, and even though he's still in wolf form, the look he gives me sends a shiver down my spine and makes my fur prickle.

Kara! You shifted! Kai's shocked voice floats through my head.

I did. Apparently, Zander in a life-or-death situation was all I needed to break the wall down. I cock my head and Zander approaches, nuzzling my side, and it's the best feeling in the world.

The other enforcer groups have all checked in, and all remaining wolves have either submitted or fled. We lost six enforcers. Fifteen more are injured and will be at the healers soon. Zander, you need to be seen, as well. Damien's no-nonsense report is comforting and upsetting in turn.

Tell one to meet us at the pack house. We need to get Kara back there. With this being her first shift in a long time, I have a feeling that once her adrenaline crashes, she's going to need healing. Just like when the pups get their wolf the first time, Zander tells him.

Agreed. Kai will lead. You and Kara in the middle. I'll follow. Damien takes up position, never stopping his scan of the trees.

We break into a run and head home, staying in wolf form for added protection and speed.

Chapter Fifty-Four

You should be resting

ZANDER

As we break through the tree line back at the pack house, Marge, Carmen, and Callum are all waiting for us on the back patio with clothes for us. They all have a mix of excitement and shock on their faces. We didn't speak much on our run back, but I know Damien being Damien made sure they would be ready for us.

Kara fucking shifted. She's back. My beautiful mate. Her rich, auburn coat and matching eyes took my breath away just like they did the first time I saw her wolf. She's perfect. But I know she's got to be close to burn out. We kept a brutal pace on our way back, and she hasn't been running, let alone shifted, for weeks.

"Holy shit, Kara!" Carmen squeals. She's practically vibrating as we stop in front of the patio and I shift back. Damien and Kai shift and grab their clothes from Callum while Marge hands me mine.

I finish putting my shorts on and turn to see that Kara hasn't shifted back. From the way she's holding herself, it looks like she's about to collapse. She's wavering on her feet just like pups when they shift for the first time. She's burned through what little energy she had. It probably wasn't smart to make her stay in wolf form for so long, but we needed to get back quickly.

Shifting for the first time in a while can be tricky for anyone, let alone someone this tired. "A little stuck there, love?" I chuckle, trying to lighten the mood. I could force her to shift, but that's not pleasant, so I want to avoid that if at all possible.

What do I do? Her words drift through my mind, and I close my eyes for just a moment, savoring the sound. Opening my eyes, I refocus on Kara. She needs me right now.

Let your wolf guide you. Think about being in your human form. Focus on that. I walk over to her and reach out to stroke her fur. It's just as soft as I remember, and the feel of it comforts me. I've missed her in this form so damn much. For a moment, nothing happens, but then I feel it—the shift beginning—and step back. I let her flow through the process.

Carmen tosses me Kara's clothes to me so as soon as she shifts, I can help her dress. The shift complete, Kara stands to shaky legs before losing the fight with exhaustion and collapsing. Catching her before she hits the ground, I look to Carmen who is standing back with the rest. "I think this is going to be a team effort." She understands and rushes over to help me dress Kara. Once dressed, I pick her up fully and carry her inside to our room.

As I lay her down on the bed, I kiss her forehead and smile to myself. When I look up, I notice everyone has joined us in here. The healer, who must have been waiting inside for us, has joined our little party, too. Augusta approaches me, but I shake my head. "Her first."

"But Alpha, Damien said you needed attention."

"Not until I know Kara's first shift in weeks didn't do damage. I need her to be okay." I go for authoritative, but it comes out desperate.

Augusta is used to my outbursts—I'm a horrible patient—but still flinches before turning to Kara. A few minutes pass in complete silence as she examines Kara before turning to me. "She will be fine, just needs to sleep. Looks like she just burned through her energy stores. Now you." I let the healer check me over and do whatever it is that healers do. We heal fast normally, but sometimes, things heal wrong, and healers step in to make sure things heal correctly and even faster than normal for us—so basically instantly.

That done, I turn to the rest of the room. "Carmen and Marge, I want one of you with Kara if I'm not. She will probably sleep for a while, but I want someone here when she wakes. She shifted and seems like she's back to herself, but there could be residual effects." They nod and take up position next to her on the bed. Walking towards the door, I nod to the men around me, and they know without words that we need to debrief. I take one final look back at my perfect mate, and head to my office.

Stepping into my office, I don't even bother sitting at my desk. I have too much anxious energy to sit right now, so I turn and lean against it, crossing my arms over my chest and feet at the ankles. My entire inner circle files into the room—Jensen and Marek must have gotten back while we were upstairs. "Report."

Damien—as my second—takes the lead and begins, "There were a total of five points of attack. Like the other attacks, most were wolves that seem spelled in some way. They were vicious, but it wore off quickly. Enforcers were able to submit mostly. We did lose six enforcers. Four of ours, and two of David's."

"Who?"

"Sebastian, Greg, Elias, and Cole," Marek says each name with the care and respect they deserve. I struggle to breathe. Elias and Cole were young, and had only been on patrol detail for about six months. Our newest class of recruits. Greg was the one who came out of retirement when we needed the support. Sebastian, I didn't know well, but his family have been working as enforcers for years.

The thing about shifters is lineage means everything. Healers, enforcers, pack leaders—they tend to follow family lines. Just like power in the pack.

Kai steps forward this time. "As best we can, we've got Grayson's pack members that submitted barricaded in one of the barracks with guards. The ones that were killed have been collected."

"Alpha, I know this isn't the time, but what are we going to do about Black Pine?" Jensen asks.

"At the moment? We need to regroup and deal with the fall out of me killing Grayson. Since it was an Alpha Match, planned or not, I now have rights to Silver Hollow. As for Black Pine, they've been dealt a blow I don't think they saw coming. Had Kara not shifted, I'd be the one dead. Grayson was thirty years my senior. Kara being Alpha blood was the only reason she was able to step in."

"Varek assumed Kara wasn't going to be there, and Grayson would kill you." Marek nods in agreement.

I nod back and add, "Exactly. Makes me think we will have time to figure out our next steps. So, we focus on border security, rebuilding, and dealing with Silver Hollow."

"Zander..." A breathy sigh that borders on moan comes from the direction of the door, and we all look up to see Carmen supporting Kara. Within my next breath, I'm at Kara's side.

"What are you doing out of bed, love? You should be resting."

"She woke up and wouldn't take no for an answer. By the way, her Alpha aura is back. That's the only reason we're here," Carmen grumbles as she steps away from Kara and goes to sit in one of the chairs along the bookshelves.

Kara looks up at me from her position in my arms. Her eyes shine with unshed tears, and I'm not sure why. "I needed to be with you." Scooping her up into my arms, I carry her towards my desk.

"Well, I was just getting to the other good part of the evening, and it involves you." I kiss her head. "So I'm glad you're here." I'm not, but what am I going to do, stop her? I settle in my chair, cradling her close. Since I'm finally sitting, the rest of the men find their own chairs. Well, all except Damien, but that's not surprising.

I know I've already said Kara shifted, and they know but I want her to have this moment of good. "Kara shifted," I announce and the room—which was full of tension a moment ago—erupts in cheers and congratulations.

In a small voice I almost don't hear, Kara whispers, "I don't have all my memories back. Most of them, but not all. My wolf doesn't know if I'll ever get them all."

The sadness radiating off her breaks my heart. "Then we'll make new ones, starting with a mating ceremony, as soon as possible," I say to her, but speak it loud enough for the whole room.

"The full moon is in two days. We can get the ceremony together by then." Carmen jumps to her feet, clapping away. "It doesn't have to be a big and elaborate thing, but the pack needs to be there. It's the Alpha taking his mate, after all."

Groaning, Kara looks at Carmen, then the rest of the room. "Fine, but shouldn't we deal with the deaths first?"

My perfect mate, making sure the pack gets what they need before she gives anything to herself. She doesn't realize it, but that's 100% how she was before the damn curse. I think she will be back to herself more and more. We just need to give it time.

"Let's all get some sleep. I have a feeling this war is just starting. But I do think we have some time before we have to deal with the next battle." I stand and carry Kara back to our room, knowing everyone will head out to get some rest as well.

We sleep well into the next morning, and only stir when my phone rings. Kara reaches for it and answers quickly when she recognizes the caller.

"Hey, Dad. You're on speaker."

"Hello there, firefly. Everyone okay? I got a report early this morning from Damien, and there was a lot in it."

"David, I'm sorry about your two men. They were good shifters who fought hard. We were overrun." I hate losing anyone, especially those who weren't mine. It hurts more for some reason.

"They knew the risks when I asked for volunteers to go." There's a pause before David continues, "Kara, Damien said you saw action last night, but said you and Zander would elaborate. What happened?"

"I shifted and helped take down Grayson," Kara says with actual pride in her voice. I'm so proud of her. As she cradles the phone in her hands, I wrap my arms around her and smile into her hair, breathing her in.

"You did? You shifted?" Away from the phone, he practically yells, "Franny, Kara shifted!"

"We will be holding our mating ceremony in...well, tomorrow night now. It's been long enough."

"We will be there. You can give me a full report at that point. I'm assuming Black Pine is still in the picture, and you haven't made a decision about Silver Hollow?"

"I'm hoping we have some breathing room for a bit, but yes on both counts," I say as I hear Franny in the background, knowing the business part of this call is over.

I kiss Kara's shoulder and get up to shower while she and her mother talk for a bit. I know we're nowhere close to the end of this. We can officially say war has come back to our region.

I step out of the shower and wrap a towel around myself just as Kara saunters into the bathroom, completely naked. My reaction is immediate.

"My parents will be here tomorrow morning. We have a lot to get done before then."

"Oh yeah." I reach for her, pulling her close. "I think I'm going to start that list right at the top." Swooping in, I take her mouth in a brutal kiss and show her just how happy I am that she's finally whole again.

Chapter Fifty-Five

You didn't need your memories

Kara

THE LAST TWENTY-FOUR HOURS have been a complete blur. Telling Carmen I don't want a big ceremony got old after the fifth—or was it sixth?—time. Zander's still in debriefs with his inner circle, and I'm running out of energy what feels like every twenty minutes. I feel like we haven't really had time to breathe, but I get it. The full moon peaks tonight, and it's either do the ceremony tonight or wait a month. I don't want to wait. Neither does my wolf.

We get to fully mate tonight, she tells me for the hundredth time. She's a bit more excited than I am. What I've come to realize is our wolf halves don't get to fully mate until we complete all the steps.

It might be our wolves that lead us to our mate. They force proximity and cause the symptoms to drive us towards mating. But, ultimately, it's the human side that gets to accept or reject the bond.

Ceremony. Mate marks. Sex after—or during. Who am I to slow the process down?

Once the human side joins together, the wolf side does, as well. We become one unit, tied in a way that only other bonded mates truly understand. There's no *if one dies, the other will follow* BS that you find in books or movies. We just get to be closer than the regular pack bond. Our power will also increase since we're both Alpha by birth.

Come to think of it, that's probably the reason Varek and his minions didn't want this bond to happen. According to my dad, it's been over a hundred years since two Alpha bloodlines mated. It creates a massive power shift. With Zander now having to deal with the aftermath of killing Grayson, there's technically three packs involved. I've decided to not take over for my father. My younger brother, Kade, will become Alpha. Both my parents and Zander support that decision. It's Kade who's still coming to terms with it. Poor guy.

My parents and brother came this morning in a whirlwind of chaos. I didn't think they would ever stop fussing. Dad and Kade immediately went into another meeting with Zander, getting full reports and trying to game plan the next steps. I wanted to join—this is my pack too—but Mom whisked me away to get ready for tonight.

Mom brought the dress she wore to her ceremony over fifty years ago. Apparently, we had already started updating and altering it for me, so all that was needed were finishing touches. Now it's nighttime, and I'm here in front of the mirror, staring at myself in this dress. Lace flowers and vines decorate the bodice and flow down the small train. The color is a beautiful light green with a plunging neckline and crisscross straps. It creates a perfect silhouette for me. In keeping with the tradition of Zander's pack, I have flowers throughout my hair as it cascades down my back.

"You look beautiful." Mom walks up behind me, placing her hands on my shoulders and squeezing. Her eyes meet mine in the mirror, love and warmth shining in their depths. "Everyone is waiting outside, you ready to go finish this bond?"

"I think so, I'm glad we're just doing the bare minimum of lines needed for this." I wither under the weight of what I need to do.

"If you forget, no one will care. It's just tradition. As long as you are both under the moon when you speak your vows, you both mark the other before it sets, and you have some fun later..." she winks and I roll my eyes, "everything will work out." Her smile helps me calm down, and I turn and give her the biggest hug I can, dislodging a few flowers in the process. We laugh as she fixes them before turning for the door.

I get to the top of the stairs and look down to see Zander standing in his brown suit pants and no shirt. Whoever made the tradition in our pack that males don't wear shirts, I need to personally thank them. This man is what people mean when they say delicious. Am I drooling?

I make my way down the stairs into Zander's waiting embrace and realize how crazy the last few months have been. From finding my mate—which I slightly remember but mostly know from what Zander and my wolf have told me—to Zander ending Grayson and all the things in between, it's been a wild ride.

"Ready, love?" Zander breaks me out of my thoughts with a kiss to the top of my head.

"I'm ready for the end of the night." I give him a sly smile and he groans.

"If we didn't have to do these steps, I'd take you right back up those stairs."

"But you do, so let's get going. There's three hundred people waiting to party!" Carmen breaks the spell we're under as she pops up right next to us.

Outside on the lawn, most of the pack creates a ring around the center point of a circle of the same flowers that adorn my hair. My heart bursts to overflowing as I look around at the gathered pack. Almost every member of Moonrise is here. There's even a small group from Shadow Creek.

The inner circle stands at key points around the circle of flowers in what makes a five-point star. They stand as witnesses to the right. Carmen, as my lady in waiting, stands at the end of the aisle before the circle. Since my parents and brother are the only family alive, they stand directly behind Carmen.

Zander, as the higher-ranking pack member, begins the ceremony. "Under the moon and in front of these witnesses, I pledge my life and being to my mate, Kara Lancaster."

Staring into his eyes, I repeat the words to him, "Under the moon and in front of these witnesses, I pledge my life and being to my mate, Zander Holt."

"From this night, I mark you as mine. Our wolves will be forever one."

I blink back tears that threaten to spill, and attempt to continue, "From this night..." the tears spill over, "I mark you as mine. Our wolves will be forever one." In my mind, my wolf whoops, *yes we will!* I smile at that.

The words done, the only thing left in front of the crowd is to kiss and run off into the woods. We could go back to the pack house. Except the pack house is where the mating ceremony parties always take place. So we made the decision to complete the bond in the same place we made the decision to complete the bond in the first place.

The lake.

Zander swoops down and kisses me long and hard, and the world falls away as he devours my mouth. *It's time for the fun to really start, love.* God, I love being able to hear him again.

To the whoops and hollers of our pack, we take off into the woods. Zander quickly strips out of his pants and hands them to me so he can shift. We didn't think it was wise for me to shift so quickly again when I'm still recovering my energy stores, so I climb onto his back and Zander takes off through the woods.

While we head off for the night, the rest of the assembled guests part. A massive party tent was put up in record time, complete with a huge bar, buffet, and dance floor. The word spread that the lake was off limits to everyone this evening. The weather is beautiful, so discouraging anyone who thinks a midnight swim is a good idea was priority.

You seem in a hurry to get to our destination, I tease him from his back. My hands are curled deep into Zander's fur, and the feel of him is amazing.

The growl I get in response makes my whole body shiver. With his speed, we arrive at the lake in record time. I climb down and he shifts back so fast I'm not even settled on the ground.

I pull the straps of my dress off my shoulders and let the dress pool at my feet. I stand here, suddenly nervous. I'm not nervous to be with him. Sex with him is as natural as breathing. I'm nervous I'll not know how or when to mark him.

You'll know. My wolf all but flips her tail like it's the most obvious thing in the world. In the two days she's been back, I've realized she's one opinionated, sassy wolf. It's fitting, because I am too.

Approaching me like the predator he is, Zander swoops down to pick me up and place me on the rock outcropping. He lays me down on the blanket we placed there ahead of time. Not giving me any time to think or process, he descends on me.

His kisses are hot and wanting, driving my need higher and higher with each touch of his lips and hands. On and on, he explores my whole body. Taking his time like there isn't an end goal—just a deep need to know every inch of me.

My hands wander all over his body, exploring and learning every inch of him, too.

"Z, please. I need you inside me. This is torture!" I moan as he kisses my neck.

"As you wish, love. I live to please you." He lines himself up and enters me fully in one thrust. The gasp I let out is one part pleasure and one part delicious pain.

Setting a pace that's much slower than I want, but wonderful all the same, he growls into my ear, "Do me a favor, scream my name when you come." With no other warning, he bites on the mark he's already made, re-marking me, and I explode.

Stars flash across my vision as he continues to keep this steady pace and I come down from my high. Once I feel a bit more in control, I tell him on another gasp, "I feel like I need to return the favor."

Without dislodging himself, Zander flips our positions so I'm straddling him, and I take control of everything. Moving on him, I set a much quicker pace and he begins to lose himself to the feeling of us.

Just when I think he's close, I lean down and bite him in the same place he marked me. The roar he unleashes would be terrifying if I wasn't lost in the feel of his blood entering my mouth.

Grabbing my hips, Zander holds me steady as he fills me with his seed, and I lick his wound closed at the same time.

I fully collapse on top of him and we lay there, just breathing each other in for what seems like hours, but I'm sure is only a few minutes. Finally finding my strength, I roll off Zander and he pulls me into his side.

Laying under the stars together feels unbelievable, and honestly, one of the craziest moments of my life. But I wouldn't change it for the world.

Hours pass in comfortable silence until Zander breaks it with the sweetest words, "See, love? You didn't need your memories to know we were right together."

I smile, knowing he was absolutely right. But don't tell him that.

Epilogue

THE FIXER

THE ONLY REASON I was able to sneak into Moonrise Pack lands is because tonight is Alpha Zander Holt's mating ceremony. For the last months, I've been contracted by just about every pack in the region to get information on the brewing war. The crazy part? It's been next to impossible to get info from the source. Moonrise is locked down tight. They must have one hell of a tech guy.

I haven't had to physically infiltrate a pack in months. But here I am, hiding in the tree line, watching the biggest party I've seen in a long time. I've been collecting bits and pieces of conversations as shifters get close. This new scent-masking spray works really well, because no one has noticed me.

That is until one shifter catches my attention. No fucking way. I am a lone wolf for this specific reason. My mate is here, and I think he knows I am, too.

I turn and move as quickly as I can through the trees until I make it across the border. Looks like I'll be using other methods to get the intel my clients asked for, because finding my mate is not happening. Ever.

Acknowledgements

To my husband, Brandon. Thank you for giving me the space and freedom for this passion project. You're always in my corner and you know you're my rock and my humor. When I told you I wrote two chapters than random day in February I expected you to question me. Instead you nodded and said, "Of course you did." In that tone you use when I say something extremely obvious. You never questioned my ability. You probably won't read this but that's okay. Love you!

To my best friend, Stacey, I love you girl. You're my biggest cheerleader and without you being my sounding board for things I don't think I'd actually have written this book. You weren't shocked either when I said I was writing a book. If anything you were shocked it took me this long. The amount of times you've told me your proud of me alone can't even be quantified.

To my Mother in law, Nancy. Thank you for jumping on this ride with me and believing in me. But mostly, thank you for reading and raving about this story before I even edited it. You're encouragement and excitement really helped!

To my online writing community. Y'all are the reason I got words on the page consistently every week. Having other people doing exactly what I was doing when I was doing it made the whole process (including the editing wasteland) tolerable.

To my editor and proofreader, you guys are stuck we me for life–pleased don't quit. You've made what I wrote ten times better!

To my beta readers, thanks for finding the holes and being excited about the book. Cause without you I never would have caught some of that shit.

To rest of the family. Y'all took finding out I wrote a book and made me go best seller (within the family at least). I hope you will still make eye contact with me after this.

Finally, to you, my readers. Thanks for taking a chance on me. I hope I met–maybe even exceeded–your expectations and you'll be back for more. Without you, this little debut indie author wouldn't have any kind of reach.

About the author

R. A. Beckem mentally lives in the Paranormal Romance world and loves that just off reality vibe to pull you into a new place. With one of her favorite sub-genres being shifter romance it was a natural conclusion that her debut novel would fall deep into wolf shifter territory. She has a voracious reading habit that only rivals her obsession with collecting pretty books.

On a any given day you can find her reading, writing, if the weather is good in one of the gardens her and her husband maintain, or preserving the veggies or herbs she pulls from the garden.

Born and raised in Southern Illinois, and currently living in town with her husband and two Australian Shepherds. Her neighbors affectionately call her a hermit and that her and her husband have made their home into a bit of an rural oasis in pseudo urban life.